W9-CIK-320

MELODY OF MURDER

*Recent Titles by Stella Cameron from
Severn House*

The Alex Duggins series

FOLLY
OUT COMES THE EVIL
MELODY OF MURDER

Other Titles

SECOND TO NONE
NO STRANGER
ALL SMILES
SHADOWS

MELODY OF MURDER

Stella Cameron

Severn House Large Print
London & New York

This first large print edition published 2017
in Great Britain and the USA by
SEVERN HOUSE PUBLISHERS LTD of
19 Cedar Road, Sutton, Surrey, England, SM2 5DA.
First world regular print edition published 2016 by
Crème de la Crime Ltd, an imprint of
Severn House Publishers Ltd.

British Library Cataloguing in Publication Data
A CIP catalogue record for this title is available from the British Library.

ISBN-13: 9780727895127

Severn House Publishers support the Forest Stewardship Council™
[FSC™], the leading international forest certification organisation. All
our titles that are printed on FSC certified paper carry the FSC logo.

MIX
Paper from
responsible sources
FSC
www.fsc.org FSC® C013056

Typeset by Palimpsest Book Production Ltd.,
Falkirk, Stirlingshire, Scotland.
Printed and bound in Great Britain by
T J International, Padstow, Cornwall.

Prologue

'When did you become so attached to this house?'

Elyan rested his fingers on the piano keys and said nothing. He avoided his father's pale hard eyes.

'Elyan, this behavior is unacceptable,' Percy Quillam said in his deceptively soft tones. A nerve twitched under his right eye, a twitch Elyan knew too well. 'You've told me far too often that this house is pretentious and you hate it. For you, I've secured a perfect property in the Cotswolds for the next six months. You have a concert tour to prepare for and we need to remove you from any distractions. We need peace, and nothing must disturb our concentration. Folly-on-Weir is the perfect solution.'

Fury tightened Elyan's throat. As always, his father was manipulating him, advancing the grand Percy Quillam plan for total control of his son.

'I never heard of this place you're talking about until now, Father. I'd rather stay here. And in case you haven't noticed, I don't need any reminders to practice. You know I'm comfortable in Hampstead. It's a bad idea to change the routine now.'

'Not possible to back out. The arrangements have been made and I've signed a contract. I've discussed everything with Sebastian and he absolutely agrees with me. So does Wells. So does

1

your mother. She's the one who found the property we'll move into.'

Sebastian Carstens had been Elyan's piano teacher since Percy decided ten-year-old Elyan had outgrown his first teacher. His training started at age four. Wells Giglio was his agent and assigned wholly to the whims of the Quillams with whom he spent an inordinate amount of time.

Sebastian was one of the few adults Elyan trusted. To hear that he had a part in this sudden dramatic change shook Elyan.

'Why is this the first time I've heard of it?' *As if he didn't know*. His father wanted him away from London. Here it was too easy for him to escape and even a few hours of freedom was more than his father could allow him with any grace. Had Percy found out about his son's night-time excursions from the house? Percy Quillam was afraid his son, the center of all his own ambitions, might throw everything up for freedom. Elyan wished the thought brought him satisfaction but he had to deal with his own demons, especially the one that made him afraid of what his father would do if he lost the focus for his existence. 'Father,' Elyan prompted quietly, 'why the secrecy?'

'You are so highly strung, my boy. Which is only to be expected. We thought it best to deal with the details and present them without worrying you with any decisions.' Those light blue eyes flickered toward the windows, and back. 'We're having Annie's parents to dinner tomorrow evening. I've already had a word with her father.

That was something else I wanted to do before speaking to you.'

Sliding to the end of the piano bench, his heart thudding at his eardrums, Elyan deliberately let his hands hang relaxed between his knees as he faced his father.

A solid man of medium height, his thick gray hair slicked back into a tail at his nape, Percy seemed unshakably sure of himself, but Elyan had come to see his parent as more thwarted artist living through his child than the artist's proud father, the image he had worked so hard to perfect.

Percy favored long velvet jackets of a studied, outmoded, relaxed cut with silk cravats, loosely tied at the necks of his collarless shirts. Streaked by sunlight through Venetian blinds and floor-to-ceiling diaphanous white draperies, he stood with head bowed, hands clasped behind his back. In the ivory and white music room, stark but for the formal, gilt-trimmed, gold damask chairs and a couch grouped around an empty marble fireplace – and Elyan's Steinway – the man resembled a subject from an early nineteenth-century painting.

He was waiting his son out as usual, waiting for him to break the silence with the wrong response, or better yet, a passive acceptance. Acceptance became harder for Elyan to utter without feeling weak and a failure.

Let him have part of his way, it wasn't time to rock the boat. 'And?' Elyan said when he thought he could control the urge to shout. 'What else is it you want to say?'

3

The eye tick returned. 'I wish you would give me credit for wanting only the best for you, my son. You are something rare and brilliant. Everything I do, I do to nurture your talent. You are not ordinary. You never will be – but you must be led. You have a public. They are the ones who fill every seat at your concerts and cry in awe at the very sight of you in the flesh. We, your closest confidants and supporters, Sebastian, Wells and I *live* to smooth your way and make sure you need only be concerned with your magnificent music. This entire household adores you.

'Eighteen is a difficult age. We have to balance your . . . urges for the mundane with the fact that music, serious music, is your past, present and future. Maturity will show you I've been right.'

How often, Elyan wondered, must he be embarrassed by Percy's extravagant declarations? Sometimes he thought his father might be mad, but then he would hear and see him interact with those who had nothing to do with all this and the doubt faded a little, at least for a while. 'You were telling me about the Bells coming to dinner,' he said, deliberately pleasant. The news didn't bode well. They were his girlfriend, Annie's, parents and Percy would undoubtedly prefer the entire family to disappear. Such an invitation had never been made before.

He would see Annie tonight, just as they had planned, and some of the anger and fear would disappear. 'I thought we didn't have dinner parties. You don't like them.' The Bells were too ordinary for the Quillams and there was nothing to be gained from encouraging them.

'This will be simple,' Percy said, absently tugging on today's mossy green and black cravat. 'A simple meal among friends. You see, I understand you better than you think I do, and I also remember being a very young man myself. These fleeting friendships seem more important than life at your age, but I don't criticize you for that. I want you to indulge in . . . whatever. As long as it doesn't interfere.'

Fleeting friendships? What he and Annie had wasn't fleeting, it was real. The urge to tell his father what he thought of him and walk out was more than appealing. 'You were talking about the Bells, Father?' And it wasn't as if Percy Quillam was more immune to women now than he always had been. He'd married Elyan's mother only weeks after his first wife died. Shortly after the marriage, Elyan, already four months old, had been whisked back from a supposed lengthy hospitalization for some mythical newborn ailment and hidden away in Percy's household until the man decided it was safe to allow his son to be seen in public. Elyan had deduced this sequence – easily – from dates of death and birth. So dear Percy had been bedding Sonia while his first wife was dying.

Percy's cravat suffered another yank. 'The Bells have accepted my invitation and, at least in theory, the suggestions your mother and I have made.'

Had there ever been a time when his father's smile had not brought Elyan out in a rash of goosebumps? His mother, as subservient as she was with Percy, didn't tend to keep from Elyan anything she decided he would want to know. That she'd kept quiet this time was another sign that there were difficulties to come. Sonia Quillam was twenty-five years younger than her husband and as hard as it was to admit, Elyan knew she was afraid of Percy, not physically, but because he held the power in every facet of her life . . . and her son's. Taken in by Percy's dazzling court-ship, Sonia had given up a career as a promising orchestral violinist, or so their longtime house-keeper, Meeker, had confided in one of her 'moments'. Meeker's moments usually loosened her tongue when she was out of sorts with Percy.

Whatever Percy wanted, Percy got.

If Elyan broke away he might set his career back but he would climb out of that in time. It was his mother who would suffer most.

'Your mother and I are hoping the Bells will allow Annie to spend a day or two each week, or perhaps every other week, with us at Green Friday.'

He frowned. 'What's that?'

Percy gave his inevitable two barks of laughter. 'Foolish name. Ridiculous. But that's what the house is called and the new owner apparently thinks it's fetchingly different. It's a beautiful place and we've got it for the rest of the spring and the summer. You and Annie will be able to walk and enjoy the lovely surroundings. And there is always riding.'

'That would be nice if we could ride. I don't know about Annie, but I've never been on a horse.' He gave his most guileless smile. 'Never too late to learn, Father?'

His father studied his hands and made a noncommittal sound. He did his best to keep Elyan from any activity that could cause injury.

'Is there a tennis court?'

Percy frowned, narrowed his eyes then let out a little puff of air. 'Yes, yes, your mother said so. I remember now. She mentioned wanting to play again herself.'

So his mother played tennis – or had at some point. 'Is it a good court? You might want a game yourself.'

'Not my thing.' Percy looked peeved. 'I didn't go into the grounds for a good look around. You and Sebastian can play. Wells, when he comes down. And Annie, of course.'

Elyan raised his brows but said nothing. He knew he was loved – as much as his father was capable of loving anyone. It was natural for an eighteen-year-old to need a little room for his growing wings, but that wouldn't stop Father's anxiety. 'Where's Mother? Shouldn't she be in on this?' Not that she was ever included in serious discussions. 'And Laura?'

'Your mother's joining us as soon as she gets in. She'll be thrilled you're happy about what we've decided. I'll speak to Laura.'

It cost so little, almost nothing, to beat back the temptation to be sullen. A smile was a cheap price for peace. And this evening he'd see Annie. They would laugh and kiss a little, maybe a lot. Elyan was glad of his long cotton sweater. His body had a mind of its own and he spent a lot

7

of time thinking about being alone with Annie, really alone.

A day or so each week, or every other week, with Annie? What did they have in mind? That she would drive or be driven there and back in the same day? That they would have no private time? Probably. So far he and Annie had managed to conceal the hours they spent together, usually in one of the less trendy Hampstead coffee houses that had become their special places. Sebastian helped them, although he made sure to drop casual warnings against 'getting carried away' and the horrors that would follow if they did. In other words, sex is evil and could ruin your life. Elyan doubted Annie's welfare entered into the cracked equation. Holy hell.

Why hadn't Sebastian warned him about the Cotswolds plans? Wells thought of nothing but squeezing the money cow and staying on the right side of Percy, but Sebastian?

Father cleared his throat. 'I've been thinking that your sister is too much alone.'

'Laura?' Laura was Elyan's half-sister, his father's child by his first wife. Her mother had died and although Sonia was careful to include her, Percy scarcely seemed to notice his daughter unless he was out of sorts and she made a convenient target. Of late she had grown more distant, as if she was always following her own secret thoughts. She still liked to join Elyan on his stealthy escapes from the house to meet Annie. They liked her enough, felt sympathetic enough, not to resent her being there – or not obviously. 'Yes, I think so too, Father. She's so much more

confident now. I can tell. She wants to sing professionally. That would be great. She's so good.
With some encouragement—'

'Absolutely not.' Percy waved a dismissive
hand. 'How could you suggest such a thing. She
isn't strong and you know we have been concerned
about her recently. Her heart condition is serious
and no daughter of mine would be encouraged
to sing the sort of popular rubbish she's interested
in anyway.'

He thought a lot about Laura. Four years his
senior, she 'wasn't strong', as Percy put it. A
childhood illness had left her with a compromised
heart. It was true that she went through low times
when she seemed to deteriorate, but she improved
again. She was in a good place now. Laura had
things she wanted to do and she wasn't listened
to, other than by Sebastian and Elyan – and Wells
Giglio whom Elyan suspected had a less innocent
interest in Laura than was commonly supposed.
Wasn't it better to do what you loved for as long
as you could, rather than exist in a sort of
emotional twilight? Her life seemed on hold.
Perhaps she would come this evening – he looked
away; he and Annie needed more time alone,
especially now.

'But blues isn't what you think. It's real. Some
of the best clubs in the world are in London
and—'

'Your sister will never be well enough for the
kind of life you're talking about, dammit!' He
dragged a chair from beside the fireplace, arranged
it to face Elyan and sat down with elbows on
knees and fingers steepled. 'Don't mention it

again. Our thinking is that to give Annie a more leisurely time with us at Green Friday, she could share Laura's room and occasionally spend the night if she wants to. It would be lovely for both of them. They get along well and they could go about together while you're practicing. That way you wouldn't have to think about entertaining Annie whenever she's there.'

Not even subtle. If he protested that he wanted to be with her, would be with her every moment if he could find a way, he would work against himself.

'What do you say?'

Look into his so innocent eyes . . . and lie. 'Laura will love that.' Laura was tired of being used or ignored. 'And Annie.' He and Annie would make it work for them, and he would take trips into London whether his father liked it or not.

'Good, good.' Percy's little smile was the one the world saw when the man was triumphant. 'I should leave you to your practice, Elyan. You're a good boy. You have always understood that I know what is best for you. Now you must never forget that.'

Pearl pink streaked the sky and a strengthening wind whipped against Elyan's back, pushing his dark hair forward. One of the benefits of curly hair was that it looked much the same whatever you did to it. His mind had raced even faster than his feet while he slipped rapidly through the back exit from the house on Lawn Road to Belsize Park tube, took a train to Hampstead station and burst up to the street again. Sebastian had made sure Elyan could get away without being seen. There had been no opportunity to discuss his father's bombshell, but that would have to come. He kept jogging the hilly streets until he reached the alley off Heath Street where Slider's, a small blues club, occupied a tucked away corner.

He saw Annie's long, coppery hair and remembered to breathe again. She stood against the gray stone wall that faced the club. From the other side of the wall, new branches of a laburnum tree loaded with yellow blossoms bounced above her head sending faint shadows over her face. His favorite face. Big, serious brown eyes, a sharp nose and a mouth that belied those serious eyes, full, soft lips tilted in the perpetual hint of a smile.

She saw him and waved. Elyan ran faster and didn't stop until he swung her against him and held her in one arm. 'Did your parents tell you about my father's plans for the Cotswolds?'

'Yes, all of it. Look at me, please.' She shook him until he stared into her eyes. 'We've always known there were going to be obstacles. This is just the latest and it won't be allowed to change a thing between us. You agree?'

Looking at her, listening to her voice, he believed anything she said. 'Of course I do. I'm ticked at the underhanded stuff, that's all. Do you trust Sebastian?' That wasn't what he meant to say next. He usually had better control over his concerns than that, especially with Annie.

'What do you mean?' Annie leaned away to see his face. 'He's your friend. He's our friend.'

11

A jostling, laughing group filed past them and he looked at the ground. Dull grey cobbles. 'Let's get inside.' He guided her up stone steps so old they were worn down in the centers. Inside Slider's, shiny brown-painted walls were covered with taped or pinned-on hand-lettered ads for flatmates, flyers for bands appearing in the area, or sessions in an array of the less traditional arts. Elyan quickly eased Annie through sagging green curtains into a darkened alcove he'd noticed before. Draped boxes and unidentifiable shapes crowded against each wall like ghost impersonators.

'Something's wrong,' Annie said breathlessly. 'Tell me now.'

He had to smile. His Annie was a quiet, composed young woman but she was no good at mysteries or guessing games. 'You're smiling,' she whispered. 'I can see it. Where would we be without Sebastian – and Laura? How would we see each other at all? Without them we wouldn't be here right now.'

'I know that and I understand Laura, she's something special, but have you ever wondered why Sebastian helps us?'

Annie gathered her long coppery hair into one hand and pulled it forward over her shoulder. 'I don't want to stay in this . . . cupboard. Laura was probably right behind us and if we aren't out there, she might leave.'

'Would that be so bad?' Damn, but this was a night for saying things that could be thought but never said aloud. 'I mean—'

'I don't believe you said that.' Annie looked

12

away. 'Is that how you feel about Laura, Elyan?'

There were times when honesty, even if it hurt a bit, was the only best course. 'Sometimes. I'd like us to have more time alone. But don't listen to me. I'm in a shit mood after today. Sorry. It's fine she's coming, you know that. We'll go in and get a table.'

'Sebastian reserves a table for us.' Light caught her eyes.

'You mean he's arranged for the same table to be available whenever we want to come. This isn't a place where you telephone to reserve tables.'

She caught his hand. 'He knows Slider. They're friends. He does it for us so we'll be close to the music.'

'Yes and I could be all wet on this, but I'm sick of being manipulated. We'll sit somewhere else.'

'Why?' She tugged on his arm. 'This is our place. We . . . this is the only place I get to hear you play your blues. We're safe here, Elyan. Please?'

There wasn't a reasonable answer. What did he think, that the table was bugged? 'Forget it. I'm overreacting.'

He let her lead him back into the passage. At the entrance to the single long, narrow room where the bar ran along most of one exposed brick wall, he ducked through the stream of people coming and going. They went to their usual table only feet from a battered upright piano where Slider, the owner, played a medley of jazz and blues.

As if magically summoned, the waitress they knew as Nancy plopped two half pints of lager on the scarred black tabletop before they were even settled. 'On the house,' she said, raising her voice above the music. 'I'll be back with Laura's.'

Slider segued into an old favorite, 'Bayou Blues', and played with his usual bench-bouncing, ivory-hammering style, his head thrown back and rocking, eyes tightly closed. The black man's shaved skull shone in a single overhead spot. One after another, crescent furrows spread across thin cheeks from a mouth drawn back in a wide smile. Forties, fifties, sixties, who knew how old the man might be? He could hold any roomful of blues lovers rapt.

Elyan raised his glass and Annie did the same. They clinked and grinned at each other. Annie took a swallow and said, 'Let's freeze this moment – stay where we are right now. Like this. Let's never go back.'

'We'll both have decisions to make, but not without thinking everything through.' He drank thoughtfully, watching her across the rim of his glass. 'You don't know how much I want . . . I'm worried.'

'About this house in the Cotswolds? So am I but I'm not going to let it ruin what we have. We've dealt with the way things are here. We'll manage there. They can't get between us if we don't let them. And Sebastian worries almost as much about your happiness as he does Daisy's, and that's a huge statement.'

Elyan passed a hand over his eyes. 'I know.' It was true. Sebastian put his daughter, Daisy,

14

first in all things, but his prize pupil and friend came in a close second, or so it had always seemed. 'Forget I brought it up. Put it down to brain overload.'

'I'm late. Father had his eagle eyes in so I had to look as if I was settled in the den.' Her color high across her cheekbones, Laura slid into a chair between them. 'He's on a tear. Ripped into poor Mrs M.'

Maud Meeker, Mrs M., MMM – hummed in three-part harmony when she was nowhere around – was another safe harbor in the stormy seas of the Quillam household. Housekeeper and often all-purpose glue for the family, she'd been there a long time, since she arrived with Laura's mother, Audrey, when she and Percy married.

'Poor old Triple M,' said Annie. 'But she doesn't let much get to her. She's one of my favorite people. So many times she's been kind to me.'

Elyan kept a grip on his glass but aimed a forefinger at his half-sister. 'You're the one who keeps the lid on chaos, Laura.' He didn't want to say it, but he owed her the honesty. 'Are you okay? You aren't ill?' She darted glances around the room and he could see the sheen of sweat on her forehead. The movement was subtle, but she pressed a fist into her stomach.

'Father caught me off guard, is all. I've really never felt better, or more determined. We all know I've got a good reason to be antsy, don't we?' The look she gave him was almost wild and not like anything he'd seen before. 'We already knew I've got a good reason to be antsy. We all

15

do. But now I'll be making up my own mind about my own life.'

'We're going to talk about it,' Annie put in quickly, covering one of Laura's hands with her own. 'You're all clammy. Take some deep breaths. What do you want to drink? She said she was bringing you something.' She searched for Nancy and raised a hand when she saw her.

'I'm not staying till I inherit from my mum.' With jerky fingers Laura tore a beer mat into little pieces. 'Not anymore . . . Don't listen to me. I'm just babbling. I won't do anything in a hurry, but I'm making plans.'

The waitress glided by, plopping a gin and tonic in front of Laura without breaking stride. Laura drank more than Elyan wished she would. He worried about alcohol and whatever medication she took.

From photographs he knew that Laura was almost her dead mother's double. Shiny pale blond hair cut in a sleek, straight style at collar length, piercing blue eyes shadowed by dark, curling lashes, and rounded features that usually gave the impression of glowing health. Her illness was the one thing they never discussed and Elyan had sometimes wondered if Percy used the cardiac surgery she'd had as a small girl as an excuse to ignore her musical ambitions.

'When did he tell you about the Cotswolds?' Laura asked.

'Late this afternoon. Annie's parents told her today, too. They're coming for dinner at ours tomorrow.'

'I should have been spoken to before.' Laura's

color was suddenly too high. 'This is the best it's ever been for us. The best it will *ever* be for me. And he's found out we're happy so he's trying to rip us away so he can lock us up in some godforsaken house in the country where he can watch our every move. You're off to Oxford in a few months, Annie. Don't think our father isn't counting off the days until he can isolate Elyan completely, here or anywhere else.'

'Oxford isn't far enough away to isolate us, whether you're here or in Gloucestershire. Even the concerts won't keep you and Elyan apart forever.' Annie scooted her chair close to Laura's and put an arm around her shoulders.

Laura turned her face into Annie's shoulder. To Elyan's dismay, he could see her shoulders shaking as she cried. He pulled his own chair close and the three of them clung together.

'I finally have a chance to do what I want.' Laura choked on the words. 'People have heard me and I'm getting interest. I want to be here. I *need* to be here. How would I cope, isolated with him? He'd see any move I make. It doesn't matter. I'll wait for the right moment and jump. I can start to make money – maybe enough to support myself for a couple of years until I come into what my mother left me. I don't need much. A little stockpile to start and I'm off. I feel strong, and I feel angry. But I know how to play the subservient game. I'm going to be as near to invisible as you can imagine. I'm going to be so invisible, he won't notice I'm gone at first. I'm finally going to sing for my supper.'

This was the first time he'd heard his sister

sound like this. 'We'll be okay, sis, we *will*. All of us. We have to make changes but we'll be stronger for them.'

Annie put a forefinger on her own mouth and then rested it on his. She smiled and the agitation in him softened. 'The three of us,' she said. 'Until death do us part. I do like my little drama, too.'

They all laughed.

One

One month later

Alex Duggins scrunched down on her haunches and leaned against the back wall of St Aldwyn's church. Silence but for cool breeze flipping the leaves of a giant beech tree let her slip to a peaceful place in her too-busy mind.

Thick moss in every cranny of the building, between cracks in the pathways, smelled rich and damp. A scent that blended with the earth and the mulch of many seasons. She breathed in deeply. The cycle of growing things, even moss, was endlessly predictable and nowhere more so than among the permanent resting places of the dead. Inscriptions on ancient, leaning tomb stones faded beneath thick films of green and grey stains.

Summer came beautifully to the Cotswold Hills. From where she sat, in the shade of the beech, she could see the soft, early-morning sunlight shadow painting grass and clumps of tiny bright white daisies beneath the shadows of the dark gravestones.

Bogie, her gray, mostly terrier dog, ran after his earthward nose, back and forth, snuffling, black ears flapping. She dropped to sit on the ground. The area was still damp with lingering dew but she wore a long canvas jacket over jeans and it would keep her dry enough.

19

From the church came the sounds of someone playing the old upright piano used for choir practice. She looked toward the stained-glass windows overhead but couldn't see them without moving. They were not remarkable but she liked them. The music gained strength and a woman's voice rose in song. A woman's beautiful, husky, completely out-of-place voice singing in short bursts, with intervals on the piano. It sounded as if this was a new piece for the singer and she was working it out. Every few moments she fell silent, but then began again.

The voice reminded her of Madeleine Peyroux. When Alex had first heard Madeleine she'd thought of Billie Holiday. Alex loved the sound. The woman inside St Aldwyn's had the low, lazy tones of some blues singers, but also an unexpected range that let her climb high scales that made Alex grin with pleasure, even while her throat tightened with emotion. 'Loving you drives me crazy. But I ain't got no choice.' Again there was a piano interlude, practicing the same notes again and again. Alex could hear the woman hum while she played, a full, natural sound. The humming faded away. Each silence was longer until the sound ceased completely.

Wrapping her arms around her drawn-up knees, Alex rested her chin there and waited for more.

Any diversion was a good diversion these days. She lived in a muddle of decisions that needed to be made. Each one could be absolutely right or horribly wrong for her.

She could see the back windows of the Burke sisters' two row cottages that faced Pond Street.

The downstairs floors of the cottages had been combined to make Leaves of Comfort, their tea rooms, book and handicraft shop. Alex smiled toward the upstairs window where she knew the sisters would be having breakfast in their flat over the shop and chatting about the rights and wrongs of Folly-on-Weir, or more likely of the villagers. For two elderly, retired teachers who supposedly didn't get out much – other than to Alex's pub that was so conveniently close – they were a depthless treasure of local news and speculation.

But it was Tony, Tony Harrison, village vet, vet to the surrounding farms, and Alex's sometimes lover who crowded out everything else whenever she couldn't push thoughts of him away. He was her best friend. Now how likely was that combination?

She wanted to keep on making love with Tony. Recently, rather than slipping into a comfortable routine together, they had moved into a realm of experimentation and excitement she would never have thought either of them would seek out.

She gave a quiet smile behind her hands.

What neither of them seemed able to confront was their future. That could be for the best; they both had miserable marital failures in their pasts.

She wished the woman in the church would sing again but silence suggested a very long pause for thought. Or perhaps she'd finished.

The little girl Alex had lost at birth five years earlier, not long before she returned to Folly-on-Weir, had no marker here, in the place the child's mother, and grandmother, Lily, called home. Lily attended services regularly. Alex went when the mood moved her and it had moved her more frequently lately. This morning's visit to the churchyard had been with the idea of choosing a spot where a bench might be enjoyed by those who came here. A little brass plaque would say only 'Baby Lily', as the baby had been named after the grandmother who never saw her, never held her.

Why couldn't she move on from her lost child? Sometimes she didn't think about her for weeks, but then the memories returned, usually in the dark night hours when she lay awake watching for the dawn. She got up and wandered between graves, searching out the perfect spot for a bench. When she reached the lych-gate with its rose-draped canopy, she crossed her arms on a splintery cross beam, careful not to disturb a few vines curling there.

Teenagers on horseback clattered up Mallard Lane, laughing and chattering, their mounts' coats shining. Two Jack Russell terriers bustled in self-important circles close, but not too close, to the horses' hoofs. She watched the group until they crossed Pond Street, heading for a shortcut to the village green, then she turned back and made a loop around the entire, semi-circular path until she returned to sit against the wall again.

Alex had to concentrate on the Black Dog, Folly-on-Weir's village pub and her investment in the future when she'd returned after her divorce. No business ran itself and it was important to her not to be an absentee owner while her mother, Lily Duggins, and manager Hugh Rhys, ran the place. Capable as they were, customers formed a bond with the landlord, or lady. She smiled at the thought. Once she had wanted nothing more than to follow her career as a successful graphic artist; becoming landlady of a pub would never have occurred to her.

From inside the church came a mighty crash, the discordant clatter of piano keys. Probably a slam of exasperation. The singer had been silent for so long, Alex assumed she really had left.

Disappointed, after another lengthy, soundless interval, Alex pushed to her feet, whistled for Bogie to heel and set off for the side door into the ambulatory behind the organ. That was where the rather decrepit, if well-tuned upright was kept, and the choir practiced. The piano they occasionally used at the Black Dog was a better-looking instrument, but not much.

If the woman was still there, Alex wanted to say how she loved her voice and hoped she'd hear her again.

In the distance, to Alex's right, a figure in dark clothing walked on the other side of the graveyard wall. He, and she was sure it was a man, went toward the rectory and almost instantly disappeared from sight when the church blocked her view. Must be Reverend Ivor, the interim vicar who was rumoured to be leaving soon. She would miss him and his wife, Sybil – and their long-haired Dachshund, Fred.

'Sit,' she told Bogie, 'and stay.'

He flopped into a dejected heap beneath pink and coral rose bushes and turned reproachful black eyes up to her face.

Inside the church it took moments for Alex's

23

eyes to adjust to the dim light. She entered behind the choir risers and skirted them until she could see the back of the piano. The woman had gone, darn it. Disappointed, Alex wandered out into the ambulatory, avoiding stepping on memorial brasses set into large, side by side flagstones. She studied the knight and his lady depicted there, as she had often done before. Years of enthusiasts spreading their rolls of paper over the eerie likenesses, taping them down, rasping the raised images with rubbing wax to capture the images and later frame them, had taken a toll on the brasses. Rubbings were banned now.

Alex took a backward step to get a better angle on the knight. His toes were pointed and his chainmail enclosed arms crossed over his narrow, concave chest. In the stone beside him . . . Her heel caught something that shot away, her body keeled backward, one leg doubled under her, arms flailing. Alex cried out. The landing was painful as her elbows and bottom let her know, but at least she didn't jolt all the way back and hit her head.

Very carefully, she stretched flat on the cold floor and waited for her breathing to calm. She ached but moved her limbs, flexed her spine until she was sure she hadn't broken anything. All of her parts worked even if her body did throb. The leg that had bent backward felt achy at the knee but she could move the joint easily enough.

The sound of something rolling back and forth, slowing and coming to a stop, brought her to a sitting position. A red plastic thermos bottle had come to a standstill where it had slewed away from sharp contact with her trainer. 'Who would leave that here?' she muttered, gingerly getting to her feet and picking up the unintended weapon. Probably a choir member. There were one or two who carried water bottles and wrapped yards of scarf ostentatiously around their necks like opera singers protecting priceless voices.

Bending to grasp her knees, Alex waited for her heart to resume its usual position in her chest. Parts of her would definitely bear bruises. The thermos was an old, well-used one that should have a screw top that doubled as a cup, only that was missing.

Not far from the piano a stained-looking white lid, probably the cup belonging to the thermos, rested on its side.

She breathed through her mouth and squeezed her eyes shut. When she opened them again, her heart gave another huge bump. A thin trickle of blood ran like an emaciated scarlet snake from beneath a piano leg – from beneath a wing of glistening, pale blond hair spread in a blunt sweep over the feet of a brass music stand and gray flagstones.

One hand, fingers outstretched but still, appeared to reach for the lid of the bottle.

Two

Alex wouldn't appreciate finding out that Harriet Burke had called from Leaves of Comfort to suggest Tony 'might' want to walk past St

25

Aldwyn's this morning. Tony would do his best to make it believable that he'd wandered by while walking his dog, Katie.

That tale wouldn't pass the smell test. So what? He needed to spend real and personal time with Alex, and soon.

'Sitting at the back of the church, against the wall facing ours,' Harriet had told him. That had been some time ago and he hoped he hadn't missed her. He arrived at the spot. And there was no sign of Alex, but Katie took off as fast as her arthritic hips would allow, and he followed. The dog gave a single, excited bark, joined by a familiar yipping. He quickly found Katie with Alex's Bogie, gamboling joyfully through rose bushes near a side door to the church. The door stood slightly open.

He heard Alex's voice before he saw her. Her tone sent him striding into the building and past the choir risers. She spoke on her mobile, urgently, breathlessly, calling for help.

At her feet lay a young woman who seemed vaguely familiar. Blonde, her blue eyes open and dimmed, her rounded features seemed flaccid. Tony felt the emptiness of death.

He dropped to his knees and felt for a pulse. Nothing. But she was warm, soft, and he started CPR. Her head gradually lolled before he could return to her mouth for a second time and a glance at her eyes confirmed his fears. Her lips were blue, a little puffy even, and saliva had drizzled from her mouth and across a cheek. He looked more closely at her clothes. Her shirt stuck to her body as if she had sweated heavily. He sniffed and realized she must have vomited although he couldn't see any evidence. Carefully, he shifted back, stood and looked around, desperate not to move or even touch anything the authorities would want to deal with.

Alex's free hand reached for him. He squeezed her fingers and saw tears pouring down her cheeks from oval green eyes that glittered with confusion. 'Yes,' she said into the mobile. 'What? She's at St Aldwyn's, Folly-on-Weir, near the organ. Hurry, please. Yes, I'll stay here until they come.'

'Tony,' she said, slipping the phone into a pocket in her green jacket. 'How did you know to come?'

He swallowed. 'I didn't. I just came looking for you and here you are. I'm glad I'm here. Do you know who she is?'

Alex angled her head. 'I think I've seen her somewhere.'

'My dad was going to see Harriet and Mary this morning.' He pulled out his own mobile. His father was the local GP. 'We can hope he's already there.'

It was sensible Harriet Burke who answered, 'Leaves of Comfort.'

He asked if Doc Harrison was there. 'Yes,' she said promptly but couldn't resist asking, 'is there a problem over there?'

So they had been watching to see if he went looking for Alex. 'Please ask him to come to the church – use the door behind the organ, the one closest to where the choir stands,' he said firmly and clicked off.

'Tony.' Alex stared at him. 'Is this . . . Tony, did someone do this to her?'

He looked up into the rafters high above and swallowed. 'I don't know.'

'But you think so, don't you? It's her head. Oh, my god, someone hit her over the head.'

'Or she fell,' he said quickly. 'Onto the bottom of the music stand, do you think?'

Alex shook her head. 'I don't know what to think. An ambulance is coming.'

Their eyes met again and Tony grimaced. 'What's that?' He nodded to the red thermos she held.

She sniffed it. 'Smells like berries – and perhaps cloves – but it's sharp. I don't recognize the stuff. Could be a cordial. It was over there. I tripped and fell on it. I think that's the top of it near her hand.'

He nodded. 'I'd like to take a closer look at the body, but we must not move her. Dad will get here. Alex, you shouldn't have moved that thermos, or touched it.'

'It's empty.' She set the thing on the piano stool and wiped her hand on her jeans. 'I didn't think about anything like that. I hadn't noticed . . . her. Tony, why? She's so young. You're sure she hasn't just passed out and cut her head?'

'I'm sure, darling. I wish I weren't.'

'Morning,' his dad said briskly, coming through the side door, bag in hand. 'Are you two volunteering for the choir? It's been a bit thin lately but are you sure you'd be an asset, Tony? If I remember . . .' He saw the girl and didn't miss a step before going to kneel beside her. He felt her throat for a pulse and pulled his stethoscope from the bag.

28

It all felt hopeless.

'Have you phoned for an ambulance?' he asked sharply.

'Yes. She was singing in here when I was sitting out there. Then she stopped but I didn't hear her call out.'

Doc James Harrison leaned over and moved the stethoscope over the girl's chest. He pulled off the scope and set it on the ground while he felt her neck again. After a few moments he sat back and looked steadily down into her face. 'How long ago did she stop singing?'

'I don't know.' Alex looked near tears again. She checked her watch. 'I was out there a long time, I think. She stopped singing several times as if she were practicing, or trying to get the song right. That was before I went around the church-yard. I walked around for a bit, thinking, and eventually went back to sit again. It was as if she'd been in here figuring something out but she suddenly got frustrated. She banged the piano keys hard. After that it was quiet. I was thinking about something else.'

'She hasn't been dead long at all,' Doc said. He had been a physician most of his life but he hadn't lost empathy in the face of tragedy. Looking at him, Tony saw what Alex had often pointed out, an image of himself in his sixties; tall, straight-backed, his dark blond hair turned grey but still thick and wavy, and the same dark blue eyes.

Tony gave all his attention to Alex. He could almost see her thoughts. She shook her head and said, 'I wandered around out there while she died.'

29

'Best not think about that,' he said. 'There was nothing you could have done.'

His father produced his own phone. 'I need to call the police.'

Three

Soft-soled shoes squeaked on tiles in the vestibule.

'Thank goodness,' Alex said.

'If it's the ambulance they'll have to stand down until the police say otherwise,' Doc told her.

Alex breathed out loudly. The old church seemed to press in on her. Sunlight caught the very tops of the single stained- glass window and dappled incongruous cheery colors on the girl's body, her pale face. That wasn't right, bright chips like a kaleidoscope frame had no place here and now.

'Hello!' A male voice accompanied the arrival of a young man with hair as dark and curly as Alex's, although Alex's was probably shorter. When he was halfway down the center aisle, he saw them and halted. 'Excuse me,' he said, and changed an empty-looking backpack from one shoulder to the other. 'I didn't expect anyone else to be here, except . . . I mean . . .' He frowned and searched around the church.

Doc glanced from Tony to Alex and went to meet the newcomer who could be in his late teens or early twenties. His angular frame suggested he might still be a teenager, although a very tall one.

'Doc James Harrison,' Doc said, walking with his hand outstretched. 'I'm the local GP. We haven't met.'

'Elyan Quillam,' the young man said, close enough now for Alex to see intelligent dark eyes and a thin but classically handsome face.

Doc had paused. 'The pianist?' he asked.

'Yes. Pleased to meet you.' No awkward side-ways looks or heightened color here, or self-consciousness – or arrogance. 'We're staying at Green Friday for a few months. We got here a fortnight ago.'

Alex couldn't move. The body on the cold stone seemed as if it must be visible to everyone, but this Elyan couldn't see it from where he was and she desperately wanted him to leave before he did. He seemed more inclined to look around as if he were searching for something.

'That's Hugh Rhys's place,' Tony said. He looked as edgy as Alex felt. 'The house he bought above the Dimple. The Dimple is the local nick-name for the oval valley you look down at when you leave Green Friday. He said he was leasing it to a family for the summer. Hope you're comfortable there.' The Dimple was a shallow indentation in a nearby hill where both Tony and Alex had homes.

Elyan nodded and gave a lopsided smile.

Doc seemed momentarily awestruck. 'I heard you at Wigmore Hall – wonderful.' He studied Elyan. 'I didn't realize you were the people taking Hugh's house. You must lead a very busy

31

life. Green Friday will be a nice retreat for you. Beautiful grounds.'

The body. Alex's eyes flickered to the dead girl. *Where's the ambulance? Where are the police?* Her head ached. Only then did the thought of Detective Chief Inspector Dan O'Reilly come seeping in. No, not this time, not again. The first time she'd met him it had been over a dead body, frozen in the snow on a hill outside the village. She gritted her teeth. Then there had been the next time . . .

'I'll wait here for my sister,' Elyan said, walking in Tony's direction.

He went around Doc and headed straight for the piano, but from the opposite side from where his sister lay. 'Look at this—' he picked up the thermos – 'I think this has been around since primary school.' His lips started to move without sound. The glisten of congealing blood had caught his attention.

With a hand on the side of the piano, he stared at the darkening trickle, and took a slow step forward, and another.

'Best not look, Elyan,' Doc said. 'Come and sit over here.'

If the boy heard him he showed no sign. Another step, deliberately avoiding touching his sister's clothing with a shoe, and he stood looking down at the woman's lifeless face.

'Laura,' he whispered, then yelled, 'Laura. Laura. Get up. What's the matter with you? Laura.' His voice broke and he reached out as if he would try to haul her into his arms.

'We're waiting for the ambulance,' Tony said,

and more softly, 'and the police.' He went to the boy and rested a hand on his shoulder.

'It's Laura,' Elyan said vaguely, thudding to his knees.

'Best leave her be,' Tony said. He crouched beside him. 'Come and sit down. Help will be here soon.'

'No!'

They both stood up together, Elyan crashing into Tony who held the boy close as if he were a hurt child. 'I'm not going to tell you anything's okay. It's not. Just hang in with us. Please.' Tony, solid and familiar, his dark blond hair too long, as usual, his big, capable hands gripping Elyan's shoulders, sharing his own vitality and strength when the other sagged, spent and crushed . . . and stunned.

'My sister,' Elyan said. 'She's my sister. She isn't always well, but she was fine earlier.' He wrenched away, his face white and still, his eyes huge. 'Who did this? Someone's hurt her. I was going to play for her but I got late. Oh, my god, I'm late. I should have been here.'

Alex found her voice. 'This is not your fault. It's an accident.' It had to be an accident.

'Damn it all,' Elyan shouted. 'One more time. They always want me to practice one more time. If it's not Sebastian, it's my father. They won't let me live my life. Percy wanted me to . . . I hate him. I hate them all. She's been so quiet and they didn't care. Most days she doesn't leave her room. She said she'd . . . she said she would become so silent she'd disappear. They never said anything about it. But last night she was

33

happy. She called me and said she wanted to come here and sing. But . . . Why didn't I just walk out and come when I said I would? Minutes make all the difference in how an accident turns out. She's got a heart condition. Seconds could make a difference.'

And she could have made that difference, Alex thought.

Heavy shoes with loud heels clipped on stone and two uniformed police officers approached quickly from the front of the building. Two other men and a woman followed dressed in something resembling surgical scrubs. Alex saw a folded gurney and large bags of equipment.

'What have we got?' one of the men said.

'We need to keep you back till we've had a look,' a young, blond policeman said. 'Where is it?' he asked of no one in particular.

'It?' Elyan shouted. '*She*, you moron.' He clapped his hands over his face and staggered backward. Tony guided him to the nearest choir riser.

'I'm Constable Bendix,' the copper said. 'This is my partner, Constable Wicks. Sorry if I said the wrong thing.' He directed this to Elyan's hunched over form.

'Here,' Doc said, leading the way. 'By the piano.'

Tony sat beside Elyan and put an arm around his shoulders. The young man shook visibly.

Bendix bent over the body, felt for the pulse they all knew he wouldn't find. He looked around the area. 'Who found the body?'

Elyan moaned and when he lifted his face his eyes didn't seem to look at anything.

'I did,' Alex said. Her eyes met Tony's and he gave an encouraging little smile. 'She was like this. I called for the ambulance. I knew it was bad but I didn't think she was dead.' Was that true? Or had she just not wanted to believe the woman might be dead?

'I've got to call our family,' Elyan said, fumbling for his mobile. 'They need to come.' He patted his pockets with a shaky hand.

'That's not a good idea, son,' Bendix said. 'Leave everything to us. The fewer people disturbing the scene, the better. They'll want everything as it is.'

Alex didn't need to ask who 'they' were but she could hope for fresh faces, as much as she'd come to respect O'Reilly.

An accident, she kept reminding herself. She was overreacting. They didn't need detectives for an accidental death.

They were told to stay where they were and the two policemen withdrew a distance. The ambulance crew continued to hover in the aisle.

Doc paced, glancing frequently at Elyan who looked close to collapse. He pointed to his sister and struggled to speak.

'Look at her mouth.' He got out at last. 'That color. It's happened before. Something to do with her heart. She had a shock, that's what happened. I don't believe she just fell over. You don't hit hard enough to do that just by falling over and bumping your head. Someone pushed her and her heart gave out. I . . . I . . . . someone wanted her out of the way.'

'No, no,' Tony said, avoiding his father's stare.

'She could have fallen very hard, especially if she'd passed out. I think she hit the music stand and it's very solid.'

The police came back before Alex thought they should. They couldn't have explained much in that length of time. It couldn't be that it was all going to start over again, the watching, the questions, the suspicion.

'There's a team on the way. The divisional surgeon will be along shortly, too. SOCOs on their way.'

'Why?' Alex couldn't stop herself from going to Bendix and looking up into his fresh young face. 'Why the scene of the crime people? This is an accident. She fell and hit her head.'

'What sort of team?' Elyan's voice was dull and he didn't attempt to get to his feet.

'Nothing to worry about, sir. We just have to take all possibilities into consideration. This is the protocol they follow when there's anything . . . unusual.'

'Who's coming?' Alex said. She couldn't stand wondering. *Unusual meant they didn't believe they were definitely dealing with an accidental death.* 'It's okay if you tell us the names of the people coming, isn't it?'

The two officers glanced at one another. 'Detectives, miss. They'd like all of you to stay here, please.'

'Who are they?'

'You wouldn't know them. Detective Chief Inspector O'Reilly and his partner. They said he's familiar with the area.'

'Oh, my god,' Tony said.

Four

Dr Molly Lewis had bustled into St Aldwyn's with photographers and SOCO in her wake. The latter waited at a respectful distance while the police surgeon started her preliminary examination. The photographers and videographer wasted no time before setting up lights while a woman worked with recording equipment.

Alex had never been more grateful to get her marching orders. With the exception of the professionals, apart from Constable Bendix who had been appointed as keeper of the civilians, they were all sent to the rectory to wait for Detective Chief Inspector Dan O'Reilly and his partner. Unless something had changed in the past couple of months, that would be the prickly Detective Sergeant Bill Lamb. Constable Wicks had tied Katie and Bogie to the metal ring in a concrete block near the side door where they'd been waiting, which didn't make Alex happy.

Entering the rectory vestibule with its worn black- and white-tiled floor felt unpleasantly familiar. Alex had not been inside the handsome Victorian house for months and the last visit had been fearsome.

Sybil Davis stood at a distance in the hallway leading to the rest of the house. She held her dachshund, Fred, in her arms and they both looked miserable. She had evidently been told not to interact with her visitors but she raised a hand and gave a small smile.

Bendix pointed the way to the library which seemed more gloomy than Alex remembered. As a schoolgirl she'd come here with Harriet Burke – some years before she retired as a schoolteacher – to use some of the extensive collection of books packed into dark wood, floor-to-ceiling shelves. For a moment Alex felt the anticipation she'd experienced in her early teens when she came into a room that felt like an Aladdin's cave to a young book lover.

When the four of them were seated in sagging tapestry chairs with wooden arms, arranged around a pink-mottled, white, marble fireplace, they waited in awkward silence. A grandfather clock ticked sonorously in one corner. The scent of dust toasted on old radiators all but beat out liberal applications of lavender wax that shone on every wooden surface. Alex shifted her forefinger on the arm of her chair, leaving a smear behind.

She put her hands in her lap.

Constable Bendix cleared his throat. 'Sorry about this. They'll get to you soon enough.' Again his throat ground and he added a sharp cough. 'A nice cuppa wouldn't go amiss, I should think. Can't do any harm if I pop out to the kitchen and ask the vicar's wife if she can manage that.'

'No harm,' Tony said amid the others' polite murmurs.

'Right then.' And Bendix was off with a sigh of relief. He wasn't enjoying himself much more than they were.

'How are you feeling?' Doc asked Elyan,

leaning toward him. 'Say the word and I'll have them find a place for you to rest.'

'I don't want to rest,' Elyan said sharply and turned red. 'Sorry. Why won't they let me get my father, at least? He should know.' His sneak-ered feet jiggled. He wore a navy-blue sweatshirt and jeans like a million other teenage boys but he had a presence that set him apart.

'I wouldn't be surprised if the police have already spoken to him.' Tony craned around to look through the leaded windowpanes. The glass was old enough to distort the view in places.

'You can't see the dogs from here,' Alex told him, reading his thoughts. 'They'll be okay.'

He didn't look completely convinced but he said to Elyan, 'The cops like a chance to interview people alone, if they can. Before there's any chance to compare stories with someone else.'

'We're not alone now,' Elyan said. 'We could be talking about anything.'

'True, but we were already together before anyone else got there.'

'They're wasting time. We're no threat to anyone but someone out there is. I'm not staying here.'

Elyan made to get up but Doc touched his arm and he slumped in the chair again. 'If there was something that could change what's happened, we'd all go and do it. We can't. And we'll only slow things down if they have to come looking for us because we've wandered off.'

Joyful yips heralded the arrival of Alex and Tony's dogs.

'Oh, my,' Alex muttered.

Tony opened his arms to the dogs. 'Well, at

39

least we weren't the ones who tied slip knots.'

A restrained titter faded with the arrival of Harriet Burke, her nimbus of white hair awry and the usually faint pink of her cheeks considerably heightened.

'What on earth is going on?' she said. Harriet never minced words. 'Katie and Bogie were tied up outside the church and there are all sorts of those officious police types marching around out there. There was so much coming and going I thought I should come and see if I could be useful. Elyan, I didn't expect to find you here!'

'Laura's dead,' Elyan announced loudly. His voice broke when he added, 'In the church. They won't let me leave and I've got to go and be with her. She's on her own with strangers.' He looked close to tears and spread a hand above his eyes.

Harriet looked around at the rest of them with disbelief. Doc shook his head slightly and stood up to give her his chair. She sat down on the edge, her brown brogues incongruously large at the end of thin legs clad in heavy, tan-colored tights. Usually completely in command in any situation, she gave an impression of having shrunk inside her green twinset and heavy tweed skirt. 'Yesterday,' she said quietly. 'It was only yesterday the three of you came in for tea. Your sister is Laura, the blond girl?'

Elyan nodded.

'We met yesterday,' Harriet said, her voice breathy. 'And the other girl was—'

'Annie, my girlfriend.' He rubbed his eyes. 'I wish she was here – but I'm glad she's gone back. Stupid, I sound stupid.'

'Not to me,' Tony said. Against an open-necked white shirt, he already looked tanned from working outside with animals. 'I'd want the one I trusted most to understand how I felt, too – at a time like this.' He looked at Alex and she gave a little smile. They did trust each other. Too often she took that for granted.

Heavy shoes came slowly in their direction and Bendix appeared, carefully balancing a tray of teacups, saucers and a large teapot. Sybil hurried in behind him, set down biscuits, sugar and milk and scurried out again.

'What are we likely to say that Sybil shouldn't hear?' Alex said, her temper fraying.

'Just following protocol, miss,' Bendix said, lifting the teapot. He paused with the floral pot held by spout and handle and frowned first at the dogs, then at Harriet with Doc standing at her shoulder. 'No one's supposed to be hearing what's said here until—'

'The dogs aren't gossips,' Harriet said with a straight face. She was renowned for her quick powers of recovery and ability to throw any opposition off balance.

'It was you I had in mind, er—'

'Harriet Burke. Miss. I live on Pond Street with my sister Mary. At Leaves of Comfort. Silly name for a perfectly good tea shop but Mary would have it.'

If she allowed the laugh she felt bubbling up, Alex knew it would come out in a hysterical series of squeaks. She put a fist to her mouth.

'Who tied these dogs up anyway?' Harriet said. 'I knew Tony and Alex wouldn't do it. Someone should be spoken to about cruelty to animals. I won't have tea, thanks just the same. We just had some. Where would you like me to take the dogs? We'd have them at ours but the cats might torture them.'

'They're too much for you,' Tony said.

'I'd like you to stay, Miss Burke,' Bendix interjected. 'Just until the chief inspector says it's all right for you to go.'

Harriet's chin came up. 'Not Dan O'Reilly? Is he coming?' Her face had relaxed and she smiled happily. 'It's been too long since he was here. Mary and I miss him. Such a nice man.'

'He only came before because—'

'Of course.' Harriet reached for a biscuit. 'I wasn't thinking. He only comes if there's a murder but he is good company and ever so interesting.' She checked both sides of the biscuit and put it in the pocket of her cardigan. 'Shop bought, but Oliver won't mind. First cat I ever had who was partial to biscuits and cake.'

'I'll call my assistant, Radhika, Constable Bendix,' Tony said. 'You can hand the dogs over at the door and she'll take them to the Black Dog. They feel at home there.'

'Murder?' Harriet asked in an unnaturally loud voice. 'Has there been another murder?'

Bendix puffed up his cheeks. He had the look of a man who had lost control and didn't have an alternate plan.

'Oh, Elyan, you poor boy. What am I thinking of, prattling on about nothing. I got confused by all the fuss and noise. Tell me your dear sister hasn't been . . . well, you know. She was so quiet

42

yesterday.' Harriet took Elyan's closest hand in her near transparent fingers.

Elyan had sunk even deeper into his chair and lost the last vestiges of color from his face. He stared at the floor and said nothing.

'Will someone tell me what's going on?' Harriet said.

'Constable,' Alex said, 'this young man has had a terrible shock and so have the rest of us. He needs to go home and it won't do for any of us to stay here like this. The vicar must need his library – this is his study, too.'

'Some situations take precedence, miss. Anyway, the vicar isn't here.'

Alex could see the man wouldn't bend.

'I should think Reverend Ivor would want to go over to the church under the circumstances,' Harriet announced.

Bendix let out a long, exasperated sigh. 'His missus says he left yesterday. Went to see his bishop. He won't be back till Saturday so why don't we all just settle down and make it easier on everyone?'

'On you, you mean,' Tony said, not sounding at all like himself. 'I've got appointments and I'm sure my father does, too. Keeping us here is ridiculous.'

The tea was cooling but Alex drank it down while she thought hard. It seemed hours since she'd walked in the peaceful churchyard – and listened to Laura sing.

She went over what had happened, bit by bit. All so unreal.

Then she remembered her disappointment when

43

she realized Laura might not sing again. Her cup hit her saucer with a dangerous clatter. 'That can't be,' she said, getting up and starting toward the door. 'I'm going to talk to Sybil.'

Five

A pre-lunch crowd congregated in the main bar at the Black Dog. Conversation was a good-natured rumble that would go up as the beer went down.

Listening for familiar voices, and especially for anyone mentioning the police activity in the village, Tony and Alex had entered the pub by the back door. His dad came into the kitchen behind them and Tony gave him credit for having wiped the irritation from his face. Their destination was the snug where the door could be closed and the room put off limits to anyone Detective Chief Inspector O'Reilly and his sergeant didn't want around.

'I love 'em all, but we're trying to avoid that lot out there, Mum,' Alex told Lily Duggins. 'Brace yourself. O'Reilly and Lamb are likely to be here shortly. We got a command message from a plod to wait for them in the snug.'

Tony gave all his attention to Lily who had the wide-eyed look of someone anticipating doom. He told her, 'We've been kept hostage in the rectory library for well more than an hour, but apparently our old detective friends have more important fish to fry before they take us out of shackles completely.'

'James?' Lily and Doc James were old friends and enjoyed one another's company in a quiet way. At least, that's what Tony assumed. Perhaps he assumed too much.

'Can we get to the snug by going through the other kitchen, then the restaurant, Lily?' Doc asked. Another part of the building housed nine guestrooms, a restaurant and guest lounge. It also had its own kitchen, and a common wall with the one behind the bar. 'I saw Kev Winslet walking through the graveyard as if he was a frequent visitor there, pretending he wasn't scoping out what was going on, which means he already knows – at least about the police crawling all over the place.'

Lily, a much taller, more statuesque version of Alex, who was a small woman, had the same oval, green eyes and dark hair, although Lily now wore her hair longer and wound up at the back of her head. She hadn't moved her attention from Tony's dad. Her expression said she was expecting bad news. 'Kev's in the bar. I thought he was whispering to his cronies.' Winslet was gamekeeper at the big Derwinter Estate higher in the hills behind both Alex's and Tony's homes. His appetite for curiosity and gossip was legendary. 'Even Major Stroud's showing his face again, hm? Right in the thick of things, he is. Nothing like someone else's bad fortune to take attention away from your own.'

Major Stroud had been through his own brush with the law, even if indirectly, and what to him must be an almost unbearable family shame.

45

Image was everything to the major. Still Alex was glad he had found a way to return to his stomping grounds and the people who were tightly wound into his life – or as tightly as anyone could be.

Doc watched Lily closely. 'It's not good, old thing,' he told her. He wasn't given to tiptoeing around. 'There's been a death in St Aldwyn's. Obviously it should be appropriately investigated. But what I can't believe is that they've already decided it's a case for a serious crimes unit. Let's get to the snug.'

They trooped through a passageway from the pub kitchen, past an expanded area where restaurant meals were prepared, and through a door into the restaurant. There were already diners seated but with Lily in the lead, the group hurried through an archway that would take them back to the bar but went into the snug instead. Lily retrieved an open and closed sign and hung it, closed side out, on a hook facing anyone who might approach.

The instant the door was closed, Lily said, 'Who is it?'

Tony caught his father's eye. 'No one from around here,' Doc said. 'It'll all be in the open soon enough.'

Lily considered that for a moment, then nodded. She was not a woman to press for information. 'You'll want some lunch?'

'There's no hurry.' Tony wasn't hungry and he doubted the others were too interested in food.

'I'll go round and get you some sandwiches in case you find you do want something,' Lily said. 'You might feel like a shot of something?'

'Just coffee, please,' Alex said.

'Make that for three,' Doc said and Tony smiled a little. His father was accustomed to taking charge and making decisions.

Lily left and the three of them sat silently at a round oak table. Alex inclined her head to look at the tapestry cushions on captains' chairs. They needed a good cleaning or replacing.

The door opened and rather than O'Reilly and Lamb, Hugh Rhys who managed the Black Dog for Alex came in. A rangy, muscular man, good-looking and dark-haired with the well-dressed confident air of a country gentleman about him, he stayed on his feet, repeatedly running a hand through curly hair in an uncharacteristically concerned manner.

All eyes were on him but he seemed reluctant to say anything. Despite his Welsh name, he wasn't Welsh, something he'd never explained – if it needed an explanation.

'Is it true?' he said finally, pausing with his feet braced apart. He hitched back his tweed jacket and anchored his hands in his trouser pockets. 'Did something happen to one of them from Green Friday?'

Tony let out a long breath he hadn't known he'd been holding. 'Of course, that's your place. You've got tenants for the summer.'

Several months earlier, unbeknownst to any of them, Hugh had quietly bought Green Friday, an impressive estate left empty by a dwindling old family for years before it went on the market. Where Hugh got the money for such a purchase was the latest source of local speculation. The village became aware of the acquisition when Hugh started hiring contractors to deal with renovations and the supposed cost of what he was doing got larger and more outrageous by the day.

'Hugh,' Alex said. 'You're making me nervous. Sit down, will you?'

He dragged up a chair, turned it backward to the table and sat astride. 'Right, I'm sitting, boss.'

Known for being unshakably polite, this didn't sound like the Hugh they had come to like so much.

'O'Reilly's coming over to talk to us shortly,' Tony said. Hugh puzzled him, most of all because he chose to work as a pub manager. A darn good one, but still.

'What's happened?' Hugh asked. 'How come you three are involved?'

'I was unfortunate enough to find a body,' Alex said softly. 'I wish I hadn't.'

Yet again Hugh raked at his hair. 'I told them this was a good place to spend a summer,' he said. 'I should have known better.'

In the long pause that followed, Tony studied Hugh, a man he'd always liked. His reaction to a shocking death was way off. Did he really care more about whether his tenants would connect him to a tragedy he couldn't have predicted?

'Come on, Hugh,' Doc said. 'This is a good place. Some of us have spent most of our lives here. We've had a run of bad luck, that's all.'

'And we're still having it,' Hugh said explosively. 'By god, this had better not be some scheme he came up with. Half the country doesn't know what's happened here. It'd make a neat enough

48

cover for some other . . . Oh, hell.' He rested his forehead on his hands atop the back of the chair. 'Will you just tell me who it is . . . please?'

Doc frowned, his concern clear, but he shook his head, no.

'Who are you talking about, Hugh. Who is the "he" you're talking about.'

Hugh said, 'Forget it.'

'We're supposed to wait here on our own,' Alex said. 'I feel horrible. This has been a horrible day but you know how O'Reilly is. Any detectives would be the same way. They give the orders, Hugh. Hold on and everyone will know the whole thing. But who did you mean just then? Please, who were you talking about?'

'I don't know anything anymore,' he said. He looked up and shook his head. 'It's not your fault, but if it turns out the way I'm afraid it could, I'll have a lot to say.'

'Oh, Hugh. What are you trying to say? What—'

He pushed away from his chair and walked out before Alex could finish. She looked at Tony and turned up her hands. 'What did that mean? I'm not surprised he feels badly if something awful happened to a tenant in his . . . estate, I suppose. But there's something else there. Am I wrong?'

Tony grasped her hand and kissed her fingers lightly. 'No, darling. You're not wrong, there's something really strange about his reaction. But can we agree not to mention anything about it to the police?'

His father drew his brows down and nodded slowly. 'Absolutely. It's too easy to raise unnecessary suspicion.'

'You're right,' Alex agreed.

'Coffee and sandwiches,' Lily said through the hatch to the back of the bar. 'Ham and cheese. Egg salad. Cheese and tomato. Tuna mayonnaise. Let me know if you want more.'

She got a rousing 'thank you', and withdrew. Lily had a built-in sense of appropriate behavior.

Doc moved the plates and cups from the pass through to the table and sat down again.

'Okay,' Tony said, still holding on to Alex's hand. 'Why did you rush off to see Sybil Davis? Right before Wicks turned up to tell us to come here?'

'I don't want to talk about it.'

'You don't . . .' Now what? 'Why wouldn't you talk about it? To us?'

'Because I don't know what I saw or if I saw anything at all. When you've said something, you can't take it back and I don't want to get someone in trouble they don't deserve. I need to be quiet and think about it. That isn't going to happen yet, so please drop it. When I can think it through and maybe check something out, I'll explain. I promise. Okay?'

Before he could answer, Detective Chief Inspector O'Reilly and Detective Sergeant Bill Lamb came in, closed the door and seated themselves at the table.

'Elyan Quillam's father is on his way back from London,' Dan O'Reilly said. 'No point in wasting time there until he gets home.' His Irish accent was familiar.

'Where's Elyan?' Tony asked. 'I thought you wanted all of us where you could find us easily.'

'None of your business,' Bill Lamb said, in

50

character as usual. His guileless blue eyes belied the brusque voice. He continued to wear his sandy hair in a thick crewcut, but not too short even though it stood straight up.

'We left an officer at the house,' Dan said mildly. 'Elyan's probably passed out by now. Poor kid is shocked and exhausted. He didn't tell anyone in his family what happened and we only gave a bare bones explanation. With an officer sitting watch, it's likely to stay quiet. There's staff wandering around. They're shattered. When we get a call, we'll go back.'

'How have you two been?' Tony asked and thought, *The devil made me say it.*

Lamb glared but O'Reilly nodded, dug out a rumpled bag of sweets and said, 'Same old, same old. Can't complain. Sherbet lemon?'

They all demurred but O'Reilly pulled out one of his favorite sticky yellow sweets, popped it in his mouth and sucked, giving the expected wince when the sharp sherbet exploded.

Tony caught Alex's eye and they grinned. Some things didn't change and that could be comforting.

Lamb went to the hatch and ordered a lime and lemon. O'Reilly said he wanted coffee.

'Now,' O'Reilly said. 'Let's go through it from the beginning.'

For the first time, Tony heard Alex explain what had happened that morning, all the way through. He detested seeing her so deflated and sad. She finished by telling O'Reilly she thought Laura had passed out and hit her head as she fell.

'That's it, then,' Bill Lamb said. 'Case solved by the resident expert. We can all go home.'

51

'Damn, you're a sarcastic bastard,' Tony said.

His father laughed while he piled sandwiches on a small plate.

Scratching at the door got Dan O'Reilly out of his chair immediately. He let Katie in with Bogie a close second. Both dogs waggled to the policeman and when he sat down, fussed around his knees.

'Long memories,' Tony said.

O'Reilly only shrugged but he ruffled the two animals' coats and accepted licks with obvious pleasure.

'You're sure the victim was dead when you found her?' Lamb said to Alex.

'No. Or I wasn't. Not until Doc Harrison got there. She was singing and playing the piano until . . .'

'Until what?' Lamb said.

'I don't know. I walked around the churchyard. I was thinking. I had a lot on my mind.'

'Like what?' Lamb said.

'None of your business,' Tony said and enjoyed it too much to feel childish – or too childish.

'Anything in particular on your mind?' O'Reilly asked, smiling slightly. 'That might have a bearing on the incident?'

Alex hung her head back. 'Nothing like that. I was deciding on a memorial bench for someone special to me. I took a while walking around the graveyard, looking for the right spot. And there were some riders and dogs – I love to watch them. Then I went back to the church. It was quiet and I went inside to see if I could catch whoever had been singing. She had a fabulous, moody voice. A blues voice. I wanted to tell her

52

how much I enjoyed it and that I hoped I'd hear her again.'

A memorial bench, Tony thought. She'd been distant for weeks but he wasn't sure why, unless she was afraid of getting in too deep with him. Was the bench for the little girl she lost? He was fairly sure it was. He'd like to have a child, with her, but there never seemed to be a right moment to talk about it. And now he couldn't imagine ever mentioning the subject to her.

'And you, doctor?' O'Reilly said. 'You decided, what?'

'She was dead. There was a significant blow to the head, behind the left temple. The brass music stand could be involved, but I don't know how heavy it is or whether it would fall over with the impact. It was still standing when I saw it. I don't know what the police surgeon thinks, we didn't speak yet, but I imagine she'll agree we have to wait for the post-mortem.'

Lamb ate sandwiches, one after another.

'We don't expect the results of that before tomorrow, if we're lucky,' O'Reilly said. 'Depends on the backlog. But you didn't get anything else you thought might be interesting? Out of synch?'

Tony's dad looked steadily at O'Reilly, a look his son knew meant that he was making up his mind what should come next. At last he said, 'Let's wait for the surgeon's findings. I can say the young woman was dead when I got there. That she had a significant blow to the head. Anything else needs to wait.'

'He does think something else,' Lamb said, his

53

voice rising. 'You're holding back, doc. What did you see that you thought was off?'

Doc pursed his mouth, shook his head. 'Uh uh. That would be speculation. Just like Dr Lewis, I don't have anything else to give you without substantiation.' He slid back in his chair and crossed his arms. 'I'd like to stand in on the post-mortem, if that's possible.'

O'Reilly was giving Doc a measured look when his own mobile rang. He answered and listened, hung up. 'We need to go,' he told Lamb. 'The rest of you, remember, don't fuel the talk. Keep your own counsel – unless you hear what you think you already know coming from someone who wasn't there. We'll need to speak with each of you.'

Alex put down a cup of coffee that had to be cold. 'If they do tell us something new, what are we supposed to say then?'

'Nothing,' Lamb snapped. 'Come straight to us.'

Six

'Must be nice,' Lamb said. 'Just a little hovel away from home.'

'At your sarcastic best, Bill?'

'Look at it. The driveway's about five miles long.'

Dan grinned. 'Could be two. But that's long enough. Place is beautiful but people who own piles like this have the money, so what?'

'So how does the manager of a local pub own an estate like this?'

The mystery of Hugh Rhys had not eluded Dan. 'We'll find out. But don't get too excited. He won't be the first rich man who opts for a simple life.'

'If he wants it so simple, why the palatial digs?'

Dan drummed his fingers on the console. 'We've got a bit of a balls-up here. Not that it's a surprise. This lot in Folly always spell trouble and a messy case.'

'They get on my wick,' Bill said. 'I honestly think we'd shove the case to someone else if we weren't so damn curious about what they're up to this time.'

He wasn't getting into that discussion. 'It's the contamination of evidence I'm talking about. And not necessarily the physical. They've had nothing but time together. Nothing but time to shine up their *facts*. They're back there now – all cozy and comparing notes. The only one missing is the boy, so keep your ears pinned and your eyes peeled. Comparing their story with his is going to be critical.'

Bill hunkered down in his seat. 'He'd have to say something earth-shattering to be useful.'

'He wasn't there when Alex allegedly fell,' Dan said. 'None of them were. Allegedly.'

'You saw her elbows. Left one was bleeding and she didn't even know it till she pushed up her sleeves after we got there. She should have bruises in other places.'

'Yeah.' Dan wasn't worried about proving Alex had bruises, he had seen the ones on her elbows, and the grazed palms.

The house came into view. A beautiful, angular, many-roofed building of warm gold Cotswold stone. Espaliered pyracantha climbed walls on a large porch, the masses of red berries ablaze in the sun.

'Tennis courts,' Bill said, pointing to the right of the house. 'What do you bet they've got a swimming pool, too?'

'I quite like the black Bentley, myself,' Dan said, and meant it. Behind the Bentley, in the drive that circled in front of the house, a red and white mini, shiny and new as it was, looked as if it should be in some staff parking area.

'Think the Bentley's Quillam Senior's?' Bill scanned the leaded pane windows on the lower floor, some set at odd angles where different segments of the building ducked in to meet one of the recessed walls. There were stained glass brow windows in jewel colors.

'The call I got said Percy Quillam was on his way and should be home by now,' Dan said. 'Park in front of the Bentley or we're likely to get blocked in if someone else comes. You do know we have to step carefully here, don't you?'

As usual, the expression in Bill Lamb's pale blue eyes gave no clue to what he was thinking. 'I know,' he said. 'What are you going to say about the cause of death?'

'That depends. I'll size him up, first. There could be something to be said for holding back, or for the shock value of laying right out what has a good chance of being true. What's the wife's name?'

'Sonia,' Lamb said promptly. He took the parking spot Dan had suggested. 'Then there's a piano teacher called Sebastian Carstens. Sebastian's a poncy name.'

'Is it?' Rising to Bill's goading might please Dan's sergeant but it was a waste of energy. They had different views on more than they agreed about. He pulled out his notebook and leafed through a few pages. 'His little girl is Daisy.'

'Didn't know he had a kid. Do they live here?'

'They live wherever the virtuoso lives. I gather from talking to Maud Meeker on the phone that the only reason any of them bother to live at all is to mollycoddle the prodigy. There's an agent. Italian name I don't remember but he's in London most of the time.'

'Who is Maud Meeker?'

'Housekeeper,' Dan said shortly. 'They're using local casual help for other things. Barbara and Crystal, I think Edie said. Potter twins. We've sat here long enough. Off we go.'

Bill leaned on the window and spread an arm along his seatback. 'This ought to be an accident. Given the way it looks. But you don't think so. Why?'

'If the post-mortem sets me straight, we're out of here,' Dan said. 'Let's leave it at that for now.'

He got out of the unmarked Lexus and walked around the bonnet. By the time Bill slammed his door and Dan started up the front steps beneath a stone-covered porch, a heavy front door had swung open.

A stocky man with gray hair scraped back into a tail at his nape erupted toward them. He looked a bit late 1700s in a knee-length velvet coat, trousers that hugged heavily muscled calves and a gold and black striped cravat tied in a floppy bow and draping over the mostly green coat.

Puffy white sleeves flowed beneath his coat cuffs and he spread his arms like an exotic bird about to take flight. 'Come in, come in,' he boomed. 'Can't get a sensible word out of Elyan and the rest insist they don't know anything. I leave them alone for a few hours and the whole bloody lot falls apart. What's happened? All Sebastian would say was that Laura was taken ill. Where is she? Why is that any business of the police? I'm Percy Quillam, by the way. Elyan's father.'

Not Laura's father?

A broad, curving staircase overshadowed the entry hall. Paintings, all of them rather too dark and ominous-looking for Dan's taste, lined the hall walls and swathed the staircase. The walls themselves were covered in heavily woven gold silk.

Where, Dan wondered, were the flunkies who ought to be hovering?

In a room dominated by a grand piano, where white drapes pulled back from the windows fell in artful puddles on light oak floors as clear and bright as mirrors, Percy waved them toward tapestry couches and chairs in shades of rose and red that Dan assumed were antiques. He had learned the house came furnished and became increasingly interested in Hugh Rhys, the pub manager, since almost everything in sight belonged to him. It was doubtful that big money was to be made betting on dart matches but he wouldn't buy this house, or furnish the place on a pub manager's salary. He hadn't forgotten the man owned a 1939 BMW

58

Frazer Nash either. Any connection between Rhys's finances and the dead girl were unlikely, but they were titillating.

Percy had gone directly to a chinoiserie credenza old enough to show cracks in its pagodas, and lifted the stopper from a decanter. Without asking, he poured liberal measures into three glasses, turned to hand one to each policeman and took his own to a couch close to the gray marble fireplace.

'Sit,' he said, taking a hearty swallow from his own glass. 'Gad, I'm sorry. It's whisky, Macallan. Not bad, but if you'd rather have something else . . .' He let his sentence fade.

Like Dan, Bill muttered nothing in particular and sipped at what was a very tasty single malt. Dan sat and put his glass on a gilded, spindly-legged table. Bill followed suit. Neither of them drank on duty – but there hadn't been an appropriate pause to say as much.

'Your son hasn't given you the details about what happened this morning?'

'My son is apparently too upset to talk to his father. So exhausted, he's sleeping.' Quillam looked disgusted.

Bill produced a notebook from an inside pocket in his jacket and flipped it open. He waited with a pen hovering over the paper.

'Is Laura's mother here?' Dan said. He began to wonder if Percy Quillam was trying to control the situation by keeping all other family members out of the way.

He coughed. 'Audrey, her mother died years ago. While Laura was a small girl. Sonia is my second wife. Elyan's mother.'

59

'Is Mrs Quillam here?'

'She's resting.'

Dan shifted on the couch. 'I'm sure we can cover a great deal with you but we will want to talk with everyone in the household.'

'Why?' Quillam's jaw jutted.

'Because we have questions for them. At least some of them must have interacted with your daughter before she left for the church.'

Color rose in Quillam's cheeks. 'Church?'

'St Aldwyn's in the village. She went there to play the piano and sing.'

The man's eyes bulged. He swallowed, slugged down the rest of his drink and got up to refill his glass. 'I don't know what you're suggesting,' he said. 'Laura doesn't attend church.'

'She used the piano and sang,' Dan said. 'She wasn't attending church.'

'If she wants to play a piano, she need not leave this house to do that.'

'That's what she did today,' Bill told him. 'The woman who found her said your daughter was singing . . .' He looked to Dan for help. 'What was she singing?'

'Jazz. I think Alex said. Blues?'

Quillam rolled his glass back and forth across his forehead. 'Now I see,' he said. 'Defying me as usual. Always defying me. She got sick and I'm not surprised. It's too much for her. They all thought I wouldn't find out and now they don't want to admit they colluded in her nonsense – messing around with that rubbish. They know how I'm going to react. Where is she?'

Dan couldn't make himself believe the man

60

hadn't been told the truth of the situation. He looked at Quillam. A puffed-up, narcissistic tyrant. Master of his own empire and from what Dan had heard, the empire existed only because of a brilliant eighteen-year-old pianist. He supposed others in the household could be nervous at the prospect of telling him the whole story about Laura.

There was no point in pursuing that line of thought, or not unless it came to have bearing on the case.

Dan made up his mind. 'I regret to tell you that your daughter is dead, sir.'

Quillam stared at him, blinked and slid his gaze to Bill Lamb.

'Would you like to have someone with you?' The shock Dan looked at was real. 'Your wife should be here.'

'I don't need anyone. Sonia isn't Laura's mother.' He said it as if he wanted to make sure they understood that point.

Elyan Quillam came into Dan's line of sight from an open door into a shaded corridor. Barefoot, in the blue jeans and navy sweatshirt Dan had seen when he sent him home earlier, the boy carried enough grief for an army. His shoulders hunched, arms crossed tightly, and his reddened eyes were on his father.

'Why was she playing around in a church?' Percy Quillam asked, standing up. 'You knew, didn't you? You encouraged her. None of you helped me make sure Laura didn't do anything stupid. You only pretended to care about what she wanted. You never sought her out or tried to include her at home. Did you think it was funny to pretend to be on her side and encourage her to annoy me? What was it? A joke to make a fool of me behind my back? This will be all over the press – is that what you wanted, Elyan?'

Punching the man would feel so good. 'Sit down, Elyan,' Dan said. 'We are very sorry for your loss, and under such terrible circumstances. Your father has only just found out about Laura's death. He's in shock.'

'We're all in shock,' Elyan muttered. He sat down. 'Why would you say we didn't include her? We did. Annie and I love – loved her. She only wanted to sing, Dad. And she hated it here because she couldn't do that easily like she could in Hampstead.'

'What the hell do you mean, you ungrateful little arse? Everything you are comes from me. Without me, you'd be nothing. No one else would have seen your potential and made sure it was nurtured the way I have. You've had the best. You've got the best. But all you can do is bring trouble by encouraging a silly girl to have ambitions she shouldn't have. Now, just when we're getting ready for the biggest tour of your career to this point, you help stir up negative talk. Don't you know how many people there are who would love to knock you down? How many people do you think are praying you fall so they can take your place?'

'Laura's dead,' Elyan said, rubbing his eyes. 'Don't you get that? Laura died today. I don't give a damn about anything else.'

Percy half-rose but sat down hard again. 'What happened?' Finally his voice had softened, broken. He looked at each of them and back at Elyan. 'Did she have a heart attack? I tried to make sure she got the best care.'

'She was so unhappy,' Elyan said. 'She felt it was the end of her world when she found out we were coming here. Laura was happy where she was, with the friends she'd made. She was comfortable there and everything was familiar. There were places she could go to be with other people who loved what she loved.'

'What places? She didn't go anywhere.'

'That's what you think.' Elyan exhaled for a long time. His eyes had filled with more tears. 'She had people who liked her a lot for who she was . . . herself. Not who she was related to. She'd been excited about something and she was going to tell me. When we came here she wouldn't talk about it. She got very depressed.'

'Are you trying to tell me she killed herself?'

'No!' Fists clenched, Elyan glowered at his father.

Percy didn't seem to notice. 'You tell me everything, boy. Now! Was some man in London sniffing around her, giving her ideas? I want to know who he is.'

Studying his hands in his lap, Elyan said nothing.

'What does Sebastian know about this? And the others? You all knew, didn't you? You all enjoyed thinking you were making a fool out of me. You should have known better. No one makes a fool of me. I get what I want – one way or the other.'

'You're very upset,' Dan said.

'Don't slop over me,' Percy said. 'I'm stronger than that. I'm stronger than any of you. She wasn't strong. She had some sort of turn, didn't she? Look at me and say it, Elyan.'

'I don't know.'

The desperate misery in the boy's face angered Dan. The father was victimizing the son.

'She hit her head,' Elyan said, barely above a whisper. 'Hit it hard. She bled, Dad. She was dead when I got there. Oh, my god, Laura's dead. I can't stay here.'

'Stay where you are, son,' Dan told him. 'We're going to sort this out. You're all trying to cope with something unspeakable. Give yourselves time.'

'Your daughter is in the morgue in Gloucester, Mr Quillam,' Bill said in the ironed flat voice Dan only heard when his sergeant was fighting to keep calm. 'The police surgeon hopes to get to her post-mortem tomorrow.'

Quillam shook his head. 'It had to be her heart. A heart attack made her fall and hit her head. It must have. We'll have to deal with the things that have to be done.'

'Dad.' A rasping came with Elyan's word. He swallowed. 'The police are here because they think Laura may have been killed.'

Seven

The past two days, since she'd been with Dan and Bill in the snug, seemed to stretch back forever. She looked at the bar with genuine affection. Her anchor, that's what the place was.

This was how she loved to see the Black Dog, the way it should look and feel every night. *So why does everything, even the smiles and talk, the music, the warmth, feel wrong, askew?* She had all the questions but none of the answers, Alex thought. Except for the sensation that it was wrong to be happy when Laura Quillam lay dead, and perhaps some very human guilt at being alive, that whatever circumstances were involved had chosen Laura instead of someone else – like Alex.

No word had come from the police since she last saw them. After the telephone call O'Reilly and Lamb had left and neither returned or made contact. Constable Bendix had arrived while the pub was closed and asked to see Alex. He'd told her the chief inspector wanted to remind her to expect questioning. Tony had got the same message, and the rest, she supposed. She decided Dan O'Reilly was subtly keeping them all on edge and off balance.

Coming through the archway from the restaurant, Tony caught her attention instantly. She smiled, partly at the sight of him and partly from relief that he was here. They hadn't seen each other since the previous day.

She kept serving but edged in Tony's direction when he leaned on the bar, his hands clasped loosely together. Too bad she couldn't make her reactions to him match what she wanted to believe; casual comfort, that he wasn't so important in her life.

Too bad she never saw him without liking the way his dark blue eyes settled on her, and his little smile wrinkled at the corners. He was a

65

good-looking man with none of the arrogance so many good-looking men had.

'Anything?' he said. 'Other than chit-chat?'

'Nothing from the police, if that's what you mean. I'd like to be glad but I know we're only waiting for a shoe to drop. Someone died, that's not going away. I think good old Dan O'Reilly and Bill Lamb are playing one of their favorite break-them-down numbers. Waiting to see if – and hoping – we'll break for some reason and go running to them for answers.'

'Are you okay?' Tony asked, searching her face. 'I wanted to come earlier but it's been crazy. Look at me. How are you dealing with what happened?'

Yes, he really was wearing an old olive green sweater with holes where the neckband met the body. And a wrinkled, if clean, brown linen shirt underneath. The collar of the shirt rolled up at the points. Things she liked about Tony Harrison, not that they made much sense, but his casual approach to life felt like something solid and uncompromising. Sometimes he seemed all man, even infuriatingly male, but then the quiet bits came through, the caring bits – and the very grounded, self-confident bits.

'Alex, I asked you a question, love.'

She looked straight at him. The smile she gave felt phony as hell. 'See? I'm holding up very well. Remember, I'm a pro in the FDBD.'

He raised one brow and said, 'FDBD?'

'Finding Dead Bodies Department.'

Far from laughing, she got one of Tony's unmoved stares. He half turned away, one elbow on the bar.

66

'Alex, you don't have to impress me. This could get nasty. I'm not saying it won't get sorted but it's unfortunate you were the one to find the body. And that I was there by the time the police arrived. I doubt if we're some of their favorite people and until they get a solid suspect, we're likely to hear more from them than we want to.'

'Scotch? Or are you in the mood for an Ambler.'

'Ambler sounds good. Make it a pint.' He smiled and it was the genuine variety. 'Thanks to you, I've developed a taste for the stuff. You'll stand on your own two feet no matter what I say. I know that. But I care about you – *you* know *that*. Would it be so terrible to lean on me now and again?'

'I do,' she told him. 'But this is one of those times for both of us to lean a bit. You hold me up and I'll hold you up. If it becomes necessary, which it may not. They haven't clapped either of us in irons yet. Didn't we say we were ready to turn into the local private eyes? Some time ago?'

She pulled his beer and slid the glass across the bar.

'I think we did and I thought we were joking.'

'We had to use our intuition and the solid facts we found out before. I say we do that again if necessary.'

Tony made a noncommittal sound. He took a swallow and nodded across the room. 'Do you have a fire every night? Silly question, I know you do.'

'I like it and so do the customers,' she told him. 'These stone walls are thick. They keep out more heat than you think. We don't bank it at

67

night, just start over when it begins to cool off outside in the afternoon. People expect it.'

He smiled. 'I know I do.'

This was part of her home now. More her home than Lime Tree Lodge up in the Dimple, much as she was glad she'd bought the old house and put so much into it. But here the dark beams were laced with swags of hops in various stages of being dried out, depending on the season, and the Inglenook fireplace with wood stacked in on either side and it felt like safety against any storm. Anyway, Bogie and Katie expected to go there directly when they arrived, give long, satisfied sighs, and curl up on their respective woolen blankets – supplied by Lily.

Most of the time, Mary Burke brought the latest cat, Max, in a canvas shopping cart on wheels. 'If we leave him at home, Oliver might make him miserable,' was her excuse although the rangy tabby, Oliver, was too above the fray to bother with a one-eyed orange interloper resembling a beaten-up boxer – human variety, not dog.

'Look,' Tony said, unconsciously putting a hand over hers. 'Isn't that Elyan Quillam? Going to Harriet and Mary's table? And he's not alone. What the devil's he doing here?'

'I've never seen her before.' The woman with Quillam was medium height with mid-blond, shiny hair pulled loosely back into a cascade of curls. From a distance Alex could only tell she was perhaps early thirties, stylishly dressed in a deep blue dress and very high heels, and had a good figure that leaned toward being voluptuous.

68

Young Quillam bent over the Burke sisters' table, the one always kept free for them, and spoke earnestly into their upturned faces. The ladies looked equally serious and made motions for him and his companion to sit down.

'Good grief, I didn't notice him come in. Why would he be here tonight, of all nights? He may be eighteen and legal, but he should be at home with his family at a time like this. Do you know the woman with him?'

'No. Too old to be his girlfriend.'

'His mother?' Tony suggested.

'Possibly. A stunner. But she looks as if she wishes she were somewhere else.'

Elyan held a chair for his companion and slid into one himself, his back to Alex and Tony, and the three of them continued their conversation with heads close together. The woman sat back, not entering the exchange, and appearing self-conscious.

'I could take my drink over and join them,' Tony said. 'In the interest of local hospitality. And intelligence gathering.'

Alex wiped away her smile with difficulty.

'What?' Tony said. She hadn't covered that smile quickly enough.

'You're funny. Dr Reserved isn't always shy, is he?'

He leaned close and for a moment she thought he would kiss her – which would be very unlike Tony in public. Instead, his gaze skewered her and he said, 'If I need to forget about being reticent, I forget. When I can, I do what needs to be done. Can you think of a reason why Elyan and his friend would come in here to talk to Harriet and Mary?'

'Nope.' She shook her head and swiped at beer splatters with a counter beer cloth proudly stamped, Knights in the Bottom. A souvenir one of the regulars had brought back from a pub tour. 'Can't think of a single reason.'

'Neither can I. But it could be important. So I'll just meander over there.'

'I'll come with you.' She caught Hugh Rhys's attention. 'You okay here on your own? Liz is in the back cutting sandwiches if you need her.' Liz was part-time help who came in when needed.

Staring at Harriet and Mary's table, squint lines at the corners of his eyes, Hugh polished a glass in slow motion. He hadn't heard Alex's question. His mouth pressed together in a tight line.

'Hugh?' She tried again. 'Hold down the fort for a bit, please. Liz is in the back if you need her.'

All she got from him was a brief nod. Hugh's stroppy mood wasn't fading.

She caught up with Tony as he reached the Burkes, Elyan and his friend. 'Hello,' she said with a cheerful smile. 'Can I get you two something to drink, Elyan?'

'I'll get something if we want it,' he said. 'We're not staying long.'

Tony dragged a free chair to the table for Alex, and got one for himself. 'How has it been since yesterday?' he asked Elyan.

The young man took a deep breath. 'How do you think it's been?'

'Rotten,' Alex said, sitting down. 'I can only

70

imagine how rotten. I'm so sorry about your loss. What an awful shock. I can't get over it.'

'This is my mother,' Elyan said. 'Sonia Quillam. We both needed to get out into fresh air. Things are pretty tight at home.'

'And very sad,' Sonia Quillam said in a low but strong voice. Up close, she was beautiful. Golden eyes, smooth, light olive skin and regular features.

'Of course they are,' Alex said. 'I should have brought a drink for myself and I insist you and Elyan have something.' She turned to get Hugh's attention.

Hugh didn't appear to have moved. He continued to watch the group by the fire although he had given up working his way toward wearing a hole in a perfectly good glass with his cloth. Alex beckoned him with a big smile.

Elyan laced his fingers together on the table. She noticed they were long, but more muscular and blunt than the descriptions of pianists suggested. Or should that be, than she imagined a pianist's fingers to be? Alex put a hand on his shoulder. 'Is there anything you need, other than platitudes? I feel useless.'

'So do I,' he responded with no hesitation. 'The world comes belting down around you and you're supposed to feel, what? Anything? I want to cry about every five minutes but it won't bring Laura back. She wasn't supposed to die.'

'No,' Tony said.

She wasn't supposed to die? Alex met Tony's eyes, unsure if he had heard the potential nuance. She couldn't afford to push for Elyan's meaning, not now.

71

'Poor, poor little love,' Sonia Quillam said. 'A bright light, even if things sometimes got dark.' She shifted and colored a little as if embarrassed.

Hugh came to stand beside Alex. 'Get you something, Alex?'

He still sounded overly crisp. 'Yes,' she said, smiling up at him. 'I'll have a Courvoisier. How about you, Elyan? And Sonia.'

'Nothing . . . well, a beer, then. Lager.'

'Anything in particular?' Hugh asked.

'Whatever you suggest. I expect Mother will have a Prosecco. You like that sometimes, don't you?' he said, his eyes on her and filled with concern.

'That would be nice.' She kept her attention on the fire.

'Could you do a half-n-half with Jenever?' Elyan added. 'Mother's favorite plonk since she had a really good holiday in Amsterdam.' Elyan laughed and the relaxing atmosphere was palpable.

His mother smiled. 'Dutch courage, they call it.' She turned her face up and looked hard at Hugh. 'Don't worry. I should have thought. You won't have it.'

'As a matter of fact, I do,' Hugh said and left. Women in particular glanced at him as he passed on his way back to the bar.

Mary and Harriet each had a mostly full sherry glass. The ladies loved their sherry.

'Harvey's?' Alex asked, smiling.

'Only the best,' Harriet said, but her mouth turned sharply down at the corners. 'It's our one weakness.'

'And who do you have with you?' Alex asked, indicating the enclosed shopping trolley Mary often brought with her, and knowing the answer.

'Max,' Mary said. 'Can't leave him there with Oliver. They don't always get along.'

Alex almost laughed at the explanation about the resident cats at Leaves of Comfort. Bogie lay close to the shopping trolley, behaving as if he had no idea a cat was only the thickness of plastic-lined plaid away from him. He would do anything, put up with anything, to keep his place at the fireplace beside the sisters.

Mary unzipped the cart and tipped it toward the table. One gold eye gleamed from the darkness. Max had lost an eye to infection. Tony, with Alex's questionable help, had operated on the then very young cat.

'What were you saying after you arrived?' Mary asked Elyan. She glanced furtively around, reached inside the wheeled bag and gently removed the very healthy and sleek looking Max who went contentedly into Tony's arms.

Turning red, Elyan glanced around and across the room. 'Here comes Hugh with those drinks. They're on me, Alex.'

Rather than argue, she said, 'Thank you,' and let him pay. He needed his masculine pride, and a way to draw attention away from whatever he might have been talking to the sisters about before she and Tony arrived.

'Elyan?' Mary prodded, and Alex wanted to groan.

'We can get to that another time,' Elyan said. 'I'll be over for tea soon. Annie gets back tomorrow. I'll bring her with me. Will you come, Mother?'

Sonia nodded and Alex felt sorry for her. She

73

didn't want to be here but neither did she want to be at home. It wasn't hard to imagine the atmosphere there.

They all gave attention to their drinks.

Harriet regarded him from beneath partly lowered eyelids. 'Annie knows about Laura, does she? How did she take it?'

'Alex, it would be nice if you and Tony came back to the house with us this evening,' Elyan said, as if Harriet hadn't spoken. He smiled at her. 'I've asked Harriet and Mary to come soon, too. For tea.'

He had tried a diversion, but it wasn't subtle. Harriet and Mary nodded anyway and Mary said, 'That will be nice. Thank you.'

'Triple . . . I mean, Mrs Meeker is a fantastic cook. You'll probably think she could use lessons . . .' He laughed and dug into the side of a beer mat with a thumbnail, prying loose a layer of soggy paper. 'I mean, she won't put on the kind of tea you do. But she grew up in Italy. We get a lot of terrific pasta and everything else she makes tastes good to me but, well, there's nothing like English cakes, is there?'

'I don't know about that,' Harriet said, unexpectedly prudent, then ruined her effort by saying, 'but we'll be complimentary, regardless.'

They all drank in silence, listening to the rise and fall of conversation around them. From the game room came the ping and cascading bells of fruit machines. Alex had no idea what was pounding over the audio, but it sounded like hip hop squeezed through an icing bag. Or was that just because she still had cakes on her mind?

74

Max purred audibly, his nose tucked inside the collar of Tony's shirt.

'How's Radhika?' Harriet asked about Tony's Indian clinic assistant. A great favorite in Folly. 'When I heard Bill Lamb was back in the village, well, you know . . .'

'Yes.' Alex grinned and leaned closer to Tony. 'Has the prickly sergeant come calling on Radhika? The only time I ever saw him at a loss for words, or behaving like a human being, was around her. Not that I blame him. She's a love.'

'If he has, she's said nothing about it. But you know how quiet our Radhika is.'

Quiet, beautiful, and able to reduce Bill Lamb to silence. Silence while he watched her like a fine piece of art.

'Bill's got better taste than you might think,' Alex said.

Tony leaned toward Mary. 'We should stay until you're ready for a ride home.' His expression showed discomfort.

'No,' Harriet said. 'Thank you, Tony, but we aren't ready to go yet. And we need the walk home. We have to get in our steps, y'know.'

Tony frowned.

'Our cousin Molly in Florida sent us Fitbits,' Mary said. 'We clip them on somewhere and they tell us how many steps we take each day. We have goals but of course, they're secret.' She dimpled, sending a web of lines across her powdered pink cheeks.

Elyan downed his beer like a seasoned sailor. 'I'll be in to see you,' he told the sisters again.

75

'I should get back. I'll drive you both,' he said to Alex and Tony and pushed back his chair.

'You go on.' Harriet put a hand on Alex's arm and leaned toward her. 'We should talk, though,' she said, too quietly for others to hear. 'I think Elyan has a lot on his mind.' She took the cat back from Tony and gave him to her sister.

Nodding, Alex got out beside Sonia. She went to tell Hugh what she was doing before following the others across the room and out of the main door with the dogs in pursuit.

'We'll take my wheels,' Tony said to her. 'That way Elyan doesn't have to leave again and I can get you home.'

Elyan didn't argue.

When they were alone, Alex said, 'Why are we going to their house? This seems strange.'

He thought so, too, but said, 'I think Elyan wants other people around to lighten things up at home.' The windshield was filthy and it took a couple of minutes for the wipers to wash enough space to see into the tunnels of light from the headlamps.

The drive to Green Friday took them past both Lime Tree Lodge where Alex lived, and his own place which was only minutes away. Both houses were looming hulks in the darkness.

'Thanks for driving me,' Alex said after a long silence. 'My Rover's at home so you're making it easy for me. I don't want to be late in the morning.'

Didn't she feel how much he wanted her with him tonight? Wanted her with him every night? He grimaced in the darkness. If she knew, she managed to hide the fact most of the time. But he'd already asked her to stay at his place when they were through at Green Friday; she had dodged the question.

'The Mini's sweet,' she said, peering ahead at Elyan's little red and white car. 'I'm not sure it's what I would have expected him to drive.'

Tony concentrated on what she was saying. 'No, I don't think so. But people surprise you all the time. Have you ever heard him play?'

She shook her head. 'No. Or I don't think so.'

'I have. He's . . . well, he's amazing. I heard him on a recording at Dad's. When I found out that was him, I was stunned. You don't expect a teenager to have that sort of talent. He's very mature – or so Dad tells me. Dad is loving being able to know him a little. I've never seen my father showing signs of hero-worship before. It's nice in a way.' The Mini turned left into the Green Friday drive and Tony followed. 'Have you been here before?'

'No,' was all Alex responded.

He glanced at her. 'It's pretty spiffy.'

'Mum and I didn't go to many of the "spiffy" places around here,' she said. 'Not when I was growing up.'

Alex rarely mentioned her childhood, or being the child of a single mother who worked hard to keep them both as well as she could.

'I still don't know why Hugh decided to buy it,' he said. 'He's never shown any signs of moving out of his digs at the pub.'

'Have you noticed Hugh's in a funny mood?' she asked. 'Very quiet – distant.'

Tony thought about it. Hugh Rhys could be an odd duck. He didn't fit the role he'd chosen for himself, not that most of them weren't fitting into slightly odd-shaped holes as best they could. 'I suppose. Any idea what's eating him? Has he said anything?'

She didn't answer but leaned forward to watch the curving driveway between mature sycamores on either side. Low lights, set wide apart, gave only a minimal skim of a glow over the wide drive. But then they made another turn and the house came into sight – and the two police cars drawn up outside.

'As always,' Tony said, 'the boys in blue are grinding away at the case whether we notice or not. They certainly don't like to give any hints.'

'They must wish they weren't dealing with Harrison and Duggins again. I wouldn't blame them for being suspicious of us – or pretending they are. Someone pops off in unusual circumstances around here and we show up. Or I do for sure.'

Elyan had pulled in behind one of the cars and leapt from the Mini. He bounded into the house, not even glancing back to see where Alex and Tony were. Sonia followed much more slowly.

'I think we should leave,' Alex said. 'It's awkward, but this obviously isn't a good time.'

'Right. Like I said, I can't figure out why Elyan wanted us here anyway.'

Alex glanced at him. 'I found Laura. You were there, too. Maybe he wanted us to talk to the rest of the family about it.'

'Is this who I think it is?' Tony said, flopping

78

against the back of his seat. Promptly, Katie plunked her front paws on his shoulder and licked his ear. 'Very nice, girl. But sit. Now. Or it'll be the last time you ride outside your crate.'

Alex ducked to watch a dark colored saloon approach from the driveway. A Lexus, dark blue perhaps. 'Oh . . . crud,' she finished and crossed her arms heavily.

'We could just drive out,' Tony said. 'They aren't here to see us.'

O'Reilly's car stopped beside one of the patrol cars and Lamb erupted from behind the wheel, heading straight for Tony and Alex at a rapid pace.

'I could always say I hadn't noticed him,' Tony muttered.

Alex sniggered. 'Running down Lamb wouldn't increase our popularity with the constabulary.'

At a more normal rate, O'Reilly left the Lexus and came in their direction.

'What are you doing here?' Bill Lamb snapped at Tony through the half-open window.

'Casing the joint,' Tony said.

Alex groaned and whispered, '*Tony!*'

O'Reilly came to Alex's side and waited for her to roll down her window. 'Arriving or leaving?' he said pleasantly.

'Probably both,' Alex said. 'Elyan and his mother invited us up but it looks as if this isn't a good time, so we should leave.'

'Might be just as well,' Dan O'Reilly said. 'I'll let them know we didn't think it a good idea for you to come in tonight.' He smiled at her. Light and shadow showed up the scar running along his jaw. She'd never asked him about it and probably never would.

'Good night, then,' Alex said, starting to close the window again.

A policewoman jogged down the front steps and went straight to O'Reilly. 'Mr Quillam isn't having any, guv,' she said. 'Not without—' She frowned toward Alex and fell silent.

'It's okay, Frost,' Bill Lamb called. 'We figured as much. We brought the search warrant.'

Eight

The phone rang before the coffee finished brewing.

Alex turned to him with raised brows. 'Getting a bit late for calls. Who would that be now?'

'Doesn't it say?' Tony smiled. Alex didn't really expect him to know answers to her questions but there were a lot she asked anyway.

'Just a number,' she said, peering at the readout on her kitchen phone. 'Don't recognize it. I'm not answering.'

He was about to tell her she was overly careful when Elyan's voice came over the speaker. 'It's Elyan, Alex. I'd like to—'

She picked up. 'Hello, Elyan. Is everything all right at yours?'

After a pause while she listened, she said, 'Tony's here. Okay if I put you on speaker?'

'Hello Tony,' Elyan's voice came, a trifle

scratchy. 'I got your number from your mother, Alex. Look, I'm brassed off you walked into that.'

'We didn't think we should stay,' Tony said. 'Are they still there?'

Elyan gave a flat laugh. 'I think they've moved in. They haven't said what they're looking for. Dad's having heart attacks. Or temper tantrums, only don't ever tell him I said that.'

'This is another day from hell for all of you,' said Alex.

'I don't know what they're after,' Elyan said, sounding suddenly much younger. 'It's like they think we're guilty of something. Why else would they be going through everything?'

'It's normal,' Tony said, leaning forward. 'They don't know what they're looking for, either.'

'Do you think they decided to do a post-mortem?'

Alex looked at Tony, biting her bottom lip.

'Yes. It's routine with an unexpected or unusual death.' He shook his head slightly. There wasn't a good way to talk about this.

'You and Alex know all about this,' Elyan said, sounding out of breath now. 'Sebastian said you've had experience. What does he mean?'

Tony put a hand over Alex's on the kitchen table. He frowned, thinking.

'I don't know,' Alex said, but he knew from her tone that the question had shocked her.

'We're all going to have to let the police conduct their investigation,' Tony said firmly. 'But we're here for you. Let us know what happens. If it's convenient we'll get there tomorrow. We'd like to meet your family.'

81

Alex turned her hand, threaded their fingers together tightly.

'Call one of us,' Tony said, holding on to her. 'This is always the bad part, the waiting for answers.'

'See,' Elyan said, 'you do know about this sort of thing. Sebastian was right. I'll call you.' He hung up.

Alex stood upright, almost knocking her chair back. 'Have you ever met this Sebastian? Do we know him?'

He shook his head. 'Weird. Although someone could have talked about . . . well, you know.'

The light went out on the coffee pot and Alex turned it off. She filled two mugs and pushed one in front of Tony. From a cupboard she produced a bottle of Irish Cream and dumped a large slug into each of their coffees.

'We won't know anything else tonight,' Tony said. He drank some of the very aromatic coffee. 'This is good. Just what I needed.'

'Me, too.'

'Is there something you want to talk to me about?' The instant the question was in the air, he wished he hadn't asked.

Alex stood beside his shoulder. With her hands wrapped around the mug, she said, 'I'm leaning on you—' she did just that – 'and sometimes I feel so happy. So right. As if I've landed where I belong. I know I'm lucky but the shadows are still there. Tony, why can't it all be more simple?'

He didn't have the answer. 'I know what I want. At least, mostly I know what I want.'

'You do?'

82

With her he never knew if she wanted him to tell her the truth, or gloss over the surface. 'This is my place, here in these hills – with you.' He felt like a diver going off the high board for the first time . . . hitting the water took a very long time.

Very long.

'I'm difficult, aren't I?' she said at last. 'I think I want to be here for good. I know I'd fall apart if you went away and didn't come back.' She massaged the back of his neck, pushed her fingers into his hair. 'That's it, Tony. I'm not any closer than that and if it's not enough, I'll understand – in time.' She kissed the top of his head. 'Get your hair cut. If you can't afford it, I'll lend you the money.'

He wanted to laugh but couldn't. 'Yes, Ms Duggins. I'll do that. Now I should go.'

'I can feel bad stuff coming at us again,' she said quietly. 'Laura's death doesn't leave me for a moment.'

For an instant he'd expected her to say she was convinced they had no future. 'Something like that doesn't just go away.'

He stood up and put an arm around her shoulders, pulled her face against his chest. 'I'm not going anywhere.'

'Can you promise that?' she said, peering up at him. No one would be able to look away from her green eyes.

'Yes.' He rumpled her black curls. 'I'm all done running. Tried and ended up back where I started.'

She took his free hand, held it around her shoulders and made for the door. 'Okay, we'll see how all this works out.' They still carried their coffee.

'I don't like what Elyan's saying about us.'

Walking slowly, she went into the passage leading to the front door. 'We don't really know what he's saying? Or what this Sebastian is saying. It's grim when everything hinges on the outcome of a post-mortem.'

'We're over-thinking this. The girl was already ill. The death was accidental. I'm surprised O'Reilly and Lamb are hanging around. I don't know why they came at all. They must have more urgent cases to deal with.'

'I know. That's why I'm getting paranoid. It's as if they think we've been too close to other serious crimes and eventually they'll manage to pin one on us.'

Tony didn't like to think along those lines. 'Where are the dogs?'

'Where do you think? Asleep on one of the beds.'

He opened his mouth to call Katie.

'Killjoy,' Alex said. 'Let them sleep. Come on, keep me company while we finish our coffee.' She started up the stairs. 'For a start.'

It would be churlish to refuse her.

Nine

'Why is he here?' Sebastian Carstens waved his long, slender hands in the air. A clump of straight, dark hair slid over one side of his black-rimmed glasses, obscuring an eye as efficiently as a patch. 'Percy, you must have called Giglio last night for him to get here at the crack of dawn. Did you think we needed more histrionics, especially now? Wells upset everyone yesterday and that was before . . . well, before. When he went back I thought we were shot of him for a while. He'll hang around for hours, if not days, or I'll eat my hat.'

Elyan cast his eyes to the ceiling where a plaster rosette of cherubs danced, holding hands, around an elegant brass and crystal chandelier. Tiredness weighed so heavily that he only partly heard Sebastian, and even more vaguely thought that Sebastian could compete with any Italian histrionics of the kind he constantly accused Elyan's agent, Wells Giglio.

He curled on a purple and brown striped slipper chair in the living room, alternately squeezing his eyes shut, and opening them wide in an attempt to feel more awake. The gray of dawn still shaded the windows. There had been no sleep for him last night but he'd rather be alone in his room now regardless. He had ignored the pastries Meeker had rushed in on a large plate, and the coffee hadn't done a thing for him.

'Histrionics?' he said, yawning at the same time. 'Is that supposed to be some sort of Italian thing? I don't even know if Giglio is really Italian. He could just have taken drama classes like you, Sebastian.'

Father had been to bed and looked disgustingly fresh. He'd fished out his old scarlet waistcoat embroidered with black roses, and a black velvet jacket. Naturally, the neck cloth (Elyan could only think of the thing in historical terms) was also black – silk.

85

Oh, to say what would actually be fun to say: *The Prince Regent would have envied your sartorial splendor.* 'Father, did the police say anything before they left?'

'You don't have to worry about that,' Percy said with a wave of a hand. 'You need to be practicing. Off you go. The Schumann is almost brilliant. But no time to waste. I'll have Mrs Meeker bring you something calming. You can take a rest in there, too. I don't want you allowing your concentration to be upset. Should I have Mrs Meeker bring something for you, too, Sebastian?'

'I've hardly been to bed and you want me to start practicing?' Elyan sighed. His eyes stung yet again. 'My sister hasn't been dead two days. I don't feel like practicing. That means you can stay with Father, Sebastian. When Wells finally comes down from whatever he thinks he has to do for an hour or so after he arrives, the three of you can talk about my plans. Don't worry about my being here – not that you ever do. While you're about it, decide how quickly we can get back to town. This is not a good place for us, never was and now it's impossible.'

'I shall want Darjeeling, Percy,' Sebastian said, ignoring Elyan. He pulled his already sagging cotton jumper down until it hugged his lean body. 'Nothing added. And nothing added for Elyan, either.' He held up a hand toward his student. 'And you will be practicing today. Percy, Daisy is upset, poor lamb. When she wakes up, have Meeker bring her hot chocolate and some chocolate digestives. Today I want my little one with me. No child should have to go through such tragedy.'

Elyan was more than fond of Sebastian, but any crisis, no matter how small – which this wasn't – brought out this drippy, effete nonsense in the man.

'Let's take some time off,' Elyan said, checking his watch. 'I may try to sleep until Annie comes later. Wells doesn't need a reception committee. I want to think about what's happened. We can't behave as if Laura didn't die. She's lying in some morgue, goddammit!'

His vision blurred and he shot to his feet. Rage and helplessness sent blood pounding to his head and he didn't try to wipe away the tears that came. 'And you shouldn't involve Daisy in what's going on. Of course she'll know Laura has died and she'll be crushed . . . and probably frightened.'

A choked sound came from Sebastian. Elyan stared at him and realized the pain in his eyes wasn't an act although he raised his face to hide the evidence.

Elyan softened his voice. 'They spent a lot of time together. Laura loved her.'

'I think you overestimate your step-sister's ability to love others – unless they provided opportunities for her to do what she enjoyed most.'

Elyan blinked and scrubbed at his eyes to see his father clearly. '*Half*-sister. We share your blood, remember? And "others"? What the fuck does that mean? And what the fuck do you mean by "what she enjoyed most"?'

'Language—'

'Don't preach to me, Father dear. When it suits, you can sound like a stevedore on oral performance enhancers.'

'You want to goad me. You'd like me to hit

you, wouldn't you? You are angry and as usual you take it out on the one who cares about you more than any other.'

Elyan took a step toward his father. 'What did you mean about Laura?'

Percy sighed a long, long sigh, fell into a chair and closed his eyes. 'Don't pretend you didn't make me say this. Laura has always thought only of herself and if she could attract more attention by hurting someone else, she would. The way she hurt you, Elyan.' He opened his eyes and leaned forward. 'There is nothing to be gained by dwelling on that now, but never doubt that your *half*-sister did you harm whenever she could. Many small cuts, my boy, many small cuts. As to the little predilection she thought was secret, well, far be it from me to criticize her weakness.'

'Enough!'

Sebastian's tone swung Elyan around. The man's eyes glittered with rage and this time he pushed his forelock angrily away from his brow.

Percy waved a dismissive hand.

'Don't talk about Laura like that,' Sebastian said. 'She was a dear girl and deserved better than she got. She had no *predilections*, as you put it. You shouldn't have listened to spiteful tales.'

'I gave her everything,' Percy said in a low, controlled voice. 'Most of all I gave her the best care possible.'

'And love?' Sebastian said. 'Did you give her love? Did anyone except perhaps, Mrs Meeker? Elyan is . . . was fond of her but he has his own life. All you cared about was making sure she helped with the picture of your perfect – and

88

perfectly balanced – family. She was a nuisance to you, really, and you must have wished she'd never been born.'

Percy had turned pale. He took out a snowy handkerchief and wiped his face, looking close to tears himself. 'You think you can't be replaced,' he muttered. 'Have a care. And remember, if someone pokes too deep, they may find all sorts of things.'

'Meaning?' Sebastian pulled his slight frame up straight.

The smile Percy gave him turned Elyan's heart. 'Music room,' Percy said. 'Now. We have only six weeks to be ready for Vienna.'

We. Perhaps his father really did think he was the one on the stage wherever it happened to be, inside Elyan's body but controlling him, controlling his hands. And when Elyan stood to take a bow, did Percy put himself there in his son's place?

'I haven't mentioned Laura's death to Daisy yet,' Sebastian said distantly. 'I see no reason for a six-year-old to struggle with that concept. Kindly avoid the subject when she might hear.'

'This is a nightmare and getting worse,' Elyan said. 'How do you imagine we can keep the truth from Daisy? She will look for Laura and ask where she is. What then?'

'Laura is in London,' Sebastian said. He looked ill. 'She has gone up to visit friends—'

'You don't think Daisy is already wondering about the police being here?' Elyan cut him off. 'She saw them come and go yesterday. She's a very astute little girl and she's six, not—'

'Stop it!' Percy said, rousing himself from the

89

morose silence he'd gathered around him. 'You're a fool, Sebastian. A blithering idiot. How long do you think we can keep something this momentous from Daisy? No, I won't be editing what I say for anyone. And before you say I'm callous, I'm very fond of Daisy and want the best for her. She is a member of my household and that's how I think of her.'

Before Sebastian could get out whatever was about to explode from his mouth, Elyan covered the distance between them and slapped his hands on the teacher's shoulders. 'Let's calm down.' He narrowed his eyes at the man, willing him to get the message that they would gain nothing from expecting normal reactions from Percy.

'I want some news.' Sebastian's voice rose higher. 'The police have left us flapping in the wind. How long can it take to do a post-mortem? These people spend their lives doing these things—'

'Don't,' Elyan said, stepping back. 'I can't think about that. When are the police coming back? They must have said something to you, Father?'

'They haven't finished with the house,' Percy said tiredly. 'That O'Reilly fellow said they would need more time and we shouldn't go into Laura's room.'

'Annie will be here around noon,' Elyan said quietly. 'She can't use that room now.' He stopped short of saying Annie should have been given her own room from the beginning. There were plenty of empty bedrooms.

'She should have been stopped from coming but Mrs Meeker will have to deal with that.' Percy frowned deeply. He pressed an intercom on the wall, waited for a woman's voice to answer and said, 'Come in here, please, Meeker.'

He clicked off. 'Where's your mother?'

Elyan let out a shuddering breath. 'I should have thought you'd be the one to know that.' It was a deliberate dig at the connubial bliss his parents almost invariably served chilled, but he was beyond sheltering his feelings.

'Why don't you and Sebastian run along now?' Percy said.

Elyan could feel how badly the man wanted his son out of the way. 'I'm not four, Father. I don't have to be told to run along and play.' He shook his head and grinned at his own weak joke.

Rather than Mrs Meeker, it was Sonia who came into the room. She wore very flattering camel-colored satin lounging pajamas and strappy gold sandals with the high heels she favored, but not a scrap of make-up. Her eyes were puffy. She walked past them all and stood at the window, looking through goat willow branches in full leaf toward a stretch of lawn that sloped down to the swimming pool and the whimsical color-washed bath houses.

'Laura liked the pink and yellow,' she said distantly. 'I told her I couldn't understand why the owner would paint the pool buildings those colors when they're so close to a house like this. Out of place. But she liked them. I shall like them, too, now. When are we leaving?'

Her loose, gold curls were natural and fell in ringlets about her shoulders. Usually, she pulled them back, or somehow kept them away from her face.

'We're not leaving,' Percy said. 'Use your head, Sonia. How would it look if we packed up right after Laura's death?'

'How would it look? You make it sound as if we had something to do with what's happened.'

Sonia's shoulders shook and it was Sebastian who was first to comfort her. He patted her arm and rubbed the middle of her back. 'There, there, old thing. This is horrible. We've got to pull together or fall apart. At least, that's the way I see it.'

She nodded and snuffled.

'You wanted something, Mr Quillam?' Mrs Meeker, silent as ever in her black pumps with rubber soles and heels, came only far enough into the room to see Percy. Her face was another showing signs of distress.

'Darjeeling for Sebastian,' Percy said. 'And Elyan.'

'Where's Daisy?' Sebastian swung away from Sonia and went to Mrs Meeker. 'Where is she? Did she come down? She always finds her way to the kitchen. She's not to be alone.'

'Upstairs with Wells,' Mrs Meeker said. Amazingly, her pale lower lip trembled and she wound her hands together. Gray hair, in a stylishly cut gray bob, turned under below ear level. Her arched brows were still black, her eyes brown and unremarkable but for their natural brightness. Elyan had often wished he dare ask about Mr Meeker. The woman was tall and good-looking in an austere way. She had also always been an ally when Elyan needed to negotiate his way through the intricacies of the Quillam household.

'You do all know what will happen if they decide

92

Laura was murdered, don't you?' Sonia said. She turned around, her face in shadow with the light behind her. 'They'll take each one of us apart. Wells as well, of course. He was here that day. They will already have decided one of us did something to Laura – if it wasn't an accident.'

'Shut up,' Percy snapped. 'Why have you never learned to filter these errant thoughts of yours? Of course it was an accident.'

She took a few steps toward him and held out a hand. 'Be kind for once, Percy,' she said, her eyes filling with tears. 'Whatever you've been told about me isn't true. I gave up everything for you. Even my violin. I hardly ever play. Why don't you believe how much this family means to me?'

'Can we keep this about Laura,' Elyan said. He detested these outbursts between his parents, outbursts he had never understood. He got up and went to Sebastian who still faced the window, his head bowed. 'This is one time when we have to stop thinking about ourselves. Only about ourselves, I mean. We're upset – all of us – but we don't have to let that make us stupid.'

Rather than the expected growl of anger, his father said, 'Say what you mean, boy? Come on, speak up.'

'Right you are. Let's be plain. We have to use our heads. This village has a weird history and getting more so. I'm working on digging up anything we might want to know. Mother, of course I don't think Laura was murdered. But in case I'm wrong, you shouldn't be so quick to close the list of suspects.'

Ten

One of the benefits of not living in the village proper, or close enough to the road for someone driving by to see, was that an additional vehicle in her driveway overnight didn't usually become the subject of gossip.

Not that Alex really cared. But old inhibitions could be reflexive.

Trying to make as little noise as possible on the gravel in front of the house, she returned to the Range Rover with another armload of supplies to take down the hill. All of this, the ordinary stuff of living and working here, made her happy. When she first got up that morning, early wisps of gray wove through treetops on the wooded areas of the hillside between the Dimple, and Folly at the bottom. The strings of colored lights, which she kept draped around the forecourt throughout the year at the Black Dog, were still visible.

Already the misty ribbons had unthreaded and slipped away. Sun, still pale but with the promise of warmth, flicked silver sequins across the lake in the village green and with each moment, Alex's pub lights were harder to pick out from up here.

Fields rose gently over hills behind the village, divided by endless hedgerows and drystone walls. Copses of trees huddled, some tall, some stubby, like lonely guard squadrons.

There it was again, the emptiness picking at the

94

edges of the confidence she had worked so hard to make real. It *was* real – sometimes. The past few days had caught her off guard. Of late, little Lily who had also been real to her, but who couldn't live to run down this hill, or play on the green, was a visible child in her mind and increasingly vivid. Most frequently Alex saw the turn of a head, dark curly hair tossed around while she ran. Always she ran away and they did not touch. Would she have been a dolly and miniature pram girl, or a 'watch me jump out of this tree and break my leg' girl? Quiet or boisterous? Would she love books as Alex did? Would she want to read the many volumes, most of them collectible, of classic children's stories Alex had made a hobby – perhaps an obsession – of collecting?

She hadn't changed, she thought. Not really. Down deep and sometimes not so deeply, she wanted to love and be loved, to watch children grow and know they were her own.

Damn, was it the feelings she had for Tony that turned her into this maudlin creature she hardly recognized? Did she actually love him? Alex almost laughed aloud. Could she even think of reducing the unsettled issues of her life to simple questions of loving or not loving a man?

Last night had caused this, the way she felt about him when they were together. He made her feel happy, complete, but when dawn came, either the light of day or the clearing of her mind, she didn't know anymore.

And whether she faced it or not, he had never told her what he felt for her, truly felt. He'd like to be with her, he said. That didn't cover all the

95

things she needed to know before she risked trusting another man.

That miniature girl was dead. And she, so briefly a mother, was reacting to the reality of life and death and the human inability to hold on to whatever seemed to be happiness – if only for a moment.

Bogie sat at her feet, looking up into her face. He didn't make a sound, didn't move, just sat there and waited. 'Hey, boy,' she said quietly. 'My buddy, that's what you are. We'd better get going and hope we don't wake Tony. He works too hard. But we need to move on with our day.'

She lifted her newly-acquired and prized second-hand bike – dark red – from where it leaned on the side of the car, onto its rack at the back of her vehicle. Her helmet, also red, was already on the back seat with the big strap-on basket for Bogie. Her intention was to put the bike through its paces by going for a ride after lunch, then seeing how she did toiling up the hill to come back home. If that proved too ambitious, she could always coast back down and pick up the Rover. The whole plan could be mostly scuttled if Bogie didn't take to her 'flying hound' idea.

'Are you sneaking out on me, Duggins?'

Tony's voice startled Alex.

Braced against the front door jamb, he grinned when she looked at him. 'Get back in here and make my breakfast, woman.'

'Very funny.' Katie slid outside from behind Tony and joined Bogie in a chase around the front gardens. 'I want to get in early but I wouldn't say no to a coffee – if you're making it.'

'You've got a bike,' he said and put one bare foot down on the gravel before wincing and drawing back. 'You never said anything about a bike.'

Alex pretended to hide her face. 'I was embarrassed. I'm not sure I can still ride one, I haven't for years and years. It was offered on a card at the post office. Darlene Murray behind the counter said it was her daughter's but she never took to it. Remember Darlene's girl, Cynthia? When she was little she used to count out stamps and tear them off the big sheets for her mum when she was selling them. She'd go through the stiff pages in that big folder so carefully to find the right ones. That was years ago. Most of them don't come like that anymore. Don't you think a bike would be convenient around here?'

He studied her. 'Mm. Perhaps. You're a woman of surprises. I've still got my old Raleigh. It was my dad's.' He smirked. 'He keeps telling me it's an antique and will be worth something one day.'

'Good. Keep it safe. We may need the money for my defense.'

His eyebrows rose. 'When you do something bad enough, I'll bail you out anyway.' He hooked a thumb in the direction of the kitchen and disappeared back inside.

When she reached the kitchen she noticed Tony was damp from the shower, his clothes a bit rumpled, and he wore his favorite foot fashion – nothing. He turned the coffee on, gathered a couple of mugs and put out cream and sugar.

'We were up late last night,' he said, giving her a slight smile. 'What's the hurry this morning?

97

You could have used some extra sleep after yesterday.'

'This could be another full day,' she told him. 'Do you think Radhika could fit Bogie in for a claw trim?'

'I'll take him in with me. Now stop changing the subject.' He poured coffee for both of them. 'Take off your coat and sit down.'

'I was going to take the coffee with—'

'Please sit. It might be a good idea to gather up thoughts from yesterday. We haven't gone over it all, not properly. I don't mean we need a point by point but we should be on the same page if we get asked questions.'

'Always so sensible.' She rested a hand briefly on his face, but quickly removed it and sat down. 'Who is helping out at Green Friday – from the village, I mean? That house is big. They must need a couple of extra people. That's usually the first line of intelligence from the inside.'

'You make it sound like a military operation.' He opened a bag of bagels, and chose a plain one. 'I believe you do have the instincts of an investigator. I heard the Potter twins were going into Green Friday. The housekeeper hired them. They probably have professional grounds people.'

'Don't you want butter and jam or something? Cream cheese?'

'I like 'em just like this. And we do need to talk. It won't take long.'

Inside she felt jumpy, nervous. 'Could we talk later? I want to do a couple of things before I go to the Dog.'

'What things?'

'Just things, Tony. That's all. *Things.* Check out the mood in the village. Subtly, of course. See if there are any signs of media.'

'Media . . . I was going to say they don't show up for accidents like this but I'm forgetting who the dead woman's brother is.' Running his hands down his face, he fell back in his chair. 'I wonder how quiet it's been kept so far. All it takes is a word to someone who knows someone.'

'Or can use a phone,' Alex put in. 'How many different versions do you think there are of what happened by now? We've had a lot of chatter among ourselves but no details except for the death. It must have been talked about constantly at the Dog. Probably a whole lot more after we left with the Quillams last night. You can bet everyone knows who was in St Aldwyn's when Laura was found, and they'll have found out the police spent hours at Green Friday last night.'

'It isn't the same as if the girl was known here.'

'I don't see why that makes a difference.'

Tony inclined his head. 'There's a more personal interest in people you know. At least, that's the way it is for some.'

'What did the police see at the church that we didn't?' Alex drank from her mug. Tony seemed determined to minimize what had happened. 'Doc's been closed-mouthed, too, but I saw how he reacted.'

'Dad's not a talker, not about his work,' Tony said. 'But I'm not convinced they saw anything we didn't. The circumstances are bizarre. They could just be trying to get ahead of anything

99

unexpected that shows up. They're being cautious. And the church is still taped off as a crime scene.'

Multiple yips sounded outside the back door to the kitchen and Tony jumped up to let the dogs in. They both sat staring up at the table, their tongues lolling from their mouths, gulping loudly enough to encourage treats. Tony said, 'No. You're getting chubby, the pair of you.'

'I haven't forgotten what Elyan said last night,' Alex told him. 'We do get talked about because of what happened before. We forget sometimes that we'll always be "the ones who found the bodies".'

'Lightning struck more than once in the same place – more or less. But this is different.'

'If Laura died by accident, it's different. But I was still the first one on the scene.' Those horrible scenes jumped into her mind at will and she was helpless to stop them.

'We don't want to go into details, but I think we were side-by-side for . . .' He shook his head. 'Nope, we're not going there, not again.'

'O'Reilly and Lamb didn't stay in Folly again last night,' Alex said. 'That could be a positive. If they don't come back today, we can start breathing again. I hate it that Laura died like that, but for more reasons than one, I want it to be an accident.' She wished this day were over.

'You said Laura was singing blues,' Tony said. 'Elyan was going to play for her. He told us that. I wouldn't have thought he'd do that.'

Neither would Alex. She flattened her hands on the table and pushed upright. 'I can't stand this. I've got to find out what's going on in the village.'

'What was it you wouldn't tell me yesterday?'

100

Bogie was already making motions to go with Alex. 'It was just a flash, something I saw for a few moments.' It could be very important, but if it was, she might hold the key to someone else's fate. She dropped into the chair again, with a thump. 'I'd like to scream. It's all happening again. I do need to talk to you about something I saw, or thought I saw, but it could be nothing. We're bound to be interviewed – I'm surprised they didn't talk to us yesterday except they probably ran out of time and we're hardly flight risks. But you heard O'Reilly say we'd all be interviewed. I'm going to have to speak up.'

'What did you see?'

'I should have gone straight to O'Reilly and told him. But I don't know who it was, not for sure. I sort of guessed later but it's so far-fetched. I knew if I told you, you'd try to make me tell the police right away and I wasn't ready. There.' She crossed her arms but nothing felt settled or even reasonable.

'Alex,' Tony said and he stood up. 'Come on! You can't leave me on the edge like this.'

'All right, all right. While I was in the churchyard, I thought – no, I did see someone walking away from the church. Tallish, I think. A man. I only got a quick dekko at him. He seemed to be heading for the rectory but he moved out of my sight. I thought it was Reverend Ivor. It couldn't have been because he's away. Sybil would have no reason to make something like that up . . . Would she?'

'Have a bit of my bagel.' He held it to her mouth and she automatically took a bite. 'Are you ready yet?'

101

The piece of bagel turned chewy and she swallowed with a gulp. 'I saw that man walking away from the church. Ever since I've tried to reconstruct the time. Remember, I wasn't thinking, not really thinking about the singing. Enjoying it, yes, but I had my mind on other things. But I'm sure it was after the singing had stopped when I saw him. So, was Laura sitting at the piano then, or already passed out, or just standing there?'

'If she was sitting there, she wasn't pushed down. That wouldn't have been how she got the blow to her head. It was too severe.' He scratched Katie's head absently. 'Wouldn't she have cried out? While she was falling or as she hit the music stand or whatever?'

Staring at him, Alex let the possibilities roll over. 'She should have screamed, or shouted. I know I yelled when I fell. That stone floor hurts a lot when you hit it.'

'Back to the man you saw. Are you sure he was coming from the church?'

'The church, I think, yes.' Each time she put the pieces together, the possibilities shifted. 'Unless he was on the other side of the church and walked around to the path, *then* over past the rectory.'

'It could be significant, though,' he said, meeting her eyes. 'I understand why you'd think twice about saying who you thought it was. That's heavy.'

'Tony, I'm saying this to you and only to you for now. Think about it and see if you think I'm completely mad, and remember I thought I was seeing Ivor initially. Ivor's got really red hair!'

Light, sparking off the kitchen taps at the sink, caught his attention and he glanced away. 'This man didn't have red hair?'

'No.' She squinched up her eyes, visualizing. 'I would have seen that but I didn't. We aren't going to say this unless we discuss it first and agree?'

He nodded, then winced. 'That could be a discussion we don't want to have. But we do have to report the sighting.'

Alex looked behind her. She lowered her voice. 'We would have to do a lot of homework before we ever suggested this again.' With both hands on one of his wrists, she said, 'I'm sure I'm wrong but I've thought about Elyan.'

Eleven

'Don't usually see you around the shops this time of day,' Darlene Murray said cheerfully. 'Seems like yesterday my Cynthia was nagging me for that bike.'

'Lunch has died down at the Dog so I decided to practice riding before things get busy again. Don't want to make a spectacle of myself in front of too many people. Bogie likes it, see?' She'd had a hard time waiting all morning for an opportunity to test the village waters for useful whispers, or any whispers at all about what was going on. Concentrating on anything but what she'd said to Tony about Elyan was almost impossible, but she had to carry on.

'I think that dog of yours would like anything so long as he's with you,' Darlene said. 'You rode down from the Dimple? I don't think I'd do that.'

'I drove down and parked this time but I'm going to try the hill on this when I feel confident enough.'

A dark green MG drove by toward the High, coming a little too close to Alex and she jerked the bike from the gutter to the pavement. 'I'm still pretty unsure of myself,' she said, patting Bogie who didn't look at all ruffled.

Darlene was arranging a couple of boxes of local produce, tomatoes, still a bit green, very early peas that would be sweeter now than at any other time, several small punnets of strawberries and some gooseberries. She also had a bucket of tantalizing white and gold daisies, the bunches rubber-banded together. Folly's post office did duty as a bit-of-everything shop but Alex wondered how Darlene made a living even with her merchandising ingenuity.

The pungent scent of the gooseberries made Alex's mouth water. 'I'll take some gooseberries and two tomatoes. I love them green.' As a child she'd frequently got into trouble for picking unripe tomatoes and not leaving enough to ripen the way Lily wanted them to.

Darlene put the tomatoes in a slightly crumpled white bag and rolled the big yellow-green berries in a newspaper cone. Alex looking longingly at the daisies but she needed to perfect the art of bicycle shopping before loading down too much. She paid from a coin purse she carried in her pocket.

'Now what?' Darlene said in a voice that suggested she was enjoying herself. 'You've got Bogie in the basket. He'll squash these.' She had smiling blue eyes in a bony face some would have called very brittle. High cheekbones, a narrow-bridged nose and an uncompromising chin. Her blonde hair held back with a brown velvet headband was her softest feature.

Alex laughed, planted her feet more firmly and held the bike steady. 'I'm not used to this yet.'

'Looks as if he is. And the helmet's very fetching on you, I must say.'

'Down,' Alex told Bogie who had been sitting up like a hood ornament, looking around with what appeared to be a satisfied smirk. With a short chain, Alex had clipped his collar to the basket. He gave her a reproachful glance but scrunched into the bottom of the basket. 'Now stay,' she ordered.

Dubiously, Darlene put Alex's purchases on top of Bogie, who sighed and rolled his eyes toward Alex. When he let the lids droop shut it was a sign of surrender.

Not one word did Darlene say about yesterday, or anything that might have happened yesterday, but Alex hovered, pretending to study merchandise in the single shop window. Eclectic had real meaning here. The post office carried whatever Darlene came by in job lots at the local markets, or from people who stopped by with something they thought she might be interested in selling. Thus the small quantities of fruit and vegetables in front of a rack of newspapers, with several handmade baby hats looped by their ties to a pack of half a dozen colored plastic-covered wire hangers, and hung where they would have to be moved by anyone wanting a paper.

'You had some nice coloring books and crayons,' Alex said, getting desperate to expand the conversation just in case Darlene had heard something. If anything was being said in the village about Laura Quillam's death, the news would reach Holly Street and particularly the post office, in no time.

'I don't think I have any left but I'll look around and let you know. What do you want those for, then?'

No hesitation about asking questions here. 'Um, I thought it would be nice to have something around for when children are in the forecourt or the restaurant.'

Holly Street ran behind the High and friction persisted over the Holly shopkeepers wanting large signage to their establishments at the junction with the High where Holly Street forked away. The shopkeepers on the main street preferred not to draw attention away from their own businesses.

'Any progress with the sign?' Alex asked, feeling only slightly mean for raising the local hot topic of the moment.

Darlene pulled out a copy of the *Telegraph*. She insisted the papers be folded to hide the main news of the day. Her theory was that people wouldn't have the nerve to put a copy back after they'd pulled it from the rack and flattened it to see the headlines. How wrong could you be – but she kept on trying.

'I don't think anyone's much interested in our poor little sign at the moment,' she said. 'Take a look at this.'

'Mystery Surrounds Death of Pianist Elyan Quillam's Sister.'

'Nobody was supposed to say anything and certainly not to the papers?' Alex said and closed her mouth. But it was too late, she'd shown she already knew about the death.

'Oh, Alex,' Darlene said. 'It *was* you there. You're the one who found her. They don't give a name for the person but I hoped this wasn't another of your bodies.'

Your bodies. They weren't *her* bodies. And why did she have to be the one to come upon grisly scenes that shouldn't even be dreamed of in a gentle-looking village like Folly-on-Weir? Repeatedly, her suspicions about Elyan, and telling Tony about them, came back with stomach-turning force. He couldn't have been responsible for his sister's death.

'Was it really bad?' Darlene asked. She crossed her arms and shivered. 'Terrible thing. So young, too. Only twenty-three and she'd already had all that illness. I've seen him, the pianist. Very handsome young man. Did she look like him?'

'No, she didn't.' Alex looked skyward and gave herself a mental kick. All she had to do was be polite and get away, not keep tying herself to Laura Quillam's death. 'I'll take the paper.' She'd rather not, but it would be better to go somewhere quiet and read the article than go back and get the one at the Dog in front of everyone there.

She paid for the paper and rode away with a

jaunty wave that almost landed her – and Bogie – on the rough road.

What would the article say? Darlene had guessed she was the unnamed person written about. Why wouldn't everyone else? They probably already did. Where Holly Street dead-ended, a lane to the right led to a children's play area. It had been started with grand notions of expensive custom-built equipment and finished with two picnic tables, a seesaw, a row of swings and a small roundabout with a red plastic toadstool poking up through its center.

But the grass was kept mowed although few people went there, especially while most children were in school.

Alex got off the bike and pushed it through the gate. Her purchases went on the nearest picnic table and she lifted Bogie from the basket. He raced off to explore at once, ears flapping, stump of a tail wagging and all feet flying.

The table was under an acer with red-gold leaves and Alex was grateful for the shade. She took off the helmet, ruffled her hair and slid to sit on a bench where she could spread the *Telegraph* on the splintery, grey wood tabletop.

The article was horrible. Impersonal yet sensationalized. What did they say, 'If it bleeds, it leads?' Well apart from hooking readers by dropping Elyan's name – and printing a picture of him – they had certainly painted a more or less accurate picture of Laura on the cold stone flags at St Aldwyn's with blood seeping from a head wound. She, Alex, was 'unnamed, first on the scene, the woman who called the police', which

108

she hadn't. Doc had. Who, Alex wondered, had run to the press?

Getting at the personal histories of well-known people must be easy and fast. Elyan's father, Percy Quillam, had first been married to Laura's mother, soprano Audrey, an heiress, who died of a heart condition. Now he was married to Elyan's mother Sonia, once a promising violinist, and had been since shortly after Audrey died. The bones, Alex decided, got well and truly picked. All family members apart from the deceased had close ties to classical music and opera, and with the exception of Elyan's, their careers had come to a halt, including Percy's.

And about all that, Alex thought, she knew very little.

What she hadn't expected to read was that despite there being no final post-mortem report as yet, the police would be asking someone in particular to help with their enquiries into the details surrounding the death. That bit could have been put in to add drama – as if there wasn't already enough.

Barking out his warning pitch, Bogie rushed toward her and she turned around. A thin man was leading a little, dark-haired girl through the gate. The child pointed at Bogie and from the man's reaction, Alex could tell he had only just noticed she was sitting under the acer.

The girl held the man's hand with both of hers and leaned close. Alex noted she was small, her dark hair curly and reaching below her shoulders, and she wore glasses with light, green-flecked frames.

109

To bury her head in the newspaper again or to give a polite greeting, that was the question.

'Good morning.' He raised a hand in a wave, dealing with her dilemma, and carried on toward the swings.

Alex returned the wave and continued to read. This was definitely more about the famous pianist and his conductor father – who had put his own career on hold to concentrate on guiding his son's development – and Percy's (this approached slyly) reputation as an eccentric and a connoisseur of beautiful women, than the death of an unknown young woman, no matter how horrible the circumstances.

A fresh battery of barking broke Alex's concentration and she raised her face to see the man and the child walking toward her.

A tight black turtleneck accentuated his slenderness and as he drew closer, straight dark hair, black-framed glasses and a pallor that suggested he rarely saw daylight, to say nothing of sun, gave an impression of artistic affectation. Alex glanced at the beautiful child in her expensive red raw silk dress and a black angora bolero – more suited to a party than a playground – and filed the twosome away under 'foreign', possibly French and quite likely Parisian.

'Hello,' the man said. Nothing remotely French there. 'Thought we should introduce ourselves since we've invaded your peaceful territory. I'm Sebastian Carstens and this is my daughter, Daisy.'

Alex was taken aback at the approach – at any direct approach from a stranger. 'Hello,' she said, tentatively.

'I'm six and we live with Elyan and his family,' the child said seriously. Her eyes were the same green as her father's. 'Daddy's a pianist, too.'

Sebastian Carstens laughed. It was clear that his daughter delighted him. 'I have the honor of being Elyan Quillam's teacher. Not at all the same thing, I assure you.'

Alex offered her hand and he shook it firmly. 'Alex Duggins,' she said. 'The Black Dog is my place. I'm playing truant. Too nice a day to waste it all.'

'Yes,' the man responded vaguely, his eyes trained above her head as if he had already moved on from his greeting.

Alex wondered if they made a habit of talking to strangers as if they should automatically know who Elyan was, and possibly be impressed. But perhaps that wasn't fair since it had been the little girl who made the personal announcement.

Daisy was very like him; the same slender face – almost too slender for a six-year-old. She was a lovely, feminine version of her handsome father except that there was nothing of his sharp focus in her.

'You own the pub?' he said, as if such a thing were amazing and inappropriate. 'Strange for a woman.' He didn't sound rude, just puzzled.

She almost told him she was also an artist, but why should she feel she needed to justify herself? 'I like it. I never know what a new day will bring. It's perfect for someone who enjoys people.'

'And do you . . . enjoy people?' Once again she got the impression he was trying on a new idea.

111

Alex laughed. She picked up Bogie and sat him on her lap. 'Bogie loves people, too,' she said, looking at Daisy. 'Would you like to stroke him?'

The girl looked at her father, who nodded but managed a slight shrug at the same time. Daisy came to stand beside Alex and lifted a hand to hover over Bogie's head.

'Do you have a dog?' Alex said.

Daisy shook her head, no.

'He likes it if you scratch his head between his ears.'

Bogie turned his head to regard the child who put her hands on her knees, bending a little to stare closely into the dog's face. She made a humming sound.

'He won't bite?' her father said, quietly but with tight anxiety.

Alex shook her head, no, and smiled at him.

'Bogie,' Daisy said in a high voice. 'Good dog, Bogie.' She rubbed between his ears and rested her cheek there, crooning to him.

Alex could feel her dog give great sighs and she couldn't help grinning. 'A natural dog lover,' she said. 'I was just like this with animals at her age. My mother had to take cats back to their owners when I borrowed them.'

Daisy's dark ringlets were soft and shiny, loose, and there were tiny curls at her hairline. Alex swallowed and pressed her lips together. This girl reminded her of the one she saw in her dreams, in her imagination. She touched Daisy's head lightly.

'May I sit with you?' Sebastian asked.

She drew her hand back. 'Of course.' A nasty sensation crawled up her back. A familiar sensation from other moments when she'd had a premonition of something unpleasant lying in wait for her. Was this an opportunity for her to learn more about the Quillams, or a potential trap? She couldn't risk saying the wrong – or incriminating – thing. What could they possibly have to say to each other?

'Go and play on the swings, Daisy,' he said. 'Stay off the other things. You might get hurt. And just rock on the swing, please.'

An overprotective parent, and he had something to say that was not for the child's ears.

Daisy walked away obediently but looked back frequently, more interested in Bogie and what the adults might be about to say than 'rocking' on the swings.

'You're Alex Duggins?' Sebastian said, flicking a gaze at her from behind his glasses. There was nothing soft in those eyes. 'From the church – the one where Laura died?'

Swallowing, Alex held Bogie tighter.

'That was you?' Sebastian Carstens prompted, leaning toward her. He was rigid and his left hand made a fist on the table. 'Wasn't it?' This time he was sharp and demanding.

'But how do you know this is me? There's no name mentioned here.' She tapped the paper and folded it, in half, and in half again, using the time to think. He didn't pose any threat, at least not while his daughter was with him, but for an instant she'd thought he might like to strike her. His mouth was still pressed together in a straight line, the lips pale.

'Elyan knows who you are. We all do now.'

113

'Yes, of course. I'm not from St Aldwyn's, as you put it. I was in the churchyard and decided to go into the church.' She owed him no explanations.

'And decided to find Laura's body?'

'I beg your pardon?' What an outrageous question. 'I found her but that was the last thing I wanted to do. It's a terrible thing.'

'Terrible,' he said with a one-sided smile. 'We all love – loved, Laura. She was a gentle soul. Daisy loves – yes, still loves her to distraction. I think Laura's the closest she's come to a caring mother figure. She doesn't know what happened yet. I don't want it mentioned in front of her until I think she can handle the shock.'

Once again he was imperious. Alex had no doubt she was getting an order but she didn't respond.

'The police kept you together at the rectory afterwards, didn't they? You and your boyfriend? Elyan and the doctor?' Without any change in his expression, he managed to sound condescending, or insolent.

'I can't discuss any details with you,' Alex said. She couldn't understand his manner or the way he was approaching her.

'Sorry to be pushy but it's all in the family. We need explanations. We need to know what happened.'

'I don't know what happened.' She kept Bogie on her lap and knew she drew comfort from him. Daisy's presence on the swing was a relief although why Sebastian would seem threatening to her, Alex couldn't decide.

'You know what I mean. Tell me everything

that happened. Why did you decide to go into the church?'

'Because . . .' No! This sneak attack was an attempt to catch her enough off guard so that she treated him like some sort of official. She started to get up. 'No, Mr Carstens, is it?'

'Sebastian. Everyone calls me Sebastian.'

She doubted that were true. 'I've been instructed not to discuss anything about this case. Perhaps the police would answer your questions. Come on, Bogie.' She put him back in her bicycle basket with her few purchases tucked in around him. He didn't look pleased. 'I must get to work. Goodbye.'

'I'll hope to see you again soon,' he said.

Not if I can help it.

For the briefest instant she thought the glitter in his eyes looked moist. He pressed his lips together.

He stood also and while she buckled on her helmet, watched her face intently. If he was expecting to find some revealing answers there, he must be disappointed.

The weight of Bogie and the groceries in the basket made the bike more difficult to balance but Alex concentrated and started walking toward the gates.

Partway there she paused and looked behind her. Sebastian stood with his back to her, hands in his pocket, watching Daisy.

She raised her shoulders. A coldness tightened her skin and she took a quick inward breath through her teeth. Sebastian was a very slim man, but he was tall, or tall enough, and dark. When he started walking away, walking toward Daisy,

Alex watched him, tightening her grip on the bicycle handlebars.

Seeing bogeymen wherever she looked would have to stop. But there was something familiar about the way he walked.

Twelve

Maud Meeker had the unsettling thought that this house she so hated would be better named Black Friday than Green Friday, and until she got out of the place, for good, every day would be Black Friday.

The kitchen was more than adequate. The owner had spared nothing in his renovations, not that she knew exactly what it had looked like before, but everything had been gutted and designed afresh, very expensively designed.

Modern black sculptures, strategically positioned where, she assumed, they were never supposed to be other than a delightful diversion, got in the way and had no place in any kitchen she had to use. Walls completely tiled with silver tinted glass behaved like distorted mirrors when she moved around and she saw herself from the corner of her eye but faded away when she looked directly at the walls. Stainless steel countertops reminded her of a mortuary, her imagined picture of a mortuary.

Every cabinet had a glass front etched with grassy scenes that continued from one to another. Wheat blowing in the wind, the stalks on one

116

door, the tassels bending toward and sometimes onto the next one. Maize dotted with floating dandelion puffs that plumed like a child's soap bubbles, shooting into the imagined sky above. The gnarled branches of an old apple tree spread from the joint of two corner cabinets.

Maud tried not to look. It could probably win design awards, such things often did, but not in her book. Dark green Scandinavian appliances jarred the senses, but although the Aga cooker matched in color, it alone was enough to make her smile and forgive most of the rest.

At the sound of hammering, almost running footsteps on the polished blond wood floors outside the door, Maud winced. She looked around for an escape route but it was already too late. Wells Giglio of the distinctive walk, and equally distinctive orange suede shoes, pushed his way into the room. His expression remained as soulful and bereft as it had been since, in her dressing gown, she had let him into the house at an ungodly hour that morning. The sight of Wells on the threshold today – before Maud had even had time to shower – had been unbearable.

All this Latin melodrama exhausted her.

'It's the middle of the afternoon and they still haven't come back!' Wells spoke in statements delivered as exclamations. His thick, reddish hair, parted in the center, waved artfully to his ears. Maud knew he was considered good-looking although she couldn't see it herself. These men who struck meaningful poses and demanded center stage made her impatient. An angular face, full, too soft mouth, and dramatically arched

117

eyebrows apparently appealed to women. He always had a female in tow, or he had until . . . She had to stop shying away from details she'd rather forget. Once Wells had decided to pursue Laura, secretly, of course, but not secretly enough for Maud not to know about it, well, then he had given up his bevy of followers. He'd kept them away from the Quillams anyway.

When enough time had passed to make it obvious she didn't intend to reply, he said, 'They went to find out about the post-mortem.' A choking sound momentarily cut him off.

'The police asked them to,' Maud Meeker said. 'It was unexpected, I think – or perhaps not if we'd thought about it.'

She clenched her hands thinking of impersonal people poking at Laura, but waited in silence. Further outbursts would come without prompting.

Tears hung along Wells's lower lashes. 'They shouldn't have let them do it.'

Wordlessly, Maud dropped a capsule into the coffee maker and positioned a cup.

'It's awful,' Wells said. 'How could they allow them to cut her up like that?'

Questions, even pointless ones, needed answers. 'If you're talking about Laura, it has to be done, so I'm told.' She wanted him to go away.

'Of course, I'm talking about Laura.' As often happened, he'd moved on to almost shouting.

Maud watched coffee pour into the cup and said, 'Cream?'

'Whisky.'

She didn't mention that he hadn't had lunch and put a bottle on the counter beside his cup.

'It's raining,' she remarked, while he all but doubled the quantity in his cup with liquor.

'Bloody rain,' Wells said, glancing at the windows. 'Look at that. I was going in the pool. Don't like to swim in the rain. It could thunder. Dear Laura. I miss her already. Oh, my god, what shall I do without her? My one true confidante. The only one I could trust with the truth from my heart. She *was* my heart.'

'She'll be missed by a lot of people,' Maud said. She made coffee for herself, then dithered. She would like to take it to the peace of her room but feared Wells might trail after her.

'Sit with me, Mrs M,' Wells said, sliding onto a stool at the counter. 'I can't bear to be alone. I didn't hear the piano. Why isn't Elyan at the piano practicing?'

'He's probably out meeting Annie.' And it wasn't his business or hers, although she liked Annie and thought she was good for Elyan.

'Annie? The accountant's daughter?' No one sneered quite like Wells. 'Hardly a suitable time for her to be hanging around. What do you think the police are looking for?'

'Looking for?' Awkwardly, she negotiated her way onto another stool and sat with her hands cradling her cup.

'Opening her up like that. She had a heart condition. It wouldn't take slashing her from stem to stern and yanking everything out to decide that.'

Maud pushed her coffee back and forth, watching it come close to slopping over. 'Who went to find out about the examination?' she said, swallowing hard. 'Who did you mean?'

'Percy, of course. And I assume Sebastian since he isn't here. I didn't go.'

'No.'

'Can't stand that sort of thing.'

'I don't think they would be at the post-mortem.' She wished he would leave. Now.

'But they'll be asked if they want to see her again and my nerves just won't take it. My darling girl dead. When I was here the other day, she was full of life. Full of life. She seemed very well – better than I've seen her in ages. Excited even.'

So now Wells was calling Laura his darling girl. From what Laura had said to Maud, and she told Maud everything, she found Wells cloying if fairly well-meaning. There were other things Maud did know, the secrets Laura confided in her. It wasn't always a good thing to share information that could hurt you, or give others power over you.

'Are you sure they haven't called you to say what's been decided?' Wells asked, leaning closer. 'You're very trustworthy, Mrs M. and I'm sure you pride yourself on that, but I was special to Laura, too. She'd want me to know what's going on.'

Maud moved a plate of croissants toward him, and a delicate flowered pot of apricot jam and wispy butter curls heaped on a double rectangular dish with ice cubes in the bottom half.

'What did Percy and Sebastian say to you before they left?' Maud asked.

She got a look that suggested Wells questioned her intelligence. 'How would I have talked to them? They left while I was lying down after my shower. I left town so damned early, I was exhausted. It didn't help to have Daisy galloping in like that, but a sweetie and money for another of those wretched rubber band kits she loves and she was dispatched.'

'Why do you think they went to the post-mortem?'

He frowned and looked toward the rain-drenched windows. 'There was a post-mortem planned. I don't know who said it, but someone did. Perhaps it was Percy. Anyway, they've both gone.'

She didn't consider it his affair that since Daisy was also gone, and Sebastian's car, he must have taken his daughter somewhere. As a surprise, of course. Sebastian was always designing surprises for Daisy. Sebastian was unlikely to take Daisy anywhere near a mortuary.

'I just knew I had to come back down today, you know. Even though there isn't a thing I can say about what happened. I decided I needed to be here in case the police want to speak with me, although I can't imagine why they would. I wouldn't want them to think I was avoiding them.'

He was talking aloud to himself.

Regarding him through narrowed eyes, Maud felt the potential of something slipping into place. Perhaps Wells and Laura had been closer than she thought. Surely Laura hadn't made the mistake of confiding a dangerous detail in Wells.

Maud had been with Laura's mother, Audrey, since before she married Percy in what Maud considered a self-destructive move. When Audrey fell under Percy Quillam's thrall she had been a talented young soprano with a bright future. Percy

121

had taken that from her. Unlike some, Maud was no fool. She knew Percy's so-called adoration of Audrey would never have bloomed had she not been an heiress.

The betrayal of Audrey with Sonia – and few, least of all Maud were fooled that it was otherwise – had started a simmering disgust she kept at bay because she considered it her responsibility to watch and wait, to make sure justice was eventually served. Despite the recent dramatic events, she intended to fulfill what she considered her duty.

'Sonia's a bit of a bitch,' Wells announced abruptly. 'She must be thrilled.'

The croissants had sat on the counter too long but Maud made a show of nibbling thoughtfully at one.

'I mean, there's never enough lovely money for that one and now there will be a fresh windfall into the Quillam coffers.'

'What do you mean?' Maud gave him a blank look.

'Come on, Maud. You know. Laura's trust will happily nestle back in with the rest of what Audrey left to Percy. And it could be that the loving papa has been too free and easy with money for too long. I think he's been worried about money. Why else does he want Elyan booked for everything and anything that comes along. The boy shouldn't be overexposed. He's too young.'

'I wouldn't know about any of that.'

'Hah, I bet you know all about everything, Maud. People talk to you.'

Like you?

'Of course, you know who'll be the most relieved.'

She didn't like the way her stomach was starting to feel. She shook her head, no.

'After Sonia, it would have to be Sebastian. If everything fell apart he'd be nowhere. He wants his cushy situation to continue. There could never be anything quite like it again. Family for Daisy. Privilege. Oh, yes, it will suit his master plan that Percy turns the money spigot on full again. Although . . .' He frowned deeply and poured whisky into his cup without bothering with coffee this time. After a mouthful he said distantly, 'Of course that could have been what he was really after, the bastard.'

Thirteen

Summer rain always lifted Tony's spirits. He grinned, pulling the hood of his Barbour back up and holding onto it. Wind drove the rain – and his hood if he tried to release it. Everything dripped.

Katie didn't like rain at any time of year so it was a good thing she didn't belong to a hunter. Rather than run ahead as she usually did, when it rained she did her best to use Tony as a shield. This evening she managed to trot behind his left heel without too many collisions.

The front car park at the Black Dog looked full and more vehicles were pulled in along the hedgerows and drystone walls. Colored lights along the rooflines shone through misty haloes. In the forecourt, benches had been tipped upside down on top of the tables.

He pushed open the door to the bar and Katie rushed past him. She disappeared in the direction of the fireplace where the Burke sisters were already ensconced at their table. One-eyed orange Max had graduated to Mary's lap where he curled up, apparently oblivious to humans and animals alike.

Live music probably accounted for the crowd. Tony shrugged out of his coat and shook it vigorously. Piano. Jazz. He recognized Bayou something and a distinctly Oscar Peterson sound that brought a broad smile. Almost no conversation interfered with this performance. Whoever Alex had hired was incredibly good, not that she enjoyed jazz so much.

Alex wasn't behind the bar, or circulating among the customers.

The piano stood in what was known as the up-room because it was one step up from the rest of the bar and used primarily by people who wanted a little quieter spot to eat their bar food and talk. Someone had pulled the old upright from its usual spot against a wall and moved it to a more visible spot.

Tony paused, letting his arm fall so the coat trailed on the floor. The jazzman was Elyan Quillam who bowed over the keyboard in a very non concert-like pose.

'I wonder if they all know who they're listening to,' Juste Vidal whispered close to Tony's ear. 'Would his papa approve, do you think?'

124

Tony heard a smile in the man's very French accented English and looked at him, raising a palm. 'How did this happen? His father would be furious, I should think.' He grinned. 'Who is the young lady with him?'

The girl had long, auburn hair and she was lovely in a wholesome way.

'Her name is Annie,' Juste said. 'His girlfriend, I think. I wish he would play all night.'

This theology student studying in Cheltenham to be a minister frequently made unexpected comments. 'So do I,' Tony said. 'Have you seen Alex?'

'She went through to the back a little earlier.'

'Okay.' Rather than walk between pianist and his audience, he would go back outside and use the door into the kitchens from the back car park. 'Any sign of O'Reilly and Lamb?' He hoped not.

'Mmm, no. Perhaps they find no reason to come back.'

'From your lips to God's ears,' Tony said and gave another, broader grin. 'Well, you do have a closer connection than most of us.'

Chuckling and shaking his head as he went, Juste threaded a path between tables to reach the bar.

They were all listening to a virtuoso, a man scarcely past boyhood with a prodigious talent that was not constrained. He played his jazz with absolute assurance and his love for the form made it, and him, magical. Yet he was known to the world for his classical concerts and would, so Tony's father had told him, also be famous for his own compositions, or so it was expected by those with inside knowledge.

Finding Alex felt even more pressing. She had yet to fully explain her reasons for suspecting Elyan of sneaking around the rectory, although Tony doubted she could look at him tonight and hold onto any doubts.

He retraced his steps, pulling on his coat by the time he opened the front door to a ferocious battering of wind and rain. The night was a wild and wonderful one.

Staying close to the building, Tony walked carefully, watching the ground beneath his feet with the aid of ground lights. The path was reduced to mush, clumps of grass surrounded by welling water.

By the time he reached the back of the building, he was moving very slowly and wishing he wore boots.

'You made me a promise. I told you coming to Folly wasn't a great idea, but you insisted. Now you have to stick to your side of the bargain and leave me out of anything to do with your issues.'

The familiar voice, Hugh Rhys's, came from nearby, probably where an overhang shielded the back path from rain for customers. Tony flattened himself to the wall and looked behind him. He needed to retreat, and absolutely quietly.

'That's not what you used to say, Hugh. We wanted each other and you would have done anything for us to be together. All I'm asking for is a little of your time, a little comfort. I still love you. I've never stopped loving you. I'm lonely and I'm afraid.'

A stranger's voice this time, a woman struggling not to cry. A desperate woman.

126

The last thing Tony wanted was to embarrass anyone with his presence.

'I should never have leased Green Friday to you.'

'Don't be like this, Hugh.' Not a stranger's voice, Tony realized. This was Sonia Quillam. And this was the first tiny window into the man's past. Alex treasured Hugh's easy and efficient management of the pub, but she wondered, as Tony did, why Hugh had chosen to bury himself in Folly. He never spoke of family or friends but obviously had considerable means. And he liked his job, that much was obvious.

'Don't worry,' Sonia said. 'I won't give away anything about us.'

'There hasn't been an "us" for a very long time. That was your choice and you made sure there could never be any turning back of the clock. I don't want to think of you being afraid, but I don't see there's any threat to you, Sonia. Your cozy world – and you chose it – is a bit upset and nasty for now. I'm sad for your loss, but why should it make you afraid? From the look of young Elyan, he's coping and he loves that girl in there. The poor dead one's been sick most of her life, I hear. It could have been expected. It'll all settle down, you'll see.'

Tony knew he should move, regardless of any sound he might make. He turned around.

'I'm not safe,' Sonia said. 'Something awful could happen to me.'

'Meaning what? Are you terrified of your own death, now? We all die.'

'Of course we do and it might be a blessing if

127

it came for me now. It might be easier than have them come after me and everything that could mean. I can't be shut away.'

'Who would come after you?' Hugh was silent for moments. 'You can't mean the police.'

'I could become a suspect. They could say I had reasons to want Laura dead.'

Grateful for the sound of rain beating on windows, Tony took long, hurried strides through the mud and didn't stop until he had passed the front of the Dog and reached the inn and restaurant entrance.

He should have thought to get to the kitchens via the restaurant in the first place.

The place was deserted on this side but Elyan still played in the bar and the music filled the building.

'Tony?' Lily came briskly down the stairs. 'Is everything all right?'

He raised his brows. What he'd overheard wouldn't be repeated – except to Alex – but he'd be a liar if he told Lily all was well. 'It will be. I'm looking for Alex. Is she still in the kitchen? I don't feel like going back into the bar to see if she's there now.'

'She went out to drive over and see you. In a hurry. She said you were working late at the clinic.'

'Blast it. And I walked over. I'd better call her.'

'I'm here.' Alex walked into the restaurant and came to stand a few feet from him. 'I went out to get in my Range Rover, but it wasn't a good time.'

He looked at her through narrowed eyes. 'What do you mean?'

Then he knew. He hadn't been the only listener in the dark.

'We can talk about it later,' Alex said. 'I was coming to tell you the reprieve is over. O'Reilly and Lamb are upstairs. They came back a little while ago and took rooms. I think we know what that means.'

Fourteen

'This won't be any simple case,' Dan O'Reilly said, stifling a yawn. The night hadn't been long enough. 'And the boss isn't amused. He's convinced we're missing something in this village. Says it'll be his neck on this one.' Dan sat on the edge of his bed while Bill took the one small, easy chair in the room. Through the mullioned window there was a view across the village green and the pond to the hillside beyond. He had opened one window, thinking some fresh air would help him wake up, but he hadn't expected the stream of cool wind that tossed the flowery curtains. Beyond the green rose the hill where a bizarre crime had first brought him to Folly. The place flooded him with an unsettling mix of emotions he'd rather not study too closely.

Up on that hill, in the shallow valley they called The Dimple, was Alex's house, Lime Tree Lodge, and he wondered if she still lived there when she wasn't staying at her pub . . . and if she lived there alone. Or at Tony Harrison's house.

'Did you hear what I said, guv?' Bill said.

He hadn't and shook his head, no.

'I asked if the boss thinks we haven't had plenty of the same thoughts he's had about this place – and what goes on here?' Bill said. 'Here we are again. Same place, different day – another dead body. But we both know the common denominators.'

The rain had stopped. Keeping company with the wind, early-morning sunshine cut a path into the room. They would have a heavy work day and had agreed to meet here for a quiet chat before breakfast. Dan was hungry now and smells of fresh brewed coffee and sizzling bacon made him salivate. 'Let's eat. With luck Alex is in and we can start our interviews with her. Works best with her to keep the approach casual. I'll invite her to join us for breakfast.'

Bill stood and checked the knot on his tie. 'You treat her with kid gloves. I think you'd be better off if you never had to deal with her again. You're not objective around Alex Duggins.'

There was a lot Dan would take from Bill Lamb because the man had a good and useful mind, but sometimes he went too far.

'Twaddle,' he said, but he didn't laugh. 'Keep your attention on the case – and giving me the support I need. When I need my head examined, I'll see a shrink. And you can add our necks to the boss's if we don't get the right result.'

'We got results in the other Folly cases,' Bill said, shrugging into his jacket.

'We did. But whether we like it or not, little jugs have big ears and you can bet every misstep we took is known to the wrong people.'

130

'Is that why you got the promotion to chief, guv? Because we didn't get results.'

Dan got up and opened the door. 'I don't believe in selective amnesia. And you won't like hearing me say this. We had help.'

Why hadn't she agreed to Tony's suggestion and gone home with him last night. Out there in the car park, in the rain, a bomb had landed in their laps. But she had wanted to think it all through before jumping in with any decisions. They had a digging job to do and she wasn't ready for what they might turn up. She had decided, but was possibly wrong, that she and Tony needed to work through what they had heard, each on their own.

Alex set a pile of plates firmly on the kitchen pass-through to the bar.

'Breakfast in the snug,' Lily said, and she wasn't smiling. 'Sounds anything but cozy to me. Good luck and be careful.'

'Careful?' She heard a crack in her voice. 'Why?'

'Lamb's the one you have to watch. He's good at tying you up in knots and you don't want to give him any ideas.'

'About what?' Alex stared at her mother, puzzled, but Lily only shrugged. 'Come on, Mum. If there's something I'm missing, tell me about it.'

'Just the obvious, really. You've heard him mention how you've been showing up at murder scenes. When he says that, what does it mean to you?'

'He's trying to stir things up, we both know

that. And we don't know if this is another murder. Not for sure.'

'Don't we?' Lily's expression made her meaning clear.

'Have they been served breakfast yet?'

'No. Almost ready.'

Alex gave Lily's arm a squeeze. 'Thanks for caring so much, Mum. I'll just have toast.'

Alex went directly to the snug where O'Reilly and Lamb were waiting for her. They already had coffee. A pot and an empty mug stood ready for her.

'Morning,' Dan said, smiling.

He was an appealing man. 'Good morning,' Alex said. She could never quite get rid of her curiosity about him but doubted she was likely to get any revelations.

'Good morning,' Bill Lamb said. 'We have questions for you – in light of recent discoveries. I know this is convenient to you – meeting here – but if you think you'd prefer to talk away from your place of business, just say the word.'

He gave her one of his pale blue-eyed, unblinking stares and her stomach flipped. Dan shifted abruptly in his seat. His expression had become serious.

'This is good for me,' she said and cleared her throat.

'You don't need a solicitor present. This is informal. But if you do want one and you can't afford—'

'I can afford one and I don't need her, thanks. Unless you're going to charge me with something

132

– like breathing.' Damn, already she was letting him get to her.

'I'll ignore that,' Bill said, but a corner of Dan's mouth tweaked up.

'Did you give in your breakfast order?' She just needed something to say. She'd been unsettled since she'd been asked to come here, now she was jumpy. And she was being silly. *Pull yourself together, Alex.*

'We've dealt with that,' Bill said. 'Let's get on with this. You know the drill – a bit too well, I should think. We'll start from the beginning, the very beginning, but first I've got a few other loose ends to tie up with you.'

She couldn't help a glance at Dan who kept his eyes on his coffee.

'Of course.' She reached for the pot and poured a full mug for herself. 'Fire away.' Careful to keep her hand steady, she added cream.

'When did you first find out the Quillam family would be coming to Folly-on-Weir?'

'I didn't, I mean I heard about them when they got here. My manager, Hugh Rhys, owns Green Friday and he leased the place to them.'

'We know that. It isn't what I asked you.'

She brought her back teeth together. 'Yes. But I did answer your question.'

'Hugh Rhys didn't run the idea past you ahead of time?'

Alex made herself wait a few seconds before saying, 'Why should he? It's none of my business.'

'Are you sure you're okay with us doing this here, Ms Duggins?'

133

He wanted to get her on edge. Well, she'd do her best to disappoint him. 'Do you have the parish hall set up already?' That's what the police had arranged the two previous times a case had brought them here.

'No,' Bill Lamb said, 'but we can take you into Cheltenham till we do get that – or somewhere else – set up in the village.'

'I appreciate how considerate you are. But we're fine here. This is a very quiet time of day for us. Is this because you've decided Laura was murdered?'

Bill Lamb glanced at his boss. 'You don't have to think about that,' he said.

He must have picked up some message from Dan since he turned back and asked, less aggressively, 'How did you come to be in the church on the morning Laura Quillam died?'

'I'd gone to the churchyard, and I—'

'That's not what I asked you—'

'You asked why I was in the church. It was because I was in the churchyard and heard singing and the piano. It was wonderful. Blues. It was Laura. She was fabulous. When she stopped singing, I was disappointed.'

Lamb drummed his fingers on the table.

A knock at the door broke the moment. 'Okay if I serve breakfast?' Lily answered Bill's bellow to 'come in'. 'Sorry to interrupt.'

'No problem, Mum,' Alex said, darned if Bill Lamb would trample even the simplest civility. 'Thanks. Just put the tray down and I'll do the rest.'

Lily slid the tray on the table, catching Alex's

134

eye as she straightened. Always sensitive, her mother had caught the atmosphere and was anxious.

'Thank you very much,' Dan said, smiling.

Lily took the breakfast plates off the tray herself and left without another word, but not without leaving an orange cat, who slipped into the snug without her noticing him.

Bill raised a hand as if to protest to Lily, but Alex scooped up Max and deposited him on her lap. 'Hey, boy,' she said, and to the detectives, 'don't worry about him. He's becoming a fixture. Not usually on his own or so early in the day, though, so I'll keep him in here till I find out if Harriet and Mary know where he is. He may have got out of their cottage.'

'The Burke sisters,' Bill said. 'Doesn't anything change around here?'

'We hope not,' Alex told him, and Dan laughed.

The two men poured brown sauce on their plates and ate in silence – apart from the scraping of their cutlery – for several minutes.

Alex put Max on the seat of a nearby chair. She moved her toast in front of her, spread butter and took a spoonful of marmalade to the side of her plate. She doubted she had ever felt much less like eating. Her coffee already had a dull film on top.

'I was in the churchyard thinking and that's when I heard Laura singing and playing the piano.' Alex pretended not to notice Bill Lamb's irritation at her interruption of his breakfast. 'I didn't know it was Laura till later, of course. I had a lot on my mind but she sang the blues the way we don't hear it around here very often. She was so good.

But then she stopped and I kept waiting for her to start again. When she didn't, I went on walking and thinking. I had a lot on my mind.'

'What?' Bill said, swallowing and drinking some coffee. 'What was on your mind?'

Murder and mahem. 'Personal things. Nothing to do with why you're here.'

'We'll decide that.' He jabbed a forefinger, the one on top of his knife, toward her. 'There's a reason for anything I ask you.'

'Right.' She reconstructed her walk in the churchyard, leaving out nothing including watching the girls riding, their dogs, and having to be careful not to stick herself on rose thorns.

With his fork, Bill made 'speed this up' motions.

'Back at the church,' she said and folded her hands together in her lap. They wanted to shake, or gesture. 'It was still quiet when I got there. Then a crash on the piano keys. Then silence.'

'Uh huh,' Bill said. 'Then?'

'I waited and thought some more for a long time about personal things.' She pulled her eyebrows together. 'I think that's the right order.'

'Be sure,' Dan told her and he didn't look amused by the minutia.

'I kept hoping she'd play again. When she didn't I left Bogie outside – under a rose bush – and went in. I wanted to tell her how much I'd enjoyed listening.' The prickling in her eyes was too familiar. 'If she was still there.'

This might be her way of dealing with Lamb's passive aggression, but she wasn't enjoying bringing back the pictures of that horrible time.

Moving through details faster, she got to when

136

she found Laura's body. 'She was lying on the floor with her head against the music stand. I didn't see her at first but when I fell—'

'You told us all about that before.' Finished with his meal, Dan put down his knife and fork.

'I've been asked to tell everything again, from the beginning. There are steps there, where the choir stalls are. You will have seen them. I put my foot down from the bottom one and landed on a thermos bottle. It shot out from under my shoe and I went down. But I wasn't hurt. Sore elbows, that's about it.'

'Thermos.' Dan made it a statement. 'You fell over a thermos? What kind?'

'One of those hot or cold insulated types. I think they're all more or less the same. This one was red with a knitted sleeve on it.'

Dan and Bill glanced at one another a little too long.

'It was there when all those people arrived,' Alex added. She reached for Max and sat him on her lap again. He stayed, which surprised her. 'Doc James. Ambulance. The police. I expect forensics bagged it.'

Bill's face whipped toward her. 'If you start sounding much more like a pro, we'll have to sign you up for the force.'

'Call in and check it, Bill,' Dan said shortly. He wasn't a happy man. 'Step out and do it now.'

Alex was confronted by two unhappy men.

Bill took out his phone and left the room.

'That cat's only got one eye,' Dan said, as if thinking of something very different.

'Tony had to take it out,' she told him, barely

137

stopping herself from adding that she'd helped with the procedure. 'It was badly infected.'

'Was it?' He rubbed absently at the scar along his jaw. 'When we got here last night someone was playing the piano. Blues. Bit of a coincidence, wouldn't you say? Did you remember the music from last night and say Laura Quillam was playing the same stuff? Just by accident?'

'I've talked about Laura playing the blues a number of times. That was Elyan Quillam playing last night. It was an impromptu thing. His girlfriend came and asked if anyone was allowed to use the piano, then persuaded him to play. I was expecting something like Bach but you heard him.'

'Talented boy – or man.'

Alex murmured agreement. 'I didn't mistake the kind of music Laura was playing.'

Bill Lamb reappeared and shut the door firmly. With absolutely no facial expression, he took the empty dishes, opened the hatch to the bar and pushed them through.

In other words, he didn't want more interruptions.

In silence, he sat and scribbled something in his notebook, tore out the sheet and gave it to Dan who read, also in silence.

'That cat's only got one eye,' Bill said. 'Doesn't he fall off things?'

'His balance can be a bit—'

'Describe the bottle,' Dan said.

The bottle. She pressed her eyes shut. 'I just did, but here goes again. Red with some sort of knitted tartan sleeve on it. The top was off – the cup, that was near Laura.'

'And there was a stopper. Screw-in type, I expect,' Dan said.

She thought about that. 'Of course there would be. I hadn't thought about that. But I didn't notice one. The bottle smelled of some sort of juice.'

'You picked it up?' Bill said at once.

'Yes.' She swallowed. 'I wondered for a second if the blood was juice from the bottle, but it wasn't.'

'No,' Bill said. 'What did you do with the bottle?'

'I put it on top of the piano bench. Tony said I shouldn't have picked it up and he was right. But it was just reflex, really.'

'Why was Tony there?' Dan asked.

'He was looking for me. We didn't have a chance to discuss why.' In the quiet moments that followed Alex began to feel trapped and as if she were being closed in more and more tightly. 'Please, tell me how Laura died. I never met her – not while she was alive – and it all feels unfinished. She was murdered, wasn't she? That's why you've come back to Folly.'

'I really couldn't answer that,' Dan said. 'But I can say forensics didn't find a thermos to match your description. Or any other description.'

Fifteen

Alex stood alone in the snug, holding Max over her shoulder, for a long time after the detectives left. The cat purred into her neck and gave her hair a lick of approval.

139

'You're growing into a sloppy date, my boy,' she told him, but her heart wasn't in it and if she wound herself much more tightly, she'd snap.

With her eyes tightly closed, she recreated the scene in St Aldwyn's. She had set the wretched bottle on the piano stool, she was sure of it. But then it was the last thing she could or wanted to concentrate on. Laura had been all that mattered, and the mad outrage of her lying there.

She thought of poor Elyan, his disbelief and obvious agony. And the man walking away from the church a bit earlier . . . even if it had been Elyan, and she had no proof, she'd seen how he fell apart when he'd seen his sister, lifeless, on the cold flagstones.

Tony appeared in the doorway and braced himself on the jambs. He raised his dark brows. 'One of my spies let me know you'd been in here with Sherlock and Watson for a long time.'

'That's supposed to be us, or have you forgotten – or dissolved our partnership?'

He was too sensitive to her mood for laughter or smiles.

'Laura was murdered,' she told him. 'I'm sure of it from the way Dan didn't say so.'

'What does that mean?'

'I asked him directly and he said he, um, he couldn't answer that. As in he didn't think he should tell me.'

Tony shrugged away from the door. 'The press are already gathering like maggots on . . . like . . . they're all over the place. Kev Winslet says there were TV crews skulking around Green Friday. And there's a couple of reporters in the bar trying to wheedle information out of Lily. They haven't figured out that they'd have better luck with the ducks on the pond.'

'Tony.' The word seemed forced past paralyzed muscles. 'They didn't find that red bottle that was on the floor, the one I picked up and put on the piano bench. Apparently forensics have no record of it.'

Red slashes rose on his cheekbones. 'That's ridiculous. It was there. Anything that was there when we arrived, was there when we left. Did you tell them you picked the thing up?'

'Of course. Why wouldn't I?'

'You're right, you're right. I want us to go somewhere and talk. Not here. Let's give Max to Harriet and Mary.'

Alex followed him into the main bar where the sisters sat by the fire as if they made a habit of spending mornings as well as evenings there. Bogie rose from his blue tartan blanket and if a dog could frown he'd be doing just that. He hurried to stand at Alex's side, head raised, teeth bared, as he glared at Max. The cat saw him but settled in more snugly.

'Here's your boy,' Alex said, giving Max to Mary.

'Before you ask,' Harriet said, 'no, we don't usually come in the mornings but we saw that lovely Dan O'Reilly and his unpleasant companion arrive last night and came over out of, well, interest. And we thought you might need some support, Alex. We saw them leave just now but they had you with them in the snug, didn't they? And that Lamb person looked in a nasty mood when they left.'

141

Alex sighed and Mary said, 'You don't have to say anything but we know they were in there with you, Alex. Don't let yourself be upset by anyone. Do you understand, young lady?'

Feeling as she might have at age eight, Alex nodded.

'We're expecting two o'clock customers,' Harriet said very quietly. 'Nice young couple who need a quiet and safe place to be together. Just thought we'd mention it in case you felt like coming by.'

Alex whispered in Harriet's ear, 'Elyan and his girlfriend?'

Harriet nodded. 'Told them how to get there by the back way along the lane. You already know.'

Tony got down on his haunches and ruffled Bogie's fur. Alex slipped into an empty chair beside Mary. They were all trying not to look at the scatter of strangers at the bar who might as well have worn 'Press' signs around their necks.

'We need a little time to ourselves, ladies,' Tony said. 'If we could come earlier than your other guests, I'd appreciate it very much. Is there an actual back door out of your place?'

'Do you think the fire department would let us operate without one?'

Alex smiled at him and rubbed his arm. 'We should know that, shouldn't we? Sometimes you don't think about those things.'

Straightening up, Mary said, 'Come by the lane. The hedges each side of the garden path go all the way to the cottages and turn right and left. Take the right fork. Beside what used to be a fuel bunker, there's a big gap in the hedge there and a door into the building. We'll make sure it's open. Just let yourselves in. I really did think you knew that was there. There's an exit sign on the inside for customers. In case of fire.'

'We don't go that side,' Alex said. 'But you're right, we should have known. When would be a good time to come?'

'Anytime. We'll be going back now so please yourselves.'

'Can I give you a lift?' Tony asked.

Harriet smiled sweetly. 'I think it would be better if we didn't draw too much attention to any relationship, don't you? And we need our walks anyway.'

'Absolutely,' Alex said, standing and starting toward the bar with Tony in her wake. Bogie bounded along beside them, clearly sensing what he probably thought of as family time.

Alex slipped behind the bar and closed the hatch. 'Ambler, or something stronger?'

'Half of Ambler,' Tony said. 'We should be off as soon as you can get away. I'm glad I left Katie at the clinic with Radhika.'

'Okay, will do,' Alex said, wrinkling her nose at him.

'You will do what?'

'Leave Bogie here. Best be able to move quickly and quietly if we have to. It wouldn't surprise me if our movements are being watched.'

Alex made a fist but stopped herself from punching it down on the counter. 'I'm sick of all that,' she said in a low voice. 'What can they possibly think either of us had to do with Laura's death?'

Tony held onto her clenched hand. 'Forget I said anything. I'm being paranoid.'

'Just got a call from Sybil at the parish,' Lily said, sliding an arm across the counter and leaning toward them. 'The police have asked to move into the parish hall. Looks as if they're ready for a long haul. And word has it the press is all a'flutter. They're rushing around to beat each other with a scoop, or whatever they call it. We've already got them poking around in here.'

'Can't be nice to have strangers dislike you,' Alex said. 'Some people have to be reporters. I'm just glad I'm not one. What bothers me most about them is that they make me expect to see them write about things I hoped would turn out not to be true.'

Lily looked from Alex to Tony and grimaced. 'We could all do without this. That poor girl. Did Dan and Bill say how they think she was killed?'

'They didn't even say she *was* killed but they didn't say she wasn't, either. Reporter heading this way.'

They switched to discussing the new Broadway Historical Society.

A stocky man with a weatherworn face and deep wrinkles around brown eyes reached them. 'You're the Alex Duggins who found the body,' he stated, notebook already in hand. Not shy or a novice.

Tony faced him with a hostile stare.

'Bart Hadden with the *Echo*.' His smile was pleasant enough. 'You are Ms Duggins?' he said to Alex.

'Yes.'

'And you found the Quillam girl's body in the church.'

'I'd rather not discuss that.'

'Why? It's been reported you were there. Reliable source, too, I saw. It could help sort things out if you gave some more details. Might jog someone's memory.'

'About what?' Tony said.

Bart Hadden puffed out his lips and shrugged. 'Ooh something they saw or heard. The police are setting up shop in the village. They wouldn't do that for a straightforward death. Not even a suicide. We know what that leaves. You must have some ideas about who might want to get rid of young Laura – how about it?'

'*You* must be kidding,' Tony said and took a long swallow of his beer. 'You think one of us is going to start accusing someone of . . . of a crime?'

'You were going to say, murder.' The reporter's grin wasn't malicious. 'Well, always worth a try. It's early days yet. Give me a jingle if you want to tell me something. You can trust me to be fair.' He drew a card from the breast pocket of his baggy tweed jacket and placed it on the bar.

None of them returned his waggle-fingered wave as he turned away.

Lily sighed and swiped a cloth across the counter. 'They're like hunting dogs. They've got the scent of the prey and they're ready to close in and tear it apart.'

'Aren't they, though?' Alex said. 'And at the moment they're hoping I'm the prey.'

145

Sixteen

The sky, grey and getting greyer, sagged to rest heavily on the hills around Folly. A misty haze rose, like steam, over the fields. Tony held Alex's upper arm – her hands were deep in her coat pockets – and set out through the warped gate from the Black Dog back car park and into the overgrown jungle of untended ground behind. He used his fists to thump the sticky gate closed again.

'We're taking this clandestine operation stuff seriously, then?' Alex asked.

'You think it would be a good idea for the plods to see us making it away together? We don't want to be followed.' Already he saw signs of strain in her face. Her eyes moved from one place to another, checking for whatever, and there was a haziness to the clear green. He hoped she wasn't losing weight but she did appear even smaller today.

She smiled at him. 'No, we don't. Why not go over that stile on the other side of the path, just down there?' She pointed ahead along the stony lane, much of which sprouted knee-high clumps of weeds. Treacherous coils of old bindweed snaked in every direction, like bleached ropes waiting for the unwary foot.

'Good enough,' he said. 'I think we should probably get our own discussion over before we get to the sisters' place. There are some things that need to be said.'

'I thought that was why we were going there. They wouldn't interrupt us.'

They reached the old stile in the hedge. Alex climbed on the cross piece with her usual assurance but a loud creak slowed her down. She had flinched at the sound.

Tony helped her over and followed, breaking off a piece of wood on his way. They both grinned. 'I'm a lot heavier than the last time when I used this,' he said. 'I was thinking more that if Elyan and Annie got there early – beat us there even – we might wish we'd gone over a couple of things first. Did you tell O'Reilly and Lamb about the man you saw?'

'No.' She raised her face to the wind and her black curls tossed. 'I didn't think of it. I know that sounds ridiculous, but I didn't. Bill seemed to be in charge of grilling me, and that's what it felt like. He threw me off balance, Tony. He can be nasty.'

Large raindrops fell, spattering their faces. Almost at once the scent of the earth rose, rich and sweet. 'Bill Lamb is a nasty son of a bitch. We aren't just discovering it, either. I think it irritates the hell out of him that Dan isn't aggressive all the time. Dan should have stepped in.'

'That wouldn't be right.' She looked at him and stumbled, but caught herself. 'There's protocol and putting a fellow officer down in front of a suspect could be disastrous. Dan can be acid, too. It's strange to think of it afterwards, but as soon as they'd left I started thinking about the morning Laura died, again. And that man. Sometimes I think I imagined him.'

'Godammit, you *are not* a suspect.' Tony stopped walking and she turned back. 'Think about this before you tell me I'm mad. Do we ask Elyan about walking away from the church? Whether it was him and why? We might be able to tell a lot by his reaction. He'd be caught completely off guard.'

She ran her fingers through her hair. 'What reason could he have for being there like that? I can't think of anything. Unless he was going to meet Laura and realized he'd forgotten something so he went back.'

'That way? By the rectory. It's a very long way around. And the path goes in all kinds of directions. It would be easy for a newcomer to get lost.'

'They could have argued. He could have got there and they fell out about something so he left.' With fingers resting on her mouth, she said, 'It couldn't have been him.'

'You're the one who thought it might have been, love. So the thought was there for some reason.'

There was rain on Alex's face. She pulled up her jacket collar and held it closed beneath her chin. Abrubtly, her eyes widened. 'Did I even tell you about Sebastian Carstens? I met him yesterday.'

Tony shook his head, no. 'Who . . . oh, he's with the Quillams, right?'

'Yes, he's the piano teacher. I wouldn't have thought someone like Elyan would still have one of those.'

'Probably always will only he'll move on to someone famous. I'm surprised he hasn't already.'

He could tell Alex was thinking about that.

'Let's get under those trees,' he said. 'The rain's getting heavier.' For once she was the one to take his hand and they went quickly to stand beneath a scraggly group of alders.

'He, Sebastian, that is, sounded as if he and his daughter were part of the family. He's got a little girl called Daisy who was with him. It was uncomfortable. I was in the children's playground. I picked up a paper at the post office and rode down there with Bogie. If I'd gone back to the Dog, they'd have started talking about what was in the paper about me finding Laura. So I sat at the picnic table to read.'

'And this Sebastian just showed up? He could always have already known about the playground, of course. With a child it's something you'd probably find out.'

She looked thoughtful again. 'I think he saw me there and came in to see if I'd say anything – about the church, about what I'd seen there. He seemed irritated when I didn't react to him.'

'He couldn't have followed you. Why would he?'

'I don't know but I didn't like him. He was talking down to me, trying to impress me.'

Tony didn't like the idea of this man following Alex. He didn't like anything about any of this.

'We shouldn't be much longer,' Tony said, 'but I've thought about the Hugh and Sonia drama. How about you?'

She slapped a hand to her brow. 'I've thought of little else and now I almost forget to bring it up.'

'It's a weird one,' Tony said. 'All we've got is a few sentences and what we make of them. But

149

Hugh and Sonia know each other, and I don't just mean from her coming to Folly and meeting him here, or renting Hugh's house.'

'Did you think it sounded as if they'd been close in the past? Really close?'

Tony looked at her. 'Of course. If I had to guess I'd say they'd been about as close as a man and woman can get. So did she somehow know about him having bought Green Friday? If so, how? It would seem as if they've been keeping in touch – or someone's passing on information to Sonia. Takes less of a brain than an M & M spell checker to work that out.'

Alex snorted. 'You never make a joke.'

'I stole it from somewhere – can't remember where.'

Tony continued, 'So Sonia knew Hugh had the house and made an excuse to her husband for thinking it would make a great rental. They may have been looking for a place in the country for the summer and she just managed to pop up with it.'

'That doesn't explain what was between them before, or where it stands now,' Alex said.

'Hugh made it pretty clear where it stands with him.'

Alex felt squirmy and rolled her shoulders. 'She sounded as if she hoped to start something with him again. It's none of our business unless it's got any part in the case.'

It was Tony's turn to laugh. 'Some might say the case hasn't got anything to do with us either, but I don't agree. We were thrown into it and I'm honestly starting to think we can be useful.

And yes, I know that sounds pig-headed, but Dan and Bill are quick enough to use whatever they can get out of us.'

'You put that so well.' Smiling, Alex straightened her back. 'I feel better already. Holmes and Watson ride again.'

'I've been meaning to ask you which of us is Holmes and—'

'Best not do that,' Alex interrupted him. 'We wouldn't want hurt feelings.'

'So, ears to the ground on Hugh and Sonia?' Tony's grin was huge.

'Mmm, probably.' She gave him an enigmatic lift of the nose. 'Shall we get across to the ladies?'

A brambly space in a hedge gave them access to the lane again and it took only minutes to reach the back of Leaves of Comfort. Harriet and Mary's hedges, one on either side of the path, ran in precisely clipped lines from a wrought iron back gate to the cottages.

'We go to the fork and turn right,' Tony said and started in that direction.

'Wait!' Grabbing his hand again, this time in both of hers, the sudden pallor in her face unnerved him.

'What's wrong?'

'It came back to me. Just like that. I wasn't thinking about it and I remembered the whole thing.'

He knew better than to interrupt. Her eyes seemed to be seeing into the distance.

'I put the thermos bottle on the piano bench. Remember?'

She had been looking at it. 'Yes. I said you

151

shouldn't have picked it up but anyone would have done the same thing. Purely a reflex.'

'Elyan came looking for Laura and saw the flask. From his angle, Laura wouldn't have been visible. He must have thought she had left so he picked it up. I think he still had it when he saw her. What did he do with it?'

He massaged his temples. 'When he saw Laura he went spare.' He looked up. 'He put it on one of the choir benches, I'm sure he did.'

'Something happened to it though, Tony.'

'It's probably still there.'

'After forensics took the place apart? Think, Tony. They didn't find it and it was never logged in. But the strangest part of this is that we don't know why it's so important.'

Seventeen

The door into the house, when they found it, was overgrown with climbing yellow roses. 'If the fire department saw this they'd have a field day,' Tony said, carefully unhitching the clinging vines and gently peeling back the roses.

When he put his fingers on the rusted door handle and started to turn it, she pulled his hand away. 'I don't want to go in there.'

Tony didn't frown a lot but when he did the effect was immediate and unsettling. He held her shoulders and lowered his face to look into her eyes. 'What are you talking about? Why would you possibly feel uneasy about going into the sisters' place? That doesn't make any sense.'

She stepped out of his reach. 'Then I'm not making sense. I'm all muddled up. We don't have the vaguest what we're dealing with but we're going in to confront a young couple about an event that's probably devastating them.'

'Yep. That's what we're going to do, only carefully – we'll be very friendly. We share how upset they must be. We're upset, too. We wish we knew something helpful – to the police.'

Alex was afraid he'd see her shivering. She felt suddenly really cold and clammy. 'Right you are. On your head be it. Lead on, he who knows the right way to do anything and everything.'

The one-sided smile, more a sucking in of a corner of his mouth, had Alex looking at her shoes. 'Sorry. That was uncalled for.'

She glanced up to see the door creaking inward, and smelled the fragrant mixture of fresh baked goodies and lavender that was a permanent part of Leaves of Comfort.

'Here we go.' Tony put an arm around her and ushered her inside, but stood between her and the rest of the shop while he dropped a kiss on her forehead, and another on her mouth. 'If you didn't come up with the darndest comments, there'd be less to love about you. Now, follow my lead.'

She was too surprised to give the sharp salute she might have and walked obediently behind him, through the archway which had been made between the lower floors of the side-by-side cottages, and to the stairs leading up to Harriet and Mary's flat.

'Haloo,' he called out. 'It's Tony and Alex, ladies. Come to cadge tea and crumpets.'

Mary's head, complete with tortoiseshell mantilla comb protruding from her high bun of white hair, popped out of the door to the flat. Leaning on a walking stick, she put a finger to her lips then beckoned them up.

Stepping as lightly as they could, Tony and Alex advanced, and Oliver the lean and lithe grey tabby, stuck his inquisitive nose around Mary's ankles. Apparently the visitors weren't too interesting since he withdrew quickly.

'What's the matter?' Alex asked when they were safely closeted in the flat. 'Is Harriet sleeping?'

'If that sister of mine ever sleeps, she makes sure I don't see her,' Mary said, *sotto voce*, and cleared her throat when Harriet came out of the kitchen. 'Elyan and Annie are downstairs. All the way in the corner at that tiny table. I didn't want you to interrupt the poor young things.'

Harriet rolled her eyes.

'We didn't see them,' Alex said. 'There wasn't a sound down there.'

'That nook is almost under the stairs,' Harriet said. 'There's barely room for two chairs, but I think they might like that.'

'No dogs?' Mary didn't look pleased about that.

'Just trying to come and go quietly,' Tony said. 'We felt a bit like burglars coming in the back way but it's pretty out there.'

'The children couldn't find the door and came in the front,' Mary said. 'Defeats the purpose a bit but we'll hope they weren't seen by someone we'd rather didn't see them at all.'

Alex gave an apologetic little smile. 'We're going to talk to them. Forgive us for using you – and that's what it feels like – but we'd like to see if there's anything they want to share with us. I know we're poking our noses in again but it all got dropped in our laps and we think we might get to the bottom of at least one or two important things that could take the police a long time.'

The sisters didn't quite hide their disappointment and Alex was sure they had hoped for a private tête-à-tête. Mary sat in her pink velvet rocker and Max jumped on her lap with a sigh that suggested he was desperate for some peaceful snuggle time. His one bright eye closed at once.

'If you'll have us, we'll come again soon and chat properly,' Alex said.

'You know we'll have you,' Harriet told them. 'Run along before it's opening time and you can't talk to them at all. There is something I want to mention, but it can wait. I've had a hard time deciding if I should say anything. Go.' She flapped them toward the door.

The table where Elyan and Annie sat was, indeed, very small. Alex realized it was the one often used for stacking boxes from George's Bakery. She noticed these were on top of the counter instead.

Elyan and Annie were sitting quite still, half-drunk cups of tea and a plate of cakes in front of them. When they realized Tony and Alex knew they were there, and had actually come to find them, their faces turned to shades of red and pink.

'Hi, you two,' Alex said, smiling. 'This is a

155

wonderful place, isn't it? I've loved it ever since Harriet and Mary opened.'

Elyan stood up, bowing his head enough to avoid hitting the underside of the stairs. 'We love it, too. Sit with us, please. Have you both met Annie Bell?'

Annie just smiled.

Tony reached across the table to shake her hand. Beautiful girl in an understated way. Chestnut colored hair in loose ringlet curls to her shoulders and warm, dark-brown eyes.

'We met at the Black Dog,' Alex said. 'I can't tell you how much clamoring there is for Elyan to make our old piano sound magical. Naturally, I tell them they were lucky to have heard you once.'

Elyan made a self-deprecating motion with his hand. 'I'll come in again and fool about. It's good for me.'

'It is,' Annie said, finally showing animation.

Chairs scraped over the stone floor and Tony settled Alex before sitting down himself. 'I was hoping we'd get a chance to talk on our own,' Tony said. 'In a weird way we've become thrown together in this horrible thing that's happened.'

So he did intend to plough in and ask direct questions – or so it seemed.

Elyan nodded but kept his eyes on the table.

Annie's eyes had filled with tears and she rubbed his arm.

'You knew Laura all your life,' Tony said. 'She's always been there for you.'

In a gruff voice, Elyan said, 'Yes. They didn't know how interesting she was, or how talented. She was always pushed away, almost kept out of

156

sight because she wasn't important enough to bother with. I hate them for that. If only—'

'You did spend time with her,' Annie said. 'She loved her music even if your father wouldn't take it seriously. Should we talk about all this now? You know the police will want to interview you again – and me. Everyone, I should think. They don't like it if the people they're interested in talk to each other.'

Smart girl. Alex smiled at her.

'As long as we don't plot out a story we'll all tell, they can't stop us from talking,' Tony said. 'When you say "they" you mean your family, don't you?'

'Yes, and most of the people we have around us.'

'She had friends,' Annie said. 'There were people who encouraged her and I think she hoped she could get away and perform professionally once she had her trust fund from her mother. Lately she'd been talking about taking off and making it on her own, but she couldn't go with nothing and Percy made sure her allowance wasn't enough to give her ideas.'

'You think that's what he was doing, Annie?' Elyan said. 'Holding her hostage? He thought her music was an embarrassment. He didn't want any part of it.'

'How long before she got her own money?' Tony asked mildly.

'Two years,' Elyan said promptly. He picked up a piece of shortbread but reduced it to crumbs on his plate without taking a bite. 'Twenty-five. Then she'd never have to ask anyone for anything again.'

'Remember the red thermos bottle on the piano bench?'

Alex almost jumped. She wound her fingers together. This couldn't be fair to Elyan, not asking him like this when he was so disturbed.

'Thermos?' Elyan frowned and let his eyes roam over the tea shop. 'Laura was dead by the piano. She'd bled there.'

'It had a tartan sleeve around it,' Tony added. 'Hand-knitted.'

Elyan drew a short, sharp breath. 'Of course. I picked it up before I saw her.' He propped an elbow and covered his eyes. 'Yes, I remember. I'll never forget.'

There was no mistaking the rigid distress on Tony's face. 'So you put it down. I remember you bending over Laura.'

'I just wanted to pick her up and make her open her eyes.' Elyan's hand shook over his eyes. He began to rub with increasing speed. 'I don't know. I don't know. I wasn't thinking about that, or anything but Laura. Why are you asking me about it?'

'The police interviewed me this morning,' Alex said quickly, anxious to stop this. 'Apparently they have no record of logging in the thermos and we can't remember what happened to it for the same reasons as you. Don't think about it, please.'

'They called Green Friday,' Annie said. 'They were on their way there so we left. We can't bear it. Elyan wants to be left alone.'

Elyan dropped his hand. 'Did they say why Laura died,' he said very softly. 'Was it because of the music stand?'

158

'They wouldn't tell me.'

'Why do they have to be the way they are? Upsetting everyone when . . . haven't we suffered enough?'

'Yes, you have,' Tony said.

'If I'd been there when I was supposed to be she wouldn't have died alone.' Elyan's eyes looked raw around the rims. 'There's always one more thing they want from me. I knew if I said I had to go somewhere, they'd have kept on trying to find out where. I didn't dare say I was meeting Laura. Oh, sod it all!'

'How did they know you'd gone back to the house? Do they watch you all the time?'

Alex felt sick. She couldn't bear the idea of trying to trap this young man, but she also couldn't blame Tony for trying to cut through the length of time protocol would keep the police going through their steps. They also needed some peace and to get away from the constant upheaval that had followed them around for months.

'I don't know what you mean,' Elyan said.

'When you left St Aldwyn's and walked past the side of the rectory, weren't you going home?'

'No.' Elyan looked at Annie. 'I don't know what he's talking about.'

'Of course you don't. Tony, I think you're making a mistake about this.'

Alex couldn't pretend to have no part in the whole thing. 'I was in the churchyard. I heard Laura singing. She was so good. But I saw a man walking away from the church. Just like Tony said. I thought it was you but I'm sorry I made a mistake.'

159

This wasn't going to help. She didn't blame Tony for trying but now they should drop the subject.

'Who could it have been?' Elyan said, composed again, and screwing up his eyes as he thought. 'Oh, god! It's what we were afraid of. The police think Laura was murdered. You told them about the man . . . but . . . did you tell them you thought it was me?' He didn't seem panicky, just intensely involved.

'No. I haven't told them about it at all. I'm not sure why except all I got was an impression, something I thought I saw, and I'm not risking what they might do with that.'

'What would some bottle have to do with anything, anyway?' Annie asked. 'Laura always had something to drink with her when she sang. Her throat got dry.'

The front door handle rattled before someone pounded with their knuckles.

'Who is it?' Annie said, and she looked frightened. 'They're angry. I can tell. Is it the police?'

'Mary or Harriet will take a look from upstairs. They'll tell us if we should open the door.' Tony got up and went to the foot of the staircase.

The walls and doors in these old buildings were thick. A man's raised voice said something and a window slammed shut.

'There's a man outside for Elyan,' Harriet called down the stairs. 'Let him in if you want him in.'

The downstairs listeners all smiled a little.

'What do you want me to do?' Tony asked Elyan.

'What do you think I should do?'

'Open the door. Looks suspicious otherwise.'

Annie murmured, 'Yes.' She was winding a long

160

chestnut curl around and around in her fingers.

'Right you are,' Tony said and went quickly to unlock the door. 'Come in, come in, whoever you are,' he said with forced jollity.

He came close to getting walloped by the ferocity of the opening door. The slim man who marched in, fairly trembling with wrath, looked ready for a fight.

'You'd better have a good explanation for this, Elyan. You knew the police were coming so you ducked out.' He spoke as if the pianist were the only one there. 'You'd better come with me so we can talk. Annie can bring your car.'

'Sebastian, we'll be back shortly,' Elyan said. Rather than nervous, he appeared angry. 'How did you know I was here?'

Instead of answering, Sebastian trained his eyes on Alex. 'You again. Always around when there's trouble. I don't think I can be the only one who's noticed.'

Eighteen

Behind drystone walls along the line of cottage gardens on Pond Street, flowers mounded between clumps of perennial plants showing off their new foliage.

Even at mid-afternoon, the night-scented stocks began to breathe their heady scent. Tony and Alex had walked determinedly away from Leaves of Comfort, leaving Elyan and Annie to decide on

161

their next moves. The very abrasive Sebastian Carstens flounced theatrically from the tearoom and by the time Tony and Alex got outside he was nowhere in sight.

'He's a horrible man,' Tony said. 'Autocratic, arrogant, rude.'

'Scared?' Alex looked sideways at him, at the way he crinkled his eyes in thought.

'Does he strike you like that?' he asked. 'Why would he be scared? Is there anything to point to him having something to do with Laura's death?'

'No, I don't think that at all. I think his perfect world has been shaken up and he's not coping. Did you watch Elyan when Sebastian ordered him around?'

Tony thought about it. 'Not really.'

'He was angry, but there was surprise mixed in, and some hurt. Those two must be pretty close. From what I got earlier, they've worked together as teacher and pupil, very closely, for years. If I had to guess I'd say Sebastian's behavior was out of character.'

A cottage at the end of the row, it's door painted duck-egg blue, sported a veritable hedge of holly-hocks, their flashy blooms waving to and fro along stalks taller than Tony. They made Alex smile. 'I'm going to put hollyhocks in my gardens next year. I want more of a typical country look. It's all lawn and tidy beds. Boring.'

Tony put an arm around her shoulders and pulled her closer. 'I'll have starts in the green-house. I'll bring some down and plant them for you.' They lived less than ten minutes apart.

162

Alex slipped her hand behind his back and held onto his sweater. 'Are you happy, Tony?'

His expression was close to stricken. He didn't immediately answer, then said, 'Yes. I've got good things in my life. Mainly you.'

She smiled at him and butted her head into his chest. 'Could be we'll have enough time without trouble one of these days, and really churn over what it all means – what it's meant to mean.'

'I hope that's soon.'

She wasn't so afraid to get onto this topic now. 'The sex is great,' she said and immediately rolled toward him to hide her burning face.

Tony rubbed her back and shook her a little to make her look up. 'Ditto. But you don't know what it means to me to hear you say it. Are we finally relaxing with each other?'

'Sometimes my mouth runs away with me,' she muttered. 'I'm so honest, I embarrass myself.'

'Good!' He gave her a strong hug. 'Interference incoming, though. Do you recognize this pair?'

Walking from the direction of the Black Dog came an elegant woman of upper middle age, gray hair styled in a sleek bob and a red-haired man with his hands in his trouser pockets. Even at a distance his clothing shrieked of studied affectedness. As the couple drew closer, his fashionable wrinkled linen jacket, linen shirt a shade darker camel and pleated trousers didn't disappoint. Nor did his amazing orange suede lace-up shoes with a layer of red incorporated into the soles. The woman was impeccable in a lightweight tweed skirt and print blouse, distinctly Liberty of London paisley. She was slender right

163

down to her narrow ankles and sensible, expensive shoes. She was also completely out of place with her much younger companion.

'They aren't more of the Green Friday . . .?' Tony let his quiet question fade away.

'They might be,' Alex said. 'They look a bit like Eskimos in Biarritz, don't you think? Must have been beamed in by mistake.' She shut her mouth firmly. Sniping at incomers wasn't her usual style.

The man tossed his center-parted hair and flashed a truly wonderful smile. 'Would you know, er . . .?'

'Elyan Quillam,' the woman finished for him. 'We tried the pub and someone said they were there but left. The barman thought they could have come this way. But forgive us. Why should you know him?'

'We do,' Tony said promptly. 'This is Alex Duggins who owns that pub. I'm the local veterinarian, Tony Harrison.'

That got mute nods which irritated Alex. 'Did we miss your names?' She turned up the corners of her mouth.

'If I had a hat, I'd sweep it off,' said the man, with a flourishing bow. 'Wells Giglio, theatrical agent specializing in the fine arts. Classical musicians, to be precise. I represent Elyan Quillam . . .' He paused waiting for . . . who knew? 'Elyan is my primary client – as well as a close friend.'

He made no attempt to introduce the woman who raised an arched and knowing brow and said, 'Maud Meeker. Housekeeper and general dogsbody to the Quillam family.'

Wells covered his mouth and sputtered, 'Dogsbody? That's rich. You run them and their homes. Seriously, people, Mrs M. has been keeping an extraordinary household in line since forever. I think she was at the signing of the Magna Carta, and Henry VIII's marriage to Anne Boleyn.'

'I did miss Boleyn's beheading.' Deadpan, Maud Meeker didn't look either amused or not amused. 'I've been with them since Percy Quillam married his first wife. Before that, I was already with her – Audrey, that is. Is that enough personal information? Really, Wells, you do go on.'

'Sorry if I offend, old thing.'

'You're looking for Elyan,' Alex said, much entertained by the sideshow but becoming sorry for Mrs Meeker. 'Last I heard, he and Annie were going home.'

With eyes suddenly open to popping and a finger rudely pointed, Wells said, 'The woman. You're the woman, aren't you? Alex something.'

She didn't respond and also didn't like the way Tony stiffened beside her.

'You poor thing,' Mrs Meeker said. In what might have been the most impulsive action of her life, she touched Alex's arm with green leather-clad fingers. She put the flattened fingers of her other hand to her brow. 'I'm sorry you had to go through that. Laura was my little chum from when she was born. I can't tell you how all this has shocked me. She seemed to be doing so well.'

'Sebastian said you're like this with the detectives on the case.' Wells held up a hand with two fingers curled around each other. 'Old friends. What have they told you? I mean, they may be

165

spilling the beans to Percy and Sonia right now, as we speak, but can you tell us what killed my darling Laura?'

My darling Laura? 'They aren't revealing that,' Alex said. 'Or they haven't told me.'

'Don't worry,' Tony said in a vaguely menacing tone Alex had heard before – and recognized as dangerous. 'They'll get to you with the questioning. You'll have your own chance to see what you can get out of them. It's bound to be public knowledge shortly, anyway. The press will see to that.'

'There they are!' Wells jumped up and down waving, then took off, loping along the pavement.

Annie and Elyan were leaving the garden in front of Leaves of Comfort.

Maud Meeker's head was bowed. 'You're sure the police didn't give any information?' she asked quietly and when they both shook their heads, she added, 'Wells would have liked to get close to Laura but she wasn't interested. She was never his "darling girl". It no longer matters who she might have cared for. It's all pointless now. I wonder, could I call a taxi from the pub? I have my mobile but I expect you have a good taxi firm you use.'

'We do.'

'Let me run you where you need to go, Mrs Meeker,' Tony said. 'You're going back to work, Alex?'

She nodded, yes.

'I couldn't put you out.'

Tony smiled at Mrs Meeker. 'Where are you going?'

'Green Friday – that's where we're living. I find I'm a little weary.'

166

'I'll take you. No bother. I've got to get to my clinic and it's in the same general direction.'

Separated by miles. Alex wondered what questions he intended to ask the poor woman. 'See you, then, Tony.'

'When are you going home? I noticed you don't have your Range Rover.'

'I'm not sure yet.' And she wanted to keep her options open. 'I'll call you this evening.'

This secretiveness over the cause of Laura's death rubbed at her. She intended to see if she could trick any lips loose.

Major Stroud had been propping up the bar for too many hours. He held his drink well enough but everyone had limits. He took a healthy swig of whisky and rolled his lips inward beneath his grey brush of a mustache. The mottling of purplish veins on his nose and cheeks glowed like trickles of hot lava.

'Do I cut him off?' Hugh whispered to Alex.

She considered the older man who swayed but only slightly and talked under his breath. He was, she knew, lonely and disappointed but she still had to do the right thing.

'Major, how is Mrs Stroud? Haven't seen her in an age.'

He squinted at her and said, perfectly clearly, 'Venetia is jolly good, thanks. She's got her plants and her ballet and all's well with her world. Not that you give a damn.'

'Whoa,' she retorted. 'That doesn't sound like your usual charming self.'

'If you don't like it, you can lump it, my girl.

167

What I want to know is how you come to be involved in every filthy thing that happens around here and I seem to be the only one who notices?'

'Time to go home, Major,' Hugh said promptly. 'I'll arrange a lift for you.'

'You'll do no such bloody thing, you jumped-up scum.'

'Did you drive?' Alex asked shortly.

''Course, I did and I'll drive back again.' His words became more slurred by the moment.

She held out a hand, 'Give me your keys, please.'

He pointed a wavering finger at her. 'You're a troublemaker – or worse. You think you run this village. Own the pub. Gobs at the ready. I'll bide my time, and time my moment for maximum damage.'

Alex's back did its old prickling act. All the way up into her hair and over her scalp, she felt tight.

'I've already got someone lined up who'll use the information I've got on you.'

'That's it.' Hugh lifted the flap in the counter and reached Stroud in a couple of strides. 'Let's get out into the fresh air, sir. And I'll have those keys one way or the other.'

He marched Major Stroud out of the building and the interested eyes turned in Alex's direction quickly darted elsewhere. The volume of talk rose at once.

Lily was quick to reassure her that Stroud was all bluster, as did Liz Hadley. Liz was a long-time employee who filled in frequently and was a trusted member of the crew. Alex just wanted to take Bogie and go home. She was grateful the Burke sisters had already left.

168

In forty minutes or so, Hugh was back and brushing off the incident. 'He's still suffering because of Harry.' Harry was the major's supposed financial wizard of a son but had shown his family up pretty badly through some of his dealings.

Alex thought about what Hugh said and nodded. 'You're right. I'm going to leave you to it now. I need a quiet night at home.' His quizzical expression made her fear he was troubled himself. She and Tony were no closer to working out what to make of Hugh's conversation with Sonia Quillam. Alex had begun to wish she'd never heard them talking, even though it was a mistake that they had.

She put on Bogie's lead and went out through the inn to say goodnight to Lily who was already back at her post there.

When she stepped through the door, misty rain met her but it was light and she didn't bother to put up her hood.

Once in the car park behind the pub she glanced around and remembered she didn't have the Range Rover. All the fuss with Stroud had stopped her from thinking about whether or not she was really – as had been her intention since that morning – going to ride home.

Pedaling uphill would be a bit of a push for her but she used to ride that hill often enough as a girl.

She wasn't going to ask anyone to take her home. Bogie plopped happily into the bike basket, eyes forward even in the failing light, and she clipped the restraining hook onto his harness, took her helmet from the handlebars and plunked it on her head.

Riding out to the road she felt excited by the wind on her face and the flowery, earthy scents that came with it. She was getting very sure of herself on the bike. One of these days she'd give it a name – like Flash, or Trigger, or Samantha (when it didn't behave), shortened to Sam the rest of the time.

And I'm losing it . . .

Oh, this was jammy. She'd always had a lot of strength in her legs and it took little time for her to start climbing the hill. The pewter sky, the dark trees rising from gullies and the whine of wind through branches were a powerful boost to her muscles – and her confidence.

She could see Bogie's ears flapping and imagine his doggy smile.

Ten more minutes and the going got harder. Alex stood on the pedals and pumped more slowly. When you usually drove, you forgot the dips and rises in the road. But over the next rise there was a fairly long dip. She'd whizz down that to pick up speed and conquer the next grade upwards like a champion.

As expected, once she had labored to the crest, the faint marking at the side of the road dropped down and soon she shot between thicker woods. The misty rain turned to sparser, heavier drops and spattered her face. Alex laughed and caught the water on her tongue.

She almost expected Bogie to whoop.

An engine sounded behind her, a smooth, powerful one that would take all this as if it was a gentle slope. Her lights were on front and back, and her reflectors had been replaced with spanking new ones. In a mad moment she'd considered streamers for the ends of the handlebar grips and a jaunty flagpole. Decorum had prevailed.

The vehicle grew closer and would flash by soon enough. Alex rode as near the edge as was safe.

One of the multitude of Range Rovers around here drew level for an instant. In the gathering darkness it could be green or dark blue. It could be Tony's.

She looked toward the driver and felt the bike bump and tip. The left handlebar bounced out of her hand but she grabbed it again.

The wheels slid sideways. The whole bike slid sideways while Alex felt herself fall toward the road. Juddering wildly she squeezed the brakes, at the same time knowing she would only make things worse that way.

'Bogie,' she yelled. 'It's all right, boy.'

It was not all right. It was all wrong.

Still on the bike, she hit the ground and continued bumping downhill toward the trees.

She started to scream, but shouted, 'Help!' instead. Everything she did was useless. Beneath her body she felt slime. It made no sense and there must be stones embedded and waiting to pound her.

A single tree, too tall for her to know what it was, loomed, separate from the rest and with a great trunk designed for bone crushing – if she hit it, her bones would crush and so would poor little Bogie's.

A jolt, and the bike swung around on its side, the back wheel pointing downhill. The front wheel had slammed into that craggy tree trunk and stopped the slide.

Alex closed her eyes and lay still, waiting for pain. Falling was becoming a habit. But her helmet was still squarely buckled under her chin and as she started to move, apart from soreness here and there, no sharp agony suggested broken bones.

'Bogie?'

She had slipped backward off the saddle but gradually extricated herself from the buckled bike, awkwardly working her lower leg free, and wormed her way forward to reach the basket.

It was empty. Bogie's restraining belt had broken in two. 'Oh, no,' she muttered, her words hoarse in her own ears. 'Bogie.' And she did scream his name. 'Bogie!'

With shaky, cold hands, she pulled the torch from its clips under the handlebars, the one hit by the vehicle bent up at a sharp angle, and turned the light on. Choosing a powerful one had been a good idea although the worst she had imagined needing it for was putting more air in a tire.

Her heart pumped hard against her ribs. What she'd thought was slime and probably filled with rocks, was long damp grass and weeds that had flattened under the weight of bike and rider.

A whimper was the best sound she remembered hearing. She swept the torch beam back and forth. 'Come here, Bogie. Come on, sweetie. You're okay, I'm here.'

She saw him, scrambled to bend over him, pulled him into her arms.

The whimper turned to yelps, then screeches

172

and Alex set him on his feet. He held the front right one curled beneath him and even if she couldn't see it, she could feel his reproachful look. He whimpered steadily.

'I'm a horrible mother,' she moaned. 'I've broken your leg and look where we are. Tony will probably call the RSPCA.' Hysterical laughter bubbled into her throat and she shielded him while she located her mobile in her back pocket and punched a number.

Five rings and Tony picked up, 'Alex? Hey. Where are you, love?'

'I don't think you want to know.'

Nineteen

'You're the best thing I've ever seen,' Alex said, leaning on a tree twenty or so yards downhill from the road. 'You're wonderful, that's what you are. Isn't he, Bogie?'

Tony slithered and slid his way down to her. He cupped his hands over his mouth and blew into them. Then he took a deep breath. 'I'm trying to stay wonderful,' he said. 'Are you injured? You must be.'

'I'm not. A bit sore but not injured. I slid all the way down on the bike. Not very comfortable but the wet grass made a kind of cushion. I tell you, Tony, if I was going to slide off the road, I couldn't have picked a better—'

'*Alex*. Stop jabbering.'

173

'Yes, of course. Bit unnerved, I expect. Bogie wasn't so lucky. His restraining strap broke and he flew out of the basket.'

He used his torch to scout the area.

'I couldn't quite manage to get all three of us up the hill again.'

'Three?' He did his best not to sound menacing.

'Bogie, Sam and me.'

With the torch aimed above her head but illuminating her face, he said, 'Who is Sam, please?'

She smiled, but her eyes darted back and forth. 'My bicycle. It wasn't her fault. Now she'll have to be fixed up.'

Tony moved closer and attempted to check her pupils. 'Did you hit your head?'

'No. And I had my helmet on.' She scowled but managed to keep her lips pressed shut.

'Bogie,' Tony said. 'I'm going to take you up to the Range Rover and get a look at you. If he needs it, I can give him something for pain.' He took him gently and draped him over his left forearm. Bogie yelped.

'He's hurting,' Alex said.

'I noticed. Now, hold my right hand and I'll get us all up. I'll come back for the bike later.'

'If we leave it here it might get stolen.'

I can only hope. 'It won't be seen in the dark.'

Alex refused to wait in the vehicle. Probably just as well since another car might come too fast to see them. Once on the road, he kept his warning lights flashing and put his own flashlight on the roof, pointing downhill.

He didn't have to give Bogie more than a cursory glance to know he'd broken his right ulna

174

but not, it seemed, the radius. The leg would have to be immobilized but it shouldn't need any pins and without setbacks, healing would be rapid.

'I'm giving him a shot. Then we'll run him down to the surgery. What caused you to slide off the road, did you say?'

She glanced down and away. 'I missed the edge somehow and just went down. The handlebar jarred out of my hands when the right one bumped on something.'

'Uh huh.' He got what he needed from his bag, prepared a shot and gave it to Bogie. 'Put your hand on him while I open a crate.'

He routinely kept two crates in the back. Katie was already in hers and keeping very quiet as she took in that something was wrong. She didn't squeak until he put Bogie, already slipping out of consciousness, through the wire door and latched it.

'Okay, girl. Okay, Katie. Your buddy is going to be fine.' To Alex he said, 'He'll be out for a while.'

'Ew,' Alex muttered. 'The law is coming up the hill.'

He closed the rear of the Range Rover and turned in time to see blues and twos come on only yards away from them. 'Stupid,' he said. 'Oh, well, I guess it's for safety.'

O'Reilly leaped from his vehicle and ran toward them.

'Overreaction,' Alex said under her breath. 'We're fine, Dan. Just a little spill and I had to call for help.'

Bill Lamb hurriedly joined his boss. 'Where's your bike?'

175

'Down there.' She hooked a thumb in Sam's direction and grimaced. 'She'll have to be mended. Front wheel hit a tree.'

'And you're not hurt?' Dan said.

'Got lucky. There's no other explanation. And the long grass gave me a softer landing. Not my dog, though. We've got to get him to Tony's surgery and fix up his leg.'

'He'll be fine,' Tony said. Alex was making him question whether she was telling the whole story. 'Alex's handlebar grip may have saved her, too. Slowed her down when it hit.'

'We were hoping to have another chat with you two,' Dan said. The look he gave Alex was worried and, not for the first time, Tony's possessive buttons got pushed. DCI O'Reilly found her appealing, maybe more than appealing, damn him.

'We could start with Alex,' Bill said, his expression hard to see outside the circle of lights. 'Take her up to her place and have you call us when you're through with the dog, Tony.'

'I have to stay with Bogie,' Alex said so rapidly the words ran into one long, urgent plea. 'He's had bad stuff happen to him. I couldn't have him go without me.'

'Come to the parish hall when you're done, then,' O'Reilly said, pulling a puff of irritation from his sergeant. 'We'd like a chance to . . . we've got the post-mortem results on Laura Quillam but you probably already guessed that.'

'Right,' Alex said. 'Will that work for you, Tony?'

'We'll get there as soon as we can,' Tony said.

176

It was probably good he couldn't race right after them. He didn't need to seem too anxious to find out what they would say, but he was more than anxious. His skin felt fashioned from flayed nerves.

Bill ducked over to pick up something too dark to see. He turned it over in his hand then held it out to Alex and dropped it in her palm. 'That's probably yours, not that it'll be of any use now.'

Twenty

'You won't try that again, will you?'

Alex kept her eyes on Bogie who lay on the steel table in Tony's surgery room. She concentrated on stroking the dog and moving some cast packing closer to Tony.

'Alex?'

'I intend to keep on riding the bike,' she said, still not looking up. 'I was doing well on the hill until I fell. I have to get better and that means more practice.'

He applied the packing around Bogie's lower leg and secured it with tape. 'Please open the cast material and hand it to me.' He had gone over the procedure before starting.

Even through her gloves, the roll of fiberglass felt damp. She pulled it from its package and put it into his waiting and gloved hand. Quickly, Tony wound the material on top of the packing and immediately went to work molding and smoothing it into a cast on Bogie's lower, right front leg.

177

'This doesn't give much time before it starts to set up,' he said, fashioning like a hand potter. Finally satisfied, he pulled away any loose pieces and stood holding Bogie's leg up. 'This takes about twenty minutes to be absolutely dry.' The dog slept peacefully on his side.

'Looking good,' Alex told him, but she didn't feel the way she sounded. She was anything but breezy.

'You'd be doing fine until a bus ran you over. Is that what you meant just now? Of course you were doing fine until you fell. What did Bill Lamb give you?'

All the way here she had feared Tony would ask that question, and when he didn't, she hoped the exchange with Bill had made no impression on him.

'Alex, for God's sake stop hedging.'

'Bill gave me a piece that must have fallen off the bike,' she said, starting to feel more defensive than was good for either of them.

He pulled down his mask. 'Which piece would that be?'

She swallowed and glanced around the sparkling room that his assistant, Radhika, kept so perfectly. 'A rubber piece,' she said at last.

'Let's have a look. You put it in your jeans' pocket.'

It was no longer an option to stonewall Tony on obvious things. And she was finally learning that losing her temper and announcing her independence, what was and wasn't her private business, sounded petulant.

She wore a green apron he'd given her and she reached beneath to get to her right pocket. 'Just this,' she said, holding out what was obviously

178

the end of a bicycle handlebar grip, probably two inches long and ripped from the rest.

'From the handlebar,' Tony said, wiping sweat from his brow and leaning over to see. He looked directly into her eyes. 'This is the handlebar that hit the ground when you were sliding down the hill?'

Mute, she looked at the scuffed lump of rubber in her hands. 'I think so.'

'But it was up on the road. Did it take wing and fly up there?'

'It could have bounced,' she mumbled.

'Something else happened, didn't it?' He took his eyes slowly from hers and checked Bogie's cast. 'Don't hide things from me. We're closer than that, or I thought we were.'

She felt cold and a little sick.

'Whatever bumped the handlebar happened before you went downhill, didn't it? It caused you to slide off the road?'

'I don't want any of this to be true, Tony. If nothing else happens we can assume it was an accident and the driver never knew. I don't think he did.'

His jaw hardened. 'Were you sideswiped by a vehicle?'

Nodding, she closed her eyes. 'It was getting really dark. I was at fault for riding up there at that time. The road was slippery.'

'All true to a degree, but you don't think it was an accident, do you.'

'I don't know.' Misery was horrible company. 'It could be he didn't see me.'

'I've seen the lights you got on that thing. At

least you did that right. Hold that piece where I can see it.'

She walked around to stand beside him and put the rubber on her palm, then rolled it back and forth. 'That grip had been new so it was hit hard – and split at the end. What shape is the handlebar in?'

'Okay! The handlebar is bent way up. Ruined. I don't think they can just mend that.'

'Okay, let's dial it back. Take a plastic bag and put it inside. There won't be any fingerprints but yours and Bill Lamb's but there could be paint from the vehicle. What was it?'

'Range Rover, I think. Dark green or dark blue, or black. I didn't realize it came so close. I'd moved all the way to the edge so I wouldn't be in the way. That's probably why I went off the road so easily.'

'When this is totally dry, I'm putting Bogie in a cage and we'll take that to O'Reilly and Lamb. It should have occurred to them that it might not have been an accident.'

Stupid tears filled her eyes and she swiped at them. 'Weak,' she muttered. 'I hate being weak. If they'd wanted to kill me they could easily have hit me and that would have been it. We're making too much of it.'

'They didn't want to kill you,' Tony said, and slid Bogie onto a dry towel. 'They wanted to scare the hell out of you. And if they didn't manage that with you, they most certainly did with me. Someone wants you to stop poking around Laura's death. You haven't done all that much, but you do show up whenever something's happening.'

180

Twenty-One

Dan O'Reilly rocked back and forth in his office chair, an improvement over what he'd used in the parish hall a few months earlier. He propped his feet on the trestle table that served as his desk and felt the familiar quiet night in the country settle around him.

One constable manned the silent phones, drinking coffee and reading a copy of *Twisted Dark* with the concentration Dan doubted he ever gave to his work. One day he'd have to look into why so many members of the force were hooked on all-but-banned comics.

Bill poured more muddy coffee. They were almost at the bottom of the latest urn from the Black Dog.

'How long does it take to set one mutt's leg?' Bill called. He piled stale doughnuts on a plate and walked slowly back with two Styrofoam cups gripped by conjoined lips.

'As long as it takes,' Dan responded, yawning. 'It's not as late as you think.'

'Did you know you're always more Irish when you're tired?' Bill asked. 'I'll need a translator shortly.'

Dan ignored him.

'We need to keep this one quiet,' Bill said, hooking his head in the direction of the engrossed constable.

'I'll make sure we do,' Dan said. 'Best you don't join us unless I give you the nod.'

Bill's irritation wasn't masked. 'Didn't I do a good job with your lady friend this morning?'

'I'll let that comment pass, or the first part of it. You didn't do badly except you gave her the rubbish about her solicitor. That was inappropriate and didn't work out so well.'

Never one to give away the last word, Bill said, 'Yeah, well, it was worth a try and it didn't do any harm.'

Dan declined the doughnuts but Bill bit into a sugar-covered jelly one with evident pleasure. 'My bed is calling me.'

'You mean your current bed. How are you and the missus these days?'

'Great,' Bill said with too much gusto. 'We went our separate ways months ago.'

Dan frowned. 'I'm sorry to hear that. I like Charlene.'

'I like her, too, but a copper's wife needs a special set of coping skills and she's worn them out. Or I've worn them out for her. Divorce will be final in a few weeks.'

'Christ!' Dan swung his feet to the floor. 'You've kept all this pretty close to your chest. How's young Simon taking it?'

'I'll get him some weekends – if I'm home. He's adjusting.'

'And you're fine with all this?'

Bill looked at him with the pale blue, unblinking eyes Dan had never quite got used to. 'I don't have a choice. Where the hell are those two?'

As if he'd summoned them up, the front door

182

to the parish hall scraped open and Alex Duggins preceded Tony Harrison into the big room. She wore the T-shirt and jeans they'd seen her in on the hill; Harrison wore a green scrub shirt over his trousers and a navy-blue jumper over the top. They were not happy people.

'Evening,' Dan called. 'Come and sit over here.' He checked the constable who continued to read. Given the nature of the case, they were getting very few calls at any time, least of all at night.

It didn't upset Dan to see the couple walking toward him with several feet between them. He cleared his throat. 'Get a couple of chairs, Bill.'

Harrison picked up two folded chairs himself and opened them in front of the trestle table. He and Alex sat down heavily.

'You'll want to see this,' she said, pushing a plastic bag across the table. 'It's the end of my hand grip from my bike. It got broken off when a Range Rover drove too close to me on the hill when I was going home. That's why I slid down the hill. I don't know if it was deliberate or not.'

Harrison patted her hand but she gave no sign of noticing.

'You're bloody kidding,' Dan said. 'Why didn't you say that up there?'

'I didn't want to. I wanted it all to go away. I've had about enough of people trying to scare me. What did I do to . . . Oh, forget it.'

'She told you what happened,' Tony said, leaning aggressively forward. He indicated Lamb. 'This one picked up the evidence – on the road – and gave it to Alex without forming a question in his mind. If she supposedly hit the handlebar

183

going down the hill, how would the grip be on the hill.'

'She lied.' Bill didn't raise his voice. No muscles appeared to move in his face. 'She should have said at once that a vehicle was involved. What vehicle? Did you get the license plate number?'

'While I was shooting downhill on my side, mixed up with my bike?'

'Range Rover,' Dan said, breathing through his mouth. 'Description.'

Alex reeled off what she remembered.

'Right,' Dan said. 'See what can be found, Bill. Give me that.' He took the piece of rubber and peered at it through the plastic bag. 'Not that fingerprints will be useful unless we're looking for you, Bill, or Alex. Damn, this is the kind of thing that drives me over the edge with you people. Half-truths and flat-out lies.'

'That's rubbish,' Alex said, rising to her feet. 'I was shocked up there. Bogie's got a broken leg. I admit I couldn't be sure if the vehicle deliberately got too close but I don't like accusing people of things. Once you do, other people get in their faces and it's hard to get them out.'

'Right,' Bill said, sneering. 'Let's keep all the sympathy for the perps. This was probably a hit-and-run driver. He knew what he was doing and intended to kill you.'

'Then he could easily have done it,' Alex said through her teeth. 'Do you think I enjoyed what happened up there? I'm absolutely frosted with all this intrigue. You could grow up and start treating us as if we've got at least one brain between us. Then who knows how far we might

184

get. It wouldn't be the first time joint effort paid off.'

Tony watched her with admiring eyes but knew she'd regret the last comment.

Bill Lamb got up and went over to the desk officer. What he said couldn't be heard, but the man swiftly moved to a computer and phones at a desk farther away from Dan.

'While I'm thinking about it, I should have mentioned seeing a man walk beside the rectory the morning Laura died. I don't know who it was, probably just someone using those lanes that go past there, but I keep forgetting to mention that.'

Dan's lips parted. He looked incredulous. 'Are you kidding . . .? Scratch that, you're not. You took your time deciding to mention this.'

Alex swallowed audibly. 'I wasn't sure it was significant.'

'I . . .' Dan raised his palms. 'I can understand you wanting to be careful about it, but it isn't your place to decide you should withhold evidence. And, no, we don't yet know who that was, but we will.'

'Why does it always get ugly with us?' Alex said. 'It's never been my choice to be embroiled in these cases.'

'Nor mine,' Tony said. 'Let's get to what you wanted to talk to us about. Alex is pretty shaken up and we need to get back to the dog.'

Dan slid open a bottom drawer. He withdrew a flask and an assortment of mismatched glasses – three of them and a plastic tumbler.

'Brandy,' he said without preamble, poured

some in a glass and stood to pass it over to Alex. 'It'll do you good and I know you like it.'

He dispensed some to the three other receptacles and handed them around. 'Not a peace offering. No need for that. It's late and this is a can of worms we've landed in here.'

Tony swallowed from his glass. Not bad and it felt good going down. 'Thanks.'

'For what it's worth,' Dan said, 'I agree that whoever tapped you up there, Alex, was trying to scare you off. What I don't know is why and I think we'd better be finding out fast before whoever did that gets more aggressive. No more riding bicycles in the dark until you get the all-clear. You understand?'

She sipped brandy. 'Understood. I didn't like it, either.'

'Where's the file we brought back?' Dan asked Bill.

Bill hopped up again, went to a desk behind Dan's and returned with a heavy brown folder. 'Guv,' he said, giving it up.

'I need to know if either of you knew any of the Quillams or their entourage before they came to Folly,' Dan said.

Shaking their heads, no, Tony and Alex's eyes met. They were both waiting for the next snippet they might get on the case.

'Damn, this place is stuffy,' Bill said. He got up and went around opening windows a fraction. 'It could use a good clean, too,' he called from the far side of the room.

No one responded.

'Do you check the gallery up there?' Tony asked.

'I forget it's sometimes but it wouldn't be hard for someone to get up there without being seen.'

'It's checked,' Dan said. 'Bill, take a quick look in the gallery, just to make sure it's empty.'

Tony thought he heard Lamb mutter, 'Tosser,' as he passed by.

'We have a list of suspects,' Dan said, shocking both Alex and Tony upright. 'We're still working on motives. Plenty of possibilities but nothing feels quite right. The thing is, you just might be able to help. These people are more likely to get careless and say something to you, than one of us.'

Bill returned and sat down again. He was obviously fit. Running up and down stairs didn't as much as make him breathe harder. 'Before we get any deeper in,' he said. 'Do—'

'Okay, Bill.' Dan cut him off. 'Sort through that folder for the post-mortem report.' He turned back to Tony and Alex. 'Is there anything at all that you can think of? Come on, is there anything? Something you've been batting around. An idea? Something you've heard? These people around here are sharp-eyed and they don't have much to do but watch other people.'

One of the windows rattled ferociously and Alex half closed her eyes. She gave her head a quick shake. But then she concentrated all her attention on Tony as if she was peering into his mind for an answer to what she – or he – ought to say.

He'd take over this one. It had to be worded with care and he could tell Alex wasn't keen on saying much about it at all. 'I think Sonia Quillam and Hugh Rhys may have known each other in

187

the past. Could be they were quite close. But that's conjecture.'

He had the two men's full attention.

'What makes you think that?' Dan asked.

'Just a very short conversation I heard outside the pub when they thought they were alone.'

'I heard it, too,' Alex said. 'I'd come around from the inn but Tony was on the path beside the pub. It was dark and it was raining. Neither of us stayed very long.'

'That's a damn shame,' Bill said. 'It's a good thing to know when honorable intentions are misplaced. If you'd stayed it could have been really useful.'

'What did they say?' Dan asked. He didn't so much as look at Bill. 'Anything you heard could be meaningful.'

Tony drank more brandy and put the glass on the desk. He propped his elbows on his knees and supported his head in both hands. 'I don't like this. It was obviously very private. You know Green Friday is Hugh's.' He didn't look up. 'Everyone in the village does. Could be Sonia used renting Green Friday as a way to get close to Hugh again. He doesn't seem interested, or didn't from the conversation they had. They were actually in the car park.'

Alex shifted in her seat. He felt her agitation.

'What did you hear?' Bill said.

'The same thing. It was embarrassing. Perhaps Sonia had had too much to drink. She seems a reserved woman normally.'

'We'll have to follow that up,' Dan said and Alex winced. 'I doubt anyone will know we've been asking questions and if they do, they'll have no way of connecting this to you.'

'It's horrible,' Alex said.

Tony nodded agreement. 'I doubt if it's got any direct bearing on the reason you're here in Folly.'

'We'll decide that,' Bill said and Tony didn't bother to indicate he had heard him.

'Laura Quillam didn't die of natural causes,' Dan said, flipping pages in the file. 'The police surgeon believes she was murdered and so do we.'

Turning in her chair, Alex gave Tony a pleading look. He heard her swallow, and swallow again.

'Then there are a couple of questions I wish you'd answer for us,' Tony said. 'Did the blow to her head come from the music stand? And is that what killed her? I don't see how someone managed to pick up the stand and hit her, then arrange her with her head on the base of the stand.'

'That wasn't what killed her,' Dan said, looking at Bill who easily slipped into one of his absolutely blank faces. 'She probably hit her head when she fell. From the evidence at the scene we know she was still alive when she went down but I doubt it was long after that she died. She would have passed out and slipped away. Too bad someone didn't get to her a bit sooner.'

'What killed her?' Tears stood in Alex's eyes but she didn't seem to notice. 'Who would do it? I haven't heard anything nasty about her.'

'We don't have the final results on some tests yet,' Dan said, scrabbling for his bag of sherbet lemons and popping one inside his cheek. 'The only people waiting for those results are Bill and me, forensics, and the killer. The killer doesn't

189

know quite as much as they think they do about what forensics can dredge up, although if everything had gone as planned, he or she might have got away with it.'

'Did someone slip something to her?' Tony said. He leaned back and clasped his hands behind his neck. 'Enough to make her pass out? Enough to kill her?'

'I really couldn't say,' Dan said, staring at each of them by turn. 'Laura was killed by someone who expected to get clean away with it. That's what we believe.'

'And now you two know,' Bill said quietly. 'So you'll be waiting for the results, won't you?'

Tony looked at him and didn't hide his dislike. 'And when the media get hold of it, as they will, and soon, everyone will know about it. You'll be facing the press and they aren't too polite to criticize police efforts.'

'So, if it's that important to keep the truth quiet until you know whatever bits are missing, you'd better get moving.' Alex didn't look anymore pleased than Tony felt.

Twenty-Two

Hardly speaking, Alex and Tony walked through the darkness toward the clinic. There was so much to talk about but Alex hadn't the faintest where to start and Tony was obviously in the same boat.

'Pretty night,' he said when minutes had passed. 'Hard to believe anything so pointless and so evil could happen in a place like this.'

'Yes,' Alex responded. 'Again and again and again. I feel so angry and so helpless. You realize this is another time when the clock was against us? If I'd gone into the church as soon as the music stopped, she'd be alive now.'

'You don't know that.'

But he knew how she felt. The sky looked like a bowl filled with tiny glass shards. Out here, without city lights, stars could strut their stuff with abandon.

'What did they mean when they said she hit her head but being hit on the head didn't kill her? Was she pushed? Would they be able to find that out?' She put an arm through his.

'Beats me.'

They jumped the tiny stream that ran in front of the row of cottages where Tony's clinic was housed and went around to the back where the garden had been turned into a car park. Tony's Range Rover was the only vehicle there.

'I hope I've got something decent to drink,' Tony said. 'Should have. I'm not here in the evening very often and I don't keep enough personal supplies most of the time. There's milk though. And tea. And biscuits. We can get our strength up before we sally forth.'

'I just want to see Bogie now. My poor little boy goes through so much with me as his mum.'

Tony laughed. 'At least you sound a bit less frazzled.' He unlocked the door and shepherded her inside and through to the room that doubled

191

as the office but also held several kennels. 'Shh,' he said. 'They're both asleep.'

He'd deliberately put a crate for Katie close to the one Bogie was using. Both dogs were breathing regularly. They lay, facing each other through the wire.

Tony backed out and pulled the door almost shut.

'Waiting room,' Tony said quietly and led the way into the next little room. 'Sit. Kick off your shoes.'

When he located a bottle of whisky in a cupboard, he grinned and Alex was reminded of the boy she'd known. He used two teacups from a tray on top of a miniature refrigerator and poured more than she thought he should for each of them. She didn't complain when she accepted the drink.

'Do you think your father could find out more details about the post-mortem?' Alex said and blushed a little. 'Sorry, that wasn't nice to suggest.'

'It was perfectly nice to suggest if he can do it. I'll call him first thing and ask. I wonder if Dan and Bill have talked to him again yet.'

'Mmm. They'd be likely to give him more specifics than us, wouldn't you think?'

'Possibly.' Tony set down his cup and hauled his jumper over his head. 'Don't need this on in here. It's too warm. But that's a good thought you just had. They could have said more to Dad. Or the pathologist might have talked to him about details relating to Laura when we found her.'

Tony's mobile rang and he felt all of his trouser pockets. 'Darn it, where have I put it?'

She reached over and lifted his sweater from the chair. 'There.' The phone was on the seat.

'Sheesh.' He punched it on, looked amazed and shook his head. 'Just a sec, I need to tell Alex something.'

He listened. 'At the clinic. Long story but Bogie broke a leg. He's just fine. Yes, she's here with me, I just said so.'

Alex watched him wait, saw him frown, 'Are you still there? Good. It's my dad, Alex, can you believe the coincidence?'

She shook her head, no, smiling and mentally reconstructing Doc's reaction to her being with Tony in the early morning. He should have accepted that much by now.

'That was the divisional surgeon who came to the church. Didn't get her title until now. Unfortunately we've met her before. Seems like a nice woman.'

Tony stared at Alex and raised his brows. He sank slowly into an old, floral-covered armchair. 'Professional courtesy? I'm glad she remembers the term. So . . . yes, I'll shut up.'

With the mobile pressed to his ear with his left hand, he slowly located and picked up his cup of whisky. From time to time he shook his head or winced.

Doc James spoke for at least ten minutes. Alex began to feel she might shed her skin altogether, it felt as if it was shrinking to a tiny size.

'I appreciate it, Dad,' Tony said finally. 'But . . . hell, I don't envy the plods trying to sort this out. Of course I'll keep it quiet. That's understood. I will tell Alex and she'll understand, too.

Do you have any ideas? Yes, yeah, we're all going to have to do that, but it does sound like a one-off.'

'Of course, I hope I'm right.' He swallowed too much of the whisky and coughed. 'I'm fine. I hadn't thought of that one yet but Alex probably has. This is like having a poisonous snake living in your herbaceous border. Thanks. Bye.'

'I didn't think I could be stunned by anything anymore, but I'm stunned,' Tony said. 'The police surgeon called Dad. She was looking for ideas, I think. That's what we're going to be doing.'

'Will you tell me what he said?' Alex almost shouted.

'Laura died of an overdose of digoxin.'

It was her turn to frown. 'How would that happen? She'd probably been on the stuff for years. She wouldn't be likely to make a mistake.'

'You've already got a bit of this in one go, or I think you do.' He pointed at her, sinking his teeth into his lower lip. Taking a big breath, he added, 'I think whoever did this hoped it would look like suicide.'

Alex got up and paced. She went to the tiny, high window and closed the chintz curtains. 'Why do they think it's murder rather than suicide?'

'Apparently Laura had plans. She was getting away from the family. Moving on. There was a man in the picture. Don't ask me who. I don't know and neither did my father. I think that could have been one of the things on the police surgeon's mind. Strictly speaking, that's not her business, but we all get involved emotionally from time to time. I think with a young victim like that I can understand not finding it so easy to let go.'

A shiver ran up her spine. 'How do they know about the man?'

'Anonymous tip. Someone called and said Laura had every reason to live because she had plans. And she was leaving soon. Also she wasn't feeling well the morning she died. I suppose that could have had something to do with too much digoxin in her system already. Mrs Meeker mentioned that. For all we know, she could have made the call. The operator didn't get a name and didn't remember if it was a male or female voice.'

'What else did Doc say?' She was too edgy to stay in one place. She kept seeing Laura on those cold stone flags – so pretty, so dead.

'He said whoever made that call to the police used what they call a burner phone. Use once and get rid of it. And it sounds as if the person's got detailed and intimate information about some of the family's private business.'

'I know what a burner phone is.' She thought she sounded like a shrew and sucked in the corners of her mouth. 'Sorry to be snippy. I'm trying to figure this out. Did someone up her dosage of digoxin? Wouldn't she have noticed something like that? And the anonymous call. I think "why" is more important than "who".'

Tony offered her his hand and she took it. He pulled her closer. 'We need a different hobby.'

'No kidding.'

'Dad said they're waiting for some final results but they think she was already taking more of the drug than she needed.' He held up his free hand.

'Don't ask me why. They think the actual overdose that killed her was in liquid form. She drank it.'

'And didn't know? I don't see how.'

'The liquid is lime flavored, but it still tastes bitter. Mix it with something that masks the bitterness, the person would drink down and that's how.'

She closed her eyes. 'Tony, the thermos. That's it, isn't it? It was in there and she drank it in the church.'

He didn't answer and she looked at him.

'What the devil happened to it, Alex? We all saw it. Now it's gone. How?'

She walked away from him. 'I want to go back into the church and search.'

'You think the police haven't already taken the place apart? Someone took it away and it had to be after we were taken to the rectory.'

'Tony, do you have any way of knowing it was still there then?'

He shook his head, no. 'But it had to be. It's got to be a mistake forensics made. It can't have just disappeared. Evidence gets mislabeled or lost. If they can find it, they can test it and they'll know what was in it. They are so much better at those things than people know.'

Her mind was blank.

Tony shoved his hands in his pockets. 'It's hard to get rid of something like that. It doesn't burn well and if it's been tossed, it's likely to be found. And they'll find any traces left behind. I'd like to look at one. They've probably changed. That was an old one but we could try finding one like it on eBay.'

'You're full of good ideas.'

196

Sebastian Carstens might have been the last person either of them expected to hear from, but the doorbell rang and when Tony answered, there stood Sebastian. One hand behind his neck, the other poised as if to push open the door himself, he took a step backward, perilously close to the stream that was barely visible in the darkness.

Hovering in the doorway to the waiting room, Alex saw Sebastian attempt to barge past Tony, who held him where he was.

'I know the police talk to you,' Sebastian said, his voice squeezed. 'Everyone says they do. I want you to help me.'

'Calm down,' Tony said.

Sebastian pointed past Tony, toward Alex. 'She knows. She knows more than anyone else in Folly. She's been involved in a lot of things around here. When we came here it was for peace. Elyan needs peace to work and so do I. And so does my little girl. It's all too much. I want to know what they're saying. If they're saying I had something to do with Laura's death, I *need* to know so I can make arrangements for Daisy.'

Alex had never expected to feel pity for this man, but she did now. She believed he was stretched to his limit and that he was concerned, above all else, for his child.

'Tony,' she said quietly, 'let him come in.' It could be that some answers were about to be dropped on them from an unlikely source.

With a brief glance at her, Tony let the man in. 'Wait here. I have a patient to check.' He gave Alex another, more significant look and she went directly into his office.

197

Tony followed her and closed the door behind her. 'What the hell?' he said, spreading his hands. 'What does he think we can do to help him?'

'We can't,' she said. 'But he might know something we don't know and I don't think he's the type to talk freely to the police.'

'We'll see.' Tony knelt to check Bogie who grunted, sighed, and settled back to sleep. Katie hadn't moved since the last time they came. 'I envy these two. Are you as tired as I am?'

'I think I'm too wound-up to be tired, not that I'd mind lying down and trying to clear my mind.'

He ruffled her hair and opened the door again. Sebastian was exactly where they'd left him. Tony led the way back into the waiting room but offered the man nothing other than a chair. 'What's got you so upset?' he asked.

Sebastian sat on a straight-backed chair and ran his fists up and down his thighs. 'They're taking Green Friday apart,' he said. 'Middle of the night and they come and start tearing things apart again. Percy's useless. He just rages. Wells is furious, but he doesn't say a word, just stands there, glaring. And the women look terrified. Damn, I hate this. I put Elyan in the music room and told him to sleep. He may be tired enough to do it. It's a good thing Annie's gone back home for a couple of days.'

'I take it you mean the police are searching the house,' Tony said.

'Of course. What else would I mean? Waving their sodding warrant in our faces. Mrs M. looked done in. She went back to bed and told them to search around her. Sonia had hysterics. She

198

wanted to call their solicitor but Percy wouldn't, said it wasn't necessary. But, god, he's horrible when things don't go his way. And my poor Daisy. She isn't used to being upset.'

'Where is she?' Alex asked. She couldn't help herself.

Sebastian looked stricken. 'Oh, my god. She's outside in the car.' He threw open the waiting-room door and rushed from the house.

'This could be a lot closer than we want to get to these people's problems,' Tony said. 'Are you all right?'

'I don't know,' she told him honestly. 'What are we supposed to say? What does he think we can do to help him?'

Footsteps returned and the front door slammed. Sebastian came into the room carrying Daisy who slept on his shoulder.

'Good grief,' Tony muttered. 'Put her on the little settee.'

Sebastian did as suggested, setting the little girl down without waking her. The child's black ringlets fell forward over her face. She sighed, wriggled, and grew still with one arm flung out. A blue cotton nightgown covered her thin form. She was smaller than Alex remembered.

'Keep your voices down or you'll wake her,' Tony said, and Alex smiled at the way he took charge in any situation.

'Just tell me who I should be looking out for,' Sebastian said. 'Who is it who's telling all these things to the police? We've got a killer running around and I don't know where to take Daisy for safety. The police keep asking the same people

199

the same questions and going in circles. They don't have any suspects. Or I don't think so.'

'The police seem to ask the same questions over and over,' Alex told him. 'But they change them a bit. They add things as they find out more. It's normal in an investigation.'

'Well, you should know,' Sebastian said, and shook both hands in the air. 'I don't mean that the way it sounds. Not anymore. I know you two have been pulled into things that were nothing to do with you. But listen to you, Alex. You know what you're talking about with this sort of thing.'

She could only look at the floor and feel useless.

Sebastian sat on the very edge of a chair. 'If you were me, what would you try to do? Even if I wanted to abandon ship and clear out with Daisy, I don't think I'd be allowed to go.'

'I doubt it.' Tony stood up. 'Is there someone Daisy can be sent to? Her mother?'

The man grew very still and stared past Tony. 'She only has me. We . . . we have each other and that's good enough.'

'Not if you want her out of this,' Tony pointed out.

'There is no one.' Sebastian's expression was stony. 'Would they put someone on guard, do you think?'

'That, I don't know,' Tony said. 'But you should put the idea to them. There's always concern for children's welfare.'

'I could take her to my mother's,' Alex said, the words popping out without passing her brain. She gulped. 'I would stay there, too, and there would always be someone with her.'

Sebastian frowned.

She avoided looking at Tony. 'Mum lives in Corner Cottage opposite the Black Dog. We can get the job done and you wouldn't have to worry.' Alex hoped that was really true.

'She'd be frightened. But it's a kind offer.' His mobile rang and he answered, his indecision about Alex's offer showing in the way he looked from her to Daisy.

'Should we leave you?' Tony said quietly.

'I can't understand you,' Sebastian said shortly into his phone. 'Slow down, Percy.'

Alex remembered Bill Lamb's warning about not missing important information. She shook her head slightly at Tony and clasped her hands behind her back.

'Why?' Sebastian's natural pallor increased. 'None of this has anything to do with me.'

As he listened, he slowly stood up. 'And if I don't come back?' He watched his sleeping daughter. 'Calm down, yes. *Yes*, I'm telling you to calm down. You're making it harder on everyone. Tell me what's happened and why O'Reilly is throwing threats around. I don't have to do anything he tells me to.'

With a hand propping his brow, he closed his eyes. 'Something horrible has happened, hasn't it?' Alex could hear the caller shouting. 'Okay, okay, okay, I'll be there.'

'Something's gone wrong at Green Friday?' Tony asked. 'Can we help?'

'I don't know . . . Can you keep Daisy here, please? Just until I can come for her.'

'Yes,' Tony and Alex said in unison.

'If I'm not back by morning . . . I'll get a message to you later anyway. They'll let me do that.'

Twenty-Three

The Quillam household would be interesting if being there weren't irritating as hell. Billeted in the dining room which Percy Quillam had allotted the police – with a dismissive flourish toward its grandeur – Dan O'Reilly glanced repeatedly to the open French windows. Rustling and an occasional shout came from the police outside.

'Tell them to go as carefully as they can,' Dan told Bill, indicating officers who searched bushes and tromped their boots through flowerbeds to do the job. 'From the look and sound of Quillam Senior, we'll get a list of every broken twig.'

On his way to spread an extra warning to the team outside, Bill said, 'They aren't his twigs.'

'I don't give a monkey's who owns the twigs. Whatever we mess up, we'll hear about it. This isn't your East End borough.' Tiredness and frustration were finally heating him up. 'Around here, they leave a car with four wheels, they expect to come back to four wheels. So just tell the Big Foot clones to be bloody careful.'

From a room that couldn't be that far away, given the volume, Elyan Quillam was playing. What, O'Reilly had no idea but it sounded as if he had three pairs of hands. No one pair could move that fast, or that furiously. Dan liked music, especially

Irish folk music, but compelling as the young man's piano feats were, the piece was a mystery to him.

Spread over the glassy surface of the dining table were the folders Dan and Bill had brought with them and a few useless pieces found outside and carefully placed on a sheet of plastic. There was far more information among the piles of paper than some of the people in this house would like, but the Rubik's cube that was the case felt stuck and with a lot of pieces out of place.

The family and entourage had gathered in a sitting room from which raised voices could be heard from time to time, although not so much since Elyan began venting on the piano. It did sound like angry music – or perhaps it was just the startling volume and the waterfalls of notes that emanated from the music room. Dan had been told Elyan was resting in there. Some rest. The supercilious Wells Giglio – a name Dan could imagine on a brand of shoes – made repeated trips to the bathroom, his hands clutching his belly and his head angled down, presumably to hide the agony on his face.

And rather than do as he'd been told and remain with the others, Sebastian Carstens had left. No one even heard him go and if Elyan hadn't finally, unwillingly, said he'd gone for a drive, they would be searching the estate for him by now.

They had discovered, unexpectedly, that there was a back entrance to the grounds. Apparently that was the escape route Sebastian had taken. Dan still felt furious that none of his men had reported it to him before.

Her backless high-heeled green shoes tapping

and slapping as she walked, Sonia Quillam came into the room, clicking her fingernails against the door on her way but not stopping to see if she was invited in.

'This is not fair,' she told Dan. This wasn't his first exposure to her but the result was the same – things male registered.

He opened a folder and flipped pages. 'What isn't fair, Mrs Quillam?'

Her green caftan, cinched under impossible to ignore breasts with a band of gold braid, swirled around her with a swishing sound, the silky material touching here and there as it found waiting curves.

'We are the ones who have suffered a terrible loss but we're also the ones you're persecuting. I'd like to know why.' Dark blond curls were caught up at the crown of her head and she looked at him with narrowed eyes a few shades darker than the hair. Under other circumstances he would like to sit back and look at her – for a long time.

This was the wrong moment to raise Hugh Rhys's name. 'I'm sure it seems like that. Having strangers all over your home in the little hours of the morning would be upsetting to anyone. I apologize for that but developments in the case make it necessary. We're waiting for Mr Carstens to get back before we start inside. We'd like everyone present.'

'Start without him,' she said.

'It's been suggested that's not a good idea, not with his child asleep in the house.'

She pressed her hands together as if in prayer. 'Daisy will be all right.'

204

What could have happened between Rhys and this woman to make the man hostile toward her? Dan made a mental note to chivvy whoever was following up that piece of history. He wondered if the two could have been an item before her marriage to Quillam, or after, or both.

A door at the back of the house slammed and Sonia jumped. 'That could be Sebastian now. He uses the back entrance like some tradesman. It's a pity he doesn't get . . . No matter.'

'Finish what you were going to say,' Dan told her, with a look that let her know he was insisting. The back entrance was being mentioned at every turn now. He willed his blood pressure to go down.

'I almost said tradesmen's wages which would be ridiculously unfair. Forget I said it, please.'

Dan didn't ask if she knew what tradesmen were worth these days. 'I'll meet him.' A sweeping glance over the table and he knew he couldn't leave everything out. 'Could you perhaps ask him to come in here? This is where my people expect to find me.'

There was no need for anyone to hunt down Sebastian Carstens. He walked into the room and gave Sonia a poor effort at a smile. 'How are you doing, Sonia? Have Mrs Meeker get you some tea. You look tuckered out.'

'I would if she hadn't decided she needed her beauty rest. Cheek.'

Sebastian nodded. 'I'd forgotten. So why has Mr Quillam summoned me back? I got the impression you might be thinking of arresting me, detective.'

'You know how Percy gets,' Sonia said. 'He's beside himself. And if he keeps drinking, he'll be unconscious soon.'

'Never rains but it bleedin' pours,' Bill Lamb said through his teeth, coming into the room and before he noticed Dan wasn't alone. He didn't look embarrassed. 'Glad you're here, Mr Carstens. I didn't know you'd come back. Come to that, we didn't know you'd left when you'd been told not to.'

Dan put a hand on Sonia Quillam's shoulder and walked her to the door. 'If you don't mind, we'd prefer to speak to Mr Carstens alone. You can report back that it looks as if we'll be starting on the house almost at once.'

He didn't watch her leave, but he heard the heels of those shoes tapping, and the slapping of leather against soft feet. Shoes easy to kick off.

Dan pushed the door to behind her but didn't close it. 'You took your little girl out of the house, Mr Carstens. You could have asked us if that was necessary.'

'I'm her father. I decide what's necessary for her. And how do you know what I did?'

Bill showed unusual restraint. 'Everything's fine, sir. But Dr Tony Harrison is in the hall and Ms Duggins is in his car with your daughter. They say they had to come after you almost at once. When you left the child with them she was asleep. It frightened her to be with strangers when she woke up. Children do get frightened by strange situations, don't they?'

Carstens showed signs of rushing past them but Dan held up a hand. 'We all do what we

206

think is best at the time. Bill, will you have Tony and Alex bring little Daisy in. It'll help if she sees her dad's okay and he's okay with the people he left her with.'

Damn and blast, those two turned up like maggots in a rubbish bin. They were inevitable. Someone or something always brought them tripping through his cases in this blighted village.

He heard Daisy sobbing before he saw Tony carrying the little girl and Alex trotting along rubbing the kid's back.

'Daisy, darling,' Sebastian Carstens said. He looked and sounded distraught. Nothing put on about that. 'I'm sorry. Tony and Alex are good friends of mine and I thought you'd be happier with them for the night. You know you don't like bother and there's a lot of bother going on here tonight.'

Good friends? Wheels within wheels.

The child settled in her father's arms and immediately quieted. 'Papa, I didn't know where I was.' She sounded cross. 'And you didn't bring my glasses so I could see properly. And I wanted to be with you.'

'Tell them to get started inside,' Dan told Bill, who left the room with speed.

Within minutes, while the dining room group stood trying not to meet anyone's eyes, the unmistakable thuds of a number of feet entered the house and Bill could be heard dispatching officers to different areas.

Alex was too pale. She chewed on her bottom lip and watched the child worriedly. 'Couldn't you get her settled down somewhere?' She came

207

close and Dan subdued the urge to put an arm around her shoulders.

'We will,' he said quietly. 'We didn't plan for things to go this way. You know that.'

She smiled at him, said, 'I do know that,' and he wished he could cut out the part of him that reacted whenever he looked at her. 'What a mess this is, Dan. Are you making any progress.'

He couldn't manage the steel he needed and rubbed her back. 'Hold in with me. I'll sort it out,' he said.

The officer he recognized as Wicks knocked and entered the room. He pressed his lips together, tried to smile at Alex but couldn't manage it. 'Sir, we need you,' he said to Dan.

Dan followed the man into the hall. The trouble in clear, dark eyes hadn't gone unnoticed. 'What is it?'

Elyan Quillam threw open the door to the music room. His hair was wild, his mouth slightly opened as he breathed hard. He passed Wicks and Dan and started for the stairs.

'Wait, please sir,' Wicks said, and his dark skin glistened with sweat. 'Where are you going?'

'I can't concentrate here,' he shouted, raking his hair back. 'Not like this. Why are you searching the house? You're agitated – who wouldn't feel it? It's something else, isn't it? Tell me what's wrong. Now.' It was the first time Dan had heard the young man raise his voice and he was yelling at full volume now.

Wicks looked to Dan for guidance.

Elyan paced a few steps in several directions, wringing his hands. For the first time Dan saw something of Percy Quillam in his son.

208

'Sir,' Wicks said. He kept looking at Elyan. 'Chief Inspector, we need you upstairs.'

Every policeman's nightmare was shaping up in front of him. The door to the sitting room had opened and the family and those close to them started to spill out, slowly, one behind the other.

'Stay where you are. All of you,' Dan said sharply, grateful that Bill appeared and stood at the bottom of the stairs like a blockade. 'Right, lead the way, Wicks.'

From his peripheral vision he saw Bill start up the stairs and Tony Harrison and Alex slide from the dining room and follow, quietly but deliberately. Whatever had happened, they'd know soon enough. He realized he would prefer them to know, and to hear what they had to say about it.

At the top of the stairs, Wicks led the way to another, narrower flight, and followed him upward to a small, square hall furnished with a table and two narrow leather armchairs. A bowl of chrysanthemums, gold, were in the middle of the table, their reflection mirrored in a highly polished surface.

'Mrs Meeker's rooms,' Wicks said. 'She chose to go to bed. She was too tired to stay up any longer. She told us to search around her. Constable Miller went in to wake her so she wouldn't be shocked.'

Dan heard Alex swallow and saw from the corner of an eye that Tony put an arm around her shoulder. Sebastian Carstens, his child still in his arms, appeared behind them.

Too late to stop this now. Ordering them all back down would only alarm the child.

The door stood wide open and another police constable, this one female, kept vigil on the far side of a damask-covered bed. Dan nodded at her. 'Come on,' he said. 'What is it. Spit it out.'

'The lady is dead, sir,' Wicks said, spreading his arms as if it were his fault. 'I'm sorry.'

With Alex and Tony, Dan went to the bedside. Maud Meeker was, indeed, dead. A tall drained cocktail tumbler, on its side, lay on the coverlet.

'I'm sad,' a child's small, shaky voice said. 'My mummy is dead like that. It made her go away. It's not nice.'

Twenty-Four

Green Friday had become a seething conglomeration of police, including those SOCO people Alex had already seen a few times too many, and a parade of equipment from the horrible white lights to metal suitcases to the kind of still and movie cameras no amateur had ever used.

In the sitting room where Percy Quillam had refused, volubly, to have the door closed on all of them, the atmosphere had passed electric some time ago and now felt as if it would crackle aloud if angry voices didn't drown everything out.

A woman in mufti, 'call me, Polly', who introduced herself as 'family liaison' came to talk to Sebastian. When she addressed Daisy, it was in a babyish voice that made Alex shudder, and Daisy frown. The little girl had cried softly since they were banished from the area of Mrs Meeker's rooms.

When Polly reached for Daisy, the girl let out a piercing shriek and clung to her father.

'Well, now,' Polly said. 'This is quite normal. Let me see if I can get some milk and biscuits for you while you sit with Daddy and get used to Polly. I expect everyone could use a nice cup of tea.'

The instant she left, Elyan exploded with, 'Oh, my, God, what an ass.'

'She means well,' Sonia said. 'Daisy shouldn't be in the middle of all this.'

'They aren't about to let me leave,' Sebastian pointed out. He glanced at Tony and Alex. 'I wish we'd been better prepared for her to stay with you until I could get away.'

Alex didn't comment on the collective term. There was nothing to be gained by sniping at the man. 'Tony,' she said quietly, pulling him as far from the others as she could get, 'do you have any idea what killed Mrs Meeker? She looked asleep apart from the color.'

'And the slackness,' Tony added. 'And the lack of breath . . . Sorry. I'm as punchy as anyone. The glass is bound to bring the obvious to mind.'

'Dan will think the same thing,' Alex said. 'I want to get out of here and start asking some questions. Why would the glass be left behind when the thermos was taken? I wish your dad was here. If he could take a look at her it would help. Would digoxin do you harm – as in kill you – if you didn't have a heart condition?'

'As far as I know, yes. I don't know how much

211

of it you'd need to do the job, though. That was a good-sized tumbler, if that's what happened and she drank the stuff. Remember how much strain she's been under and she's not a young woman. Who knows what condition she was in?'

She glanced over her shoulder at a roomful of people involved in their own thoughts and conversations. 'If the glass is significant, it was left behind because it was meant to be found.'

Alex got close to a curtain and raised her chin to whisper to him. 'We arrived after Mrs Meeker died. We don't know a thing about what happened here. Even Bill Lamb can't argue with that. I want to see if they'd let us leave on those grounds. If we could persuade Daisy we're a better alternative than Polly – and make it clear her father can't leave – she might be too tired to fight it. She could come back with us.'

'Sebastian's the only one who could persuade her. And I believe Bill could argue anything just to keep the balance of power in his own court. Sebastian's coming this way.'

They both turned to face Sebastian and Daisy who drew close. 'What do you think?' Sebastian said. Daisy twisted in his arm to look at Tony and Alex.

'I don't think this is good for a little girl,' Tony said, aiming a serious and very grown-up look at Daisy. 'This isn't much fun, is it?'

'It's very not fun,' Daisy said. 'Is Mrs Meeker going to wake up? Did they mean she's dead for certain sure?'

Tears were coming too easily to Alex. She blinked them back and shook her head.

Daisy touched her face. 'I said it makes you sad. Daddy, can we go away from here?'

'I'm going to ask to talk to O'Reilly,' Alex said quickly, with a hard stare at Sebastian. 'I want to get away from here, too, and I think we can. We're just bystanders. I'll leave you three to talk.'

A policeman was stationed outside the room, to the left of the door. Alex stood in front of him as he started into his spiel about not leaving the room, and smiled at him.

'I'd like to talk to Chief Inspector O'Reilly, please. It's important.'

The man looked pained. 'Is there a message I can pass on, madam?'

'Thank you for offering but I'd better talk to him directly about this. He'd want that.'

With a sigh, the grizzled officer used his radio, asked someone else to pass along that 'one of the family' wanted to speak to the guv'nor.

As she felt the approach of an instruction to go back into the sitting room, she heard footsteps coming down flights of stairs. The house was three stories high and there were plenty of stairs.

When Dan appeared from the hall, he pushed his hands in his trouser pockets and didn't look happy. 'Which family member?' he asked the officer, not looking at Alex.

'He means me,' Alex said. She didn't smile or feel moved to do so. 'I didn't say who I am. A moment please, chief inspector.'

Dan did smile. His jaw creased along the line of his scar but his smile was disarming. 'Of course, Ms Duggins.' He indicated for her to follow him back toward the hall.

213

'Tony and I haven't been here today. We weren't here when whatever has happened, happened.'

He looked at the sweep of gleaming banister, following it up the stairs as if momentarily lost in his own thoughts.

'Dan?'

'Yes?' he said. She got one of his penetrating stares. 'You were saying you haven't been here. Your point?'

She began to feel irritated. 'We have nothing to do with this house or anything that happens in it. Would it be okay with you if we went back to the clinic. Bogie needs checking and Katie needs to go outside – so does Bogie.'

'How interesting.'

'Whew.' She blew upward at a trailing curl. 'This isn't getting any easier. Could we please leave? We're hoping to take Daisy with us again.'

'That didn't go so well the last time.'

'She can't stay here,' Alex told him. 'Tony and Sebastian are chatting with her in there and with luck that will put her more at ease. You don't have to worry. We'll go to the clinic, bed Daisy down and stay there until her father can pick her up.'

In typical Dan fashion, he looked at his shoes before raising his face again. 'Any thoughts on what went on here tonight?'

It took a moment to register what he'd asked. 'All I got was a perfunctory glance. I bet forensics has that tumbler safely packed up and labeled.'

He wasn't amused. 'Yes. And unless that thermos took flight from the church, we'll find that, too.'

214

'I wonder if Laura and Mrs Meeker died the same way. Do you think they did?'

He took her by the elbow and led her to stand in the open front door. A policeman was on guard at the bottom of the steps.

'Maybe we'll get some sun tomorrow,' Dan said. 'It's time something brightened up around here.' He kept holding her arm. His scent was something ordinary and masculine – nice.

'I really couldn't answer your question, but you know that.'

'Have they finished the final tests on Laura?'

He considered. 'Yes.'

'So you know how she died?'

'Yes.'

'But you really couldn't tell me, could you.'

'You learn fast. I'm going to let you and Tony go to the clinic. Is there somewhere you can get some rest there?'

She looked up at him quickly, but didn't rise to the bait. 'Absolutely. Thanks for caring.'

'All right. Go and see if the child will go with you and don't go anywhere else but the clinic.'

Without a word, she left him there, staring at a sky that could easily portend a fine day to come.

Back in the sitting room she found the cheery Polly handing mugs of tea around. Daisy had taken a biscuit but preferred keeping a hand on Sebastian to holding a glass of milk.

Tony and Sebastian had both declined tea. Alex rejoined them with a deliberate smile stretching her mouth. 'Tony and I may go back to the clinic,' she told Sebastian, raising her eyebrows in question.

'Lucky you. It looks as if we remain here for the duration.'

'We have to go and see my dog, Bogie,' Alex said, widening her smile at Daisy. 'And Katie, Tony's dog.'

'I didn't see them there,' Daisy said promptly. She wore her green-flecked glasses again and they turned her into an even more serious-looking child than before. 'I liked Bogie.'

Anything they said would sound contrived but Tony took an audible breath and said, 'If you like, you can come back with us and help with the dogs. Then your daddy would come and get you when all this is finished here.'

Daisy looked at her father while Alex held her breath.

'Will you be all right if I go?' Daisy asked. 'It's not far and perhaps you won't be long.'

'Well . . . yes, I'll be all right. But you must promise me to at least lie down and rest. After the dogs go back to sleep, that is.'

A sudden bellow startled them all. Percy Quillam had risen from a corner on a couch where he had sunk into an evil mood that showed. 'What are you three babbling on about over there?' he shouted. 'How do you know each other? Sonia, have you seen them together before? Who are those two?'

'Alex owns the pub, darling,' Sonia said without registering surprise at her husband's manner and tone. 'And Tony is the local vet. If you weren't so standoffish, you'd have met them, too, wouldn't he, Elyan?'

Wanting to duck out on this conversation and

get going, Alex said, 'It's nice to meet you, Mr Quillam. I'm very sorry for your losses.'

He stared at her across the beautiful, cold room and the experience wasn't pleasant. 'Bloody strangers in a man's house,' he muttered.

'We have to leave everyone,' Tony said and Daisy held out her arms to him. He looked pleased to carry her and helped Sebastian slip her cardigan on. 'Good night to you. I'm so sorry.'

'What the fuck is that!' Quillam said, rocking up onto his toes.

'Percy!'

Percy wasn't to be chastised by Sebastian or anyone else. 'Fucking racket will wake the dead.' He smirked at his own sick little joke.

There was a racket indeed, coming from the area of the foyer. Through the open door Alex saw Wells Giglio all but fall into the hall. He hadn't spent much time in Folly as far as she knew but a good deal of that had been at the Black Dog where he was already a great favorite thanks to his willing wallet and largesse.

Sonia went to him and took his arm. 'Wells, where have you been? You said you were going to the bathroom.'

'And going, and going,' Percy intoned. 'Until he quite disappeared. Why did you come back?'

'This is the first time I've seen him since we arrived,' Alex said.

Sonia had shifted to drape Wells' arm around her shoulders while she held him up and they shuffled forward together. She was stronger than she looked.

The man's bleary eyes didn't focus. A silly grin

217

made a complete distortion of his face. 'Been in and out.' He wagged a finger. 'Tiptoed, through the tulips . . . into the rose garden and out the back way. Thank god we can park out there and get away. Only drove once, though. Just went and came back. Thought it was time.'

'Snotty upstart's been tippling all night,' Percy roared. 'Bathroom, my eye. The Bottle and Bog, what!' He giggled delightedly to himself.

'Can we just go?' Alex said. 'Before someone says we have to stay?'

Sonia and Wells were in the room where Elyan took over custody and pushed Wells into a chair.

'Life of the place, I was,' Wells said. 'You should have heard them when I spread all the news.'

'What place?' Elyan asked.

'Only place in this manure heap. Black Dog. They asked and I told them. About time someone told 'em what's going on. Only fair.' He burped, and sniggered.

'Got to go again,' he added, struggling to rise. 'Delhi belly's a hell of a thing.'

Twenty-Five

'Good grief,' Tony said, pulling into the car park at the back of the clinic. 'What are they doing here?'

'*How* did they get here,' Alex responded ducking to peer at the Burke sisters, bundled in coats and scarves and seated on folding chairs by the back steps. She looked over her shoulder at the sleeping Daisy in the car seat her father had produced. 'If we could get her inside without waking her it would be a relief. Stay with Daisy. I'll make sure our reception committee knows to be quiet.'

The two old ladies dispatched the first question before it was asked. 'Kev Winslet never says no to a bit of extra,' Harriet said. 'We got hold of him on his mobile while he was still at the Dog and he picked us up on his way.'

'There's a little girl asleep in the car,' Alex said. 'She belongs to the man who is Elyan Quillam's piano tutor. We're bringing her back here to get her away from all the activity at Green Friday. The police—'

'We know all about it,' Mary said, her headscarf propped up in the middle by her mantilla comb.

Alex frowned. 'The Black Dog closed hours ago.'

'We've been here a long time,' Harriet said. 'But we came prepared.' Each woman held a plastic mug of tea and had a blanket spread over her knees. 'That Kev Winslet is a piece of work. Why the Derwinters don't find a different game-keeper, I can't imagine. Probably too busy being important to know what any of their staff get up to.'

'Tony's going to carry Daisy in, hopefully without waking her up, and we'll try to settle her down. Follow us in and wait in the passageway until we can see which room will be free.'

She didn't wait for an answer, but didn't hear

219

one. Beckoning Tony to join her, she walked back. He was out and quietly sliding the door shut before opening the one behind his seat to unbuckle Daisy. He managed to transfer the girl, still sleeping, to his shoulder and they walked as quietly as they could to the cottage.

As he passed the sisters, Tony waggled fingers at them but didn't speak. Alex admired his discipline.

Inside, he didn't pause before going to a very narrow flight of stairs and treading softly upward. In a little bedroom with curtains drawn over the window and a single bed covered with a puffy duvet, he set her down as if she were made of crystal. Daisy promptly rolled on her side, pulled up her knees and slumbered on.

Alex stood on tiptoe and put her mouth to his ear. 'She'll be really frightened if she wakes here and doesn't see a familiar face.'

'Takes two seconds to run up those stairs and pick her up.' They both watched Daisy a while. She was obviously in an exhausted sleep. 'Let's get our ladies dealt with so we can both be listening. Why are they here?'

She took him by the hand, led him from the room and pulled the door to until it was only open a couple of inches. They left the landing light on. 'I don't know,' Alex told him, on her toes again. 'I think they've been out there for hours. Kev Winslet dropped them off – for a fee, I gather.'

'He'll wish he hadn't,' Tony muttered. 'Thoughtless bastard.'

Harriet and Mary stood against a wall in the passageway, holding scarves and coats against their chests. They'd left their chairs and provisions outside.

'Go in here with Alex,' Tony said, indicating the miniature sitting room. 'I need to see to a patient and let Katie out.'

When their visitors had taken seats, one on either side of the fireplace, Alex turned on the electric fire and immediately smelled toasting dust. The fire couldn't have been used for weeks or even months. 'Tea?' she asked quietly – heading for an electric kettle and holding up a box of tea bags.

At least they didn't grimace, but the 'No, thank you,' they both gave was loaded with disapproval.

Katie barked and Alex held her breath, waiting for a cry from Daisy. It didn't come.

'We saw that little girl at the playground,' Mary said. 'We were out walking. Seems like a nice child, but very quiet. Too grown up. We saw her with a man, probably her father, and we didn't go into the playground. Flashy car parked there. Green sports car. They all have expensive vehicles – and expensive everything else.'

With Bogie under his arm, Tony led Katie into the room. Predictably she went to sit between her chums in front of the fire. 'Sit down,' Tony told Alex. 'I'll put this one on your lap. He's fine but probably sore.'

Alex took Bogie and he gave a grateful sigh. Hands behind his back, Tony remained standing. 'You shouldn't have sat outside like that.' He looked thunderous.

'We couldn't get you on the phone at either of your houses and we decided we were better

221

waiting here than at home. Lily said you were looking after Bogie so we knew you'd be back. Poor thing. Dogs don't belong on bicycles.' Mary paused for a deep breath and carried on: 'We've heard so much, we've got to make sure you know about it all. We have a theory, don't we, Harriet?'

'Oh, yes. Money,' she replied, sitting very straight.

Tony got up and went to the cupboard where he'd found the brandy earlier. 'I think I've got a bottle of sherry,' he said, rooting around inside. 'Ha! Harvey's. I know that will warm the cockles of your hearts.'

Pleased murmurs met the announcement and Tony soon had the ladies sipping the sweet sherry. 'Now, what's this about money?'

'You know that horrible Giggles – no Giglio man. He turned up at the Dog and rambled on about all sorts of things I'm sure he wasn't supposed to mention,' Harriet said. 'One of our friends called to tell us about it. She was there. But I can't give her name. She doesn't want to be mixed up in any of it but she knew we would want to know. That man was drunk when he got there and he drank two more drinks. Could hardly stand up. Went on about "the money" and how some people didn't have what everyone thought they did. Didn't make much sense, but for what it's worth, he told the entire bar about how the Quillam's pecuniary state – I should have liked to hear him get that out in his condition – would change now. He was talking about the Quillams going through too much money. Living too high, he said. All right when they had it but their habits didn't change when they didn't. He kept on about "salvation in the nick of time".

222

Anyway, we're worried it'll all get muddled up by the time the police hear it and you're the ones to keep that lot straight.'

Alex met Tony's eyes. What the devil was it all about? Could Wells have been the anonymous tipster, deliberately trying to point the police in someone's direction? Or even away from it, as in away from himself? She felt Tony asking himself the same questions. It made sense.

'The reporters there were flapping their ears, or so we were told. One of them asked Giglio what was changing the Quillam's fortunes and he just tapped the side of his nose and said, "You wait and see. They'll be found out." Mary and I wonder if it's something to do with young Laura being dead. You never know how things are tied up, do you?' Harriet's eyes only grew brighter.

'No, you don't,' Alex said. 'I feel disaster on its way. Do you know if there were a lot of people in the bar.'

'Sounds like it,' Mary said.

Tony sat down and hung his hands between his knees. 'O'Reilly will have a fit if it's all across the papers tomorrow.'

'And on the telly,' Mary said. She didn't sound unhappy at the prospect.

'What was the reaction to the news about Mrs Meeker?' Alex said.

Blank faces met the question.

Tony gritted his teeth. 'Of course, Wells wasn't there for that. Or he was too shattered to realize anything had happened.' He saw the women's empty glasses and refilled them while they made weak protests.

'We need a couple of accomplices don't we, Tony.'

They looked at each other again and Tony nodded. 'You've got to help us keep the rest of what happened tonight from getting out before the police want it to.' With his hands pushed into his curly hair, he added, 'We owe Dan O'Reilly that much. He's a good egg and we shouldn't let him get sabotaged if we can help him. Are you with us?'

Both old faces pinned him. 'What's happened to Mrs Meeker? Nice woman. She came into the shop for some good tea. She thinks the way we do about important things.'

'Are you with us?' Tony repeated.

'Of course,' Harriet said, crossly.

'Mrs Meeker was found dead tonight,' Alex said. 'She'd gone to bed. The police have been at the house again, doing a search, and she got tired of being in a room with everyone else, so she went upstairs. That's where they found her.'

Mary shook her head slowly. 'Poor woman. She's been under a lot of strain, I'm sure.'

'Laura's death was a murder,' Tony said, meeting Alex's eyes.

She could see him wondering if she'd try to temper what he'd said. She didn't. 'Yes, and from what we saw and the police reaction, we wouldn't be out of line thinking what happened to Mrs Meeker was just about the same thing.'

'Poisoned,' Harriet said under her breath.

'What makes you so certain about that?' Alex asked.

Both ladies sipped at their sherry, careful as

224

always about what they said. 'There's been talk,' Harriet said. 'Not that talk means very much, or it doesn't most of the time. But then Giglio said at the Dog last night that Laura was poisoned. Everything we say is second-hand but do you know if Laura had a lot of her own money? Not our business, of course.'

Elyan had said Laura was waiting to leave home when she came into her trust fund. 'I don't know how much,' Alex said.

Katie had grown too warm by the fire and moved to lie on Tony's feet. He stroked her absently. 'I have a feeling it wasn't insignificant. I wonder what happens to it now.'

How, Alex wondered, did you find out something like that? She had another, more disturbing thought. Tentatively, she said, 'Dan O'Reilly and the lovely Bill will know how to find out those things. There couldn't have been provisions for it to go to Mrs Meeker, could there?'

Massaging his temples, Tony said, almost under his breath, 'It could be that Wells was romantically involved with Laura, or thought he was. He could have planned for her to be his route to big money and a permanent seat at the Quillam table. Disappointment leads to spite in some people.'

Twenty-Six

What a hell of a night. Hugh Rhys stood in his sitting-room window, watching dawn break. He

225

hadn't undressed from the night before. Below him the car park at the back of the pub was empty. There was a promise of a sunny day but cloud still shielded the gold to come.

He looked at his mobile. It had been in his hand for hours. He didn't want to call Sonia Quillam, but could he watch her being devoured by whatever was going on in that family and not attempt to do anything, or should he reach out and see if she was in trouble and, if so, if he could help in some way.

She had made sure he had her mobile number. He had not given her his.

Had they ever been happy together? He supposed so, in between the kind of misery he finally couldn't take anymore. But that had been years ago. He should have moved on by now, really moved on.

Slowly, he punched in the numbers to reach her. By now the police would have given them all some time to at least rest up at Green Friday, in which case Sonia would be fast asleep. That had been something she was good at, sleeping when she didn't want to face reality.

Her phone rang; it rang six times and he was about to hang up when her voice, hoarse and whispery, said, 'Hugh? Is it really you?'

'How are you holding up?'

Silence.

'Sonia, Wells Giglio came in last night and—'

'I know,' she said. 'Now it's like waiting for the guillotine. Please tell me the place was empty.'

The milk truck pulled in close to the kitchen door and he heard the clinking of bottles as the

226

delivery man stacked them in their crates near the building.

'It wasn't empty.' The truck made its noisy exit. 'Full would be closer. By now there will be talk about Laura being murdered – poisoned, as he put it – all over the village. We had a battalion of press, too.'

She moaned. 'It's horrible here, just horrible. I've got to keep it together for Elyan, but all I want to do is run away.'

'Keep it together for Percy, too, right.' Silently, he cursed his careless mouth. He didn't want her to think he cared. 'I can understand,' he added.

'Have you come to an understanding with your family?' The lift in her voice told him she was trying to change the subject by putting him on the defensive.

'We're fine,' he said. Not far from the truth.

'Really? Now that's a surprise.'

'Sonia, what's happened? Don't fool around or this conversation is over.'

'Hugh, be kind for once. It's hell here. I don't know what's happened except Laura's death has been ruled a murder and now Meeker has been found dead in bed.'

He sucked in a breath. 'Another murder?'

'I'm praying it was a heart attack.' She added, 'I don't mean that the way it sounds. I mean I hope they don't say it was another murder. Sebastian says they will. Wells is too drunk to have an opinion, and so is Percy. Elyan is busy suspecting everyone and hating everyone – except his Annie. I can't talk to him.'

'Calm down and think,' Hugh said. 'Think

about when Mrs Meeker died and who could have done it – the time, the opportunity.'

'I don't know. She was fed up and said she'd go to bed. She told the police they could search her rooms around her if they liked. All through that time Wells was in and out – most likely drinking in one of the bathrooms before he took off to the Black Dog. Sebastian was gone for a while but it seems obvious he was with Daisy, driving her to Tony Harrison's clinic to ask if he could offload the girl – not that I blame him. This has been no place for a child.'

Hugh took a breath. 'How about Percy?'

She was silent for a while before saying, 'Percy isn't the murdering type. He's capable of other things, but not murder.'

'And Elyan?' He hated asking but he hadn't cared for her defense of Percy, either.

Sonia took so long to answer that Hugh's heart beat faster and harder. 'Elyan couldn't have anything to do with things like this. He's really gentle and all he cares about is his music. And he loved Laura.'

'Who do you think did this?' This was pointless. He didn't think she'd tell him if she did know.

'Well, Wells has a lot to lose with Laura's death. I think he hoped they'd marry and he'd be on the inside of the Quillam family – and get his hands on Laura's money. Elyan's the gold mine Wells dips into, but this is a long season of practice and more practice, so the flow from him is more of a trickle. Laura could have changed his life, given him independence from us, and from anyone else.'

228

Hugh thought about Wells' appearance the night before. Perhaps the man had been too drunk to give any kind of accurate reading, but he hadn't behaved like a man involved in murder – quite the opposite. 'How about Sebastian?'

'Sebastian is a sweetheart, really. Daisy is the center of his life, Daisy and guiding Elyan. I don't know why he'd do it.'

'Do you have any ideas about why Mrs Meeker was killed? She wasn't likely to inherit from Laura's death, was she?'

Sonia gave a short laugh. 'She knew everything. That's the only reason I could come up with for someone killing her. It would be whoever killed Laura, wouldn't it? Trying to make sure she didn't give away any incriminating details.'

Hugh squeezed his gritty eyes shut. 'I don't know. Sounds plausible – if anything about this mess sounds plausible.'

'Is Birnam Bricht the label of your whisky?'

'My father's, yes.' As she well knew.

'But it comes to you when he dies.'

'I won't discuss that.'

She gave one of her conspiratorial little laughs. 'Why should you. You're already rich, thanks to your grandfather. Why did you choose a place like this to settle down?'

'I'd like to know how you tracked me down here,' he said.

'I always know where you are.'

Irritation could send him over the edge, only he wouldn't let that happen. 'I'll leave you to work out my reasons for coming here, Sonia. I called to see if you were all right. For old times' sake.'

'I knew you hadn't really forgotten me,' she said, her voice a whisper again. 'And I'm so proud to watch Birnam Bricht do so well.'

He shouldn't have called. 'You're fine, then, Sonia?'

'Why would you think that? Without you I can't be fine. I need you. I need you to help me keep Elyan safe. He's brilliant, Hugh, an incredible prodigy. Whatever happens, we must make sure nothing gets in the way of his reaching full potential.'

Hugh narrowed his eyes. As usual, she was trying to tie him up with the knots of her subterfuge. 'What does that mean?'

He heard her short breaths. 'I know something horrible has happened here. The blame needs to be placed where it should be. There's more than one who wanted to benefit, really benefit, out of Laura's trust. One of them killed her but I don't know why. When we find out who that was, we have the whole case solved. Will you help me?'

If he were completely honest he'd tell her he couldn't be sure she hadn't a reason for trying to get her hands on that money. 'Who gets the money now Laura is gone?'

The silence went on far too long.

'Sonia?'

'I don't know, but I'll try to find out. Percy keeps those things pretty close to him and he doesn't like it when I ask questions.'

'But we need to know, don't we?' Hugh would bet plenty that the police were already following up that question.

'Why did you call me, Hugh? What do you really want?'

He put the back of his hand over his mouth so she would not hear his irregular breathing. 'What do you mean?' he asked when he settled down a little.

'You don't care about me. You're probing, using me to get answers. Why do you want to know all this?'

He set his teeth, remembering why he'd left her. 'What possible reason could I have to call and ask you these things – if I don't care about you?'

She made an odd, choking sound and said, 'You know the truth, don't you. You've always known. Some things can be ignored for a long time – but not forever.'

Hugh cut her off.

Twenty-Seven

Alex didn't say a word while Hugh paced back and forth across the kitchen. From time to time he raked his dark hair and she realized that despite his hefty frame, he looked thinner, and very strained.

'Sebastian Carstens came for his daughter about an hour ago?' he said at last. 'He left her with you all night?'

Alex didn't know what point he was making. 'Yes. That was a good thing, right, Tony. Green Friday was no place for a child to be last night.'

Tired as he had to be, Tony watched Hugh with

231

interest. 'No, it wasn't. We're supposed to remain at the clinic until the police tell us otherwise but you know Alex. She has to make sure everything's all right here.'

Coffee was brewing. Alex sniffed appreciatively.

'Good business people keep their hands in,' Hugh said. 'That's why this place is such a success.'

He didn't seem totally present. 'You make a big difference, Hugh.'

'I forgot the milk. I saw it delivered then just forgot it. Excuse me while I—'

'It's fine where it is until some kitchen staff arrive,' Alex said quickly. She knew the milk delivery time and for him to see it meant he was up considerably before he needed to be. 'I've wanted to ask how you came by a Welsh name when you're a Scot.'

'My father's Welsh. My mother's Scottish. I was born and grew up in Scotland – it's home to me. Did you hear anything about that Wells Giglio coming in last night? He was three sheets and rambling on. It won't make anyone at the Quillams' happy, or the police.'

Alex got three mugs and filled them with coffee. She took a carton of cream from one of the refrigerators and left it out for the others to use.

'Mrs Meeker died last night, I'm told. That's turning into an unlucky place.'

'Who told you that?' Tony turned sharply toward Hugh.

He brought his hands down hard on the central chopping block. 'Loose lips,' he muttered. 'I was told in confidence. I can't say any more.'

Cops in for a pint when they came off duty had been known to say too much. Casual people who got small pieces of information could hardly wait to pass it around. Alex looked at Tony. His brows were drawn together. He gave his head the slightest shake, warning her not to pursue the topic.

Tony said, 'We all know that in a close-knit place like Folly, fresh gossip is pounced on.'

'Morning all.' Dan appeared from the passage between the main kitchen and this one behind the pub. The other end of the passage opened into the back of the restaurant and once he left his room and came downstairs, it was an easy thing for him to find his way to either kitchen. 'Stopped in for a couple of hours' kip and clean togs. Can't be falling asleep on the job. Did you not remember being told to stay at Tony's clinic?'

He ran so smoothly from one topic to the next, Alex didn't think to bend the truth. 'We remembered. I wanted to check things here, then we intended to go back.'

'I heard you mention the death last night, Hugh. I'll expect you to give me your sources a bit later. I've some things to go over with Alex and Tony first. Give me your mobile number.'

Hugh, obviously on edge, dictated and O'Reilly put the information in his own mobile.

'I'll ask you to drive over to the parish hall with me,' Dan said. 'Someone will bring you back for your vehicle later.'

'It's not here,' Tony said. 'We walked from the clinic.'

They reached the front door to the inn and went

233

outside into struggling sunshine. 'Did you talk to anyone on your way?'

'No,' Alex said.

'Have you told anyone about the events at Green Friday last night?'

'No,' Tony and Alex said in unison.

'I hope that's true. We can't have much longer before everything breaks wide open, but I'll take any time I can get.'

So Dan had not heard about Wells' fulsome soliloquy, either the one at the house and definitely not at the Dog. Someone ought to tell him.

They got into Dan's dark blue Lexus and he drove the fairly short distance to the parish hall where the front door was firmly closed. But it wasn't locked and the detective shoved it open with the usual scraping and creaking from swollen wood, and hinges in need of some oil.

'Jesus,' Dan said, confronted by harried activity and several officers working phones. 'Has there been a break in the case?'

Tony touched his shoulder. 'Just to bring you up-to-date, Dan. We thought you would have heard yourself by now. Wells Giglio went to the Black Dog – apparently while everyone thought he was on one of his bathroom jaunts – and he held forth about Laura being murdered, poisoned, he said. And someone else, I don't know who, has started leaking that Mrs Meeker was killed, too. Also poisoned. We were coming to tell you this but you beat us to it. There were members of the press in the pub last night.'

'Jesus, Mary and Joseph,' he said, letting his head fall back. The man was tired and things were not going his way. Alex took that as the reason for the Irish accent getting thicker. 'Hugh knew about Mrs Meeker. I caught the end of him saying so.'

When they didn't answer, he said, 'You're protecting someone. But I'll find out who the big mouth is. And I do thank you for sharing that with me.'

Tony inclined his head. 'Bill Lamb's not here?'

'He's back at Green Friday.' He looked around the room and raised his voice. 'Listen up. I'll want to see the latest from forensics as soon as it comes in. And what's the ruckus about?'

The room fell silent before a woman said, 'A lot of activity, guv. Tips, questions – you know how it goes.'

'Not if there're no bigger breaks in this case than we've already had.'

The female officer rose and approached carrying newspapers. 'You'll want to see these. And you're to contact the chief superintendent as soon as you get in, about a press conference. He's not expecting you in until later given you're working a crime scene.'

'Thanks, Miller,' Dan said, taking the papers. 'So much for more time to work before this lot hits.'

'The chief super also wants to know the connection to a Dr James Harrison. The police surgeon mentioned talking to him – or a tech mentioned it.'

'We'll be outside in my car,' Dan said. 'Let me know if you need me.'

They followed him without question and got

back into his car. 'You afraid the walls have ears?' Tony said.

Dan made a scoffing noise. 'They bloody do. Take one of these papers.' He gave one each to Tony and Alex. 'Your dad and Dr Molly Lewis are pals now, hm? I wonder how that happened. Have you talked to him this morning?'

'No.' Now Tony did sound weary.

Alex scanned the front page of the *Echo* and let out a long sigh. 'You've got someone feeding the press,' she said. 'Digoxin in a bottle by the bed, it says. It could have been suicide. Do they have any idea how many Mrs Meeker took?'

'No,' Dan snapped. 'If I get my hands on the weasel who leaked all this, he'll feel my hands around his scrawny neck.'

Alex laughed before she could stop herself.

'I'm only a man,' he said, looking angry.

She didn't respond.

'This is all about the Quillams,' Tony said. 'That's what the press is after. Says there was bruising on Mrs Meeker? A bottle dropped between nightstand and bed. Crikey, what a mess. This lot could be making it up as they go along for all we know. There's more: family and staff confined to house. The brilliant pianist, Elyan Quillam, said to be distraught and unable to play. Is that true?' He looked up from the paper.

'Not from what I heard last night,' Dan said. 'I don't know much about classical stuff but I do know he sounded bloody marvelous. Angry, but brilliant with it. He is knocked for six by it all, but who wouldn't be?'

'Local publican and local vet in the eye of the

storm,' Alex said, feeling a bit sick. 'We got sucked into this, that's all. Why do they keep trying to make one or the other of us sound like a suspect?'

She didn't get a response.

'The heading here is: "The Sleeping Murders. Detective Chief Inspector O'Reilly said to be *flummoxed*" – why would they use a silly word like that? – "and ready to call in many more locals for serious questioning. Sources who requested anonymity say police infuriated by lack of co-operation.

'"The picturesque village of Folly-on-Weir is virtually on self-imposed lockdown as fears grow that victim count could increase. Details of cause of death are sketchy but drug overdose is suspected. They think these overdoses are being administered against the will of the victims."'

'There's a note below the article,' Alex added. 'Watch for details of press conference later today.'

Dan leaned back in his seat, stiffening his arms against the steering wheel. 'Whoever is doing all this anonymous talking has put himself, or herself, under my microscope. And given what I'm thinking, all the chatter wasn't a clever move and it won't do what it's supposed to do.'

'Move suspicion away from the culprit?' Alex said.

'I shouldn't think out loud,' Dan responded.

'Didn't you ever hear about the value of having more than one brain working on a problem?' Tony's voice was even, and low, but Alex decided he could just be irritated with Dan O'Reilly.

As if he'd picked up the same subtle irritation

237

as Alex had heard in Tony's voice, Dan shifted sideways in his seat so he could see both of them. 'Okay. Chew on this one. Have we got one murderer, or more than one?'

Twenty-Eight

Tony watched Alex, watching Hugh.

'Can I get away with turning the TV off?' she asked, *sotto voce*.

'Not if you want to see sunset again,' Tony murmured. 'Harriet and Mary would be first in line to let you have it for interrupting the main news of the day.'

'Hugh looks ready to explode. He's tired and angry – and I can't figure out why he's so angry.'

Lily slid to stand beside Alex, opposite Tony across the bar. 'I don't like this,' she said. 'Did Doc tell you Dan O'Reilly put him through a tough interview?'

'No!' Tony said, bristling. 'The hell he did. Inappropriate fool.'

'Sh.' Alex put a hand across the bar to touch him. 'Calm down. Doc's more than capable of dealing with something like that.'

People in the bar were turning their chairs to get better views of the TV screen. Some moved to make a higgledy-piggledy line between tables. On the screen an announcer gave a warning that the press conference was about to start.

'Avid is the word that comes to mind,' Tony

said and raised a hand in welcome when his father walked into the bar. Doc came to join them and Lily quickly put a whisky in front of him.

'You okay, Dad?' Tony asked.

'Slightly amazed but okay, thanks, son. We'll talk later. Looks like the local crowd turned up early today. I wonder why that is? They'll be hanging on every word. I just hope they don't get more fodder to talk about – and that nothing's said to really frighten them. The police should try to calm things down. The papers got them all fired up.'

'Shh,' went up across the room.

Dan O'Reilly, with a balding police officer with a lot of badges and braid, and the woman Tony recognized as Dr Molly Lewis, the police surgeon, appeared on the television. Seated behind a table in what had to be a studio – Tony didn't recognize the setting – the three had papers in front of them and looked unhappy to be there, except for the braid-covered man who they soon knew was the chief superintendent. He spoke confidently and introduced the other two.

'My colleagues will each give a short statement, and then we'll take questions. Dr Lewis, you go first.'

Her short, blond hair looked as if she combed it with a hand mixer. 'In the Folly-on-Weir case, one of two recent deaths of interest has been ruled a murder. The victim died of an overdose of medication she took regularly. We believe she took the overdose accidentally – that is, it was presented to her in such a way that she simply drank it down. We are waiting for test results on the second death but have reason to believe it

239

may have happened in the same way as the first. That's all.'

The chief superintendent looked surprised at the doctor's brevity but turned to Dan. 'Detective Chief Inspector O'Reilly?'

'I'm disappointed by the quality of reporting I've seen in today's papers,' he said, drawing a frown from his boss.

'The man has courage,' Doc said.

'Speculation, information gathered from sources not prepared to be identified. Deliberate sensationalism intended not to help reveal any truths, but to sell copies and even to put the village of Folly-on-Weir on alert and to frighten the citizens. But I have news worth spreading. The people who live in Folly-on-Weir are made of sterner stuff. They aren't easily frightened, especially by half-truths or outright lies.

'Until the second batch of test results come back, the ones Dr Lewis referred to, I can't add to the physical case details, but I do have something to tell you and it gives me a lot of pleasure.'

'I think I feel sick,' Alex muttered.

This time Tony patted *her* hand.

'Right now, as I talk to you, a person of interest is being questioned.'

Twenty-Nine

Dan O'Reilly and Bill Lamb hadn't arrived back at the inn. The buzz in the bar went on, not as loudly as before, but insistently. With Doc, Tony, the Burke sisters and Lily, Alex hovered in the snug, unable to stay in a chair. Max the cat sat on Mary's lap and Bogie lay quiet, Katie sitting beside her, on the tartan blanket Lily brought from in front of the fireplace.

'We're all so quiet,' Alex said. They'd been there almost two hours.

'When do you think they'll get back?' Mary asked, her eyes drooping a little behind the very thick lenses of her glasses. 'O'Reilly and Lamb, I mean.'

'We know who you mean,' Harriet snapped. 'If they've arrested someone, they'll be questioning them, won't they? I've seen it on the telly. It can take hours. Who do you think will be the good cop?'

That brought a burst of laughter and Harriet joined in.

'I was being facetious. But, I broke the ice, didn't I? And for all you know it's O'Reilly who plays the mean one best.'

Hugh stuck his head through the hatch to the bar. 'What I want to know is who they've arrested. How can we find out?'

'We'll know soon enough,' Doc said. 'I think people really appreciated what Dan said about Folly.'

'He's a good man,' Alex said. 'I think he's come to care about all of us.'

Tony couldn't squelch a sliver of jealousy but then, as that policeman had said, he was only human and so was Tony.

'Anything I can get you?' Hugh asked.

'Wouldn't say no to a Harvey's Bristol,' Mary said and set off a round of ordering.

Talking to his father and finding out what Dan thought was important enough to question him about was uppermost in Tony's mind but that couldn't happen in front of a crowd.

'I've been trying to work out why anyone would want you to get hurt on the hill,' Doc said to Alex.

She shrugged. 'If it was deliberate there's only one possible reason. They wanted to unsettle me enough to stop me involving myself in what's happened here. This is my place, the only place I want to be. I'll never back away from doing something useful, if I can. And neither will Tony.'

For better or worse. Tony nodded, yes and made sure he looked enthusiastic. This case was getting creepier by the day.

Hugh returned with drinks and said, 'Alex? A word, please.'

She passed the drinks to the table and stuck her head through the hatch. 'What is it?'

'Surprise, surprise. Our prodigy is asking if he can use our piano. He says he has to practice because his father says so but he refuses to stay at Green Friday. No problem with that, is there?'

She thought about it. 'We should be honored. Let's hope we don't get *Ride of the Valkyries.* Nothing like a little Wagner to bring down a mood – in this setting, anyway. Yes, tell him that would be lovely. Not that he'll think our old piano is lovely.'

Back at the table, Alex pulled a chair closer among the others. 'Elyan Quillam is going to play. Getting away from the house and good old Father. The piano at the church is evidently in better tune, Sybil tells me. He ought to go there.'

Tony squeezed her elbow until she looked at him, at his quizzical expression. 'Darn, I'm stupid. Of course he wouldn't want to go where his sister died. Poor boy.'

They heard the sound of the piano's wheels scraping across the wooden floor in the up-room.

'That'll be good for the tuning,' Doc said. He locked his hands behind his neck, closed his eyes and began to smile. 'I'd listen to him on comb and paper.'

The bar had fallen silent which made all those in the snug smile at one another.

Elyan started to play. Tony expected jazz but Elyan had other things in mind. 'What is it?' he asked.

'*Nessun Dorma*!' Doc's eyes snapped open and he said in a whisper, 'On the piano only.' His eyes closed again.

Elyan's fingers seemed impossible to believe. Alex wanted to go into the bar but wouldn't risk making a noise.

He played the piece she had heard Pavarotti sing in a televised showing of *The Three Tenors*, and it was beautiful. Each time it seemed it must come to a close, he carried on, playing variations, she thought, although she didn't know for certain.

Harriet and Mary smiled over their sherry and Doc appeared transported elsewhere.

At the hatch, Alex could see that Hugh still stood there, absolutely immobile. She went close to look at his face and almost wished she hadn't.

His eyes were also closed, but tears had escaped.

Carefully, Alex backed away. There were so many things you never learned about some of the people you thought you knew well.

The piano became silent.

There was a long pause, then applause broke out and cheers.

'Ah,' said Doc, 'we're a highbrow bunch in this village. I hope he plays more.'

Shortly, after a tap on the snug door, Elyan walked in with Annie who smiled widely, like a proud and happy parent.

'That was so beautiful,' Alex said. 'What have we done to deserve this?'

'I'm the one who should thank you.' A second table was pulled to join the first and more chairs added. 'I know I'm saying too much but I needed to get away from that house – and some of the people. My sister was murdered and all they talk about is getting me ready for the tour. The tour, the tour. Sometimes it gets hard being the bread-winner for people who want everything. I – I'm sorry. Bad form.'

He looked at Annie who smiled gently and held his hand. 'He plays *Nessun Dorma* for me. I don't think it counts as real practice, though.' The pair leaned together and giggled.

Alex suddenly wished the two of them were alone in this moment.

Yet again the door opened, this time to admit Reverend Ivor Davis. 'Knock, knock,' he said. Never socially adroit, he rarely came to the pub and gave the impression he might be a 'not quite grown-up' and still gangly red-haired student.

His black cassock flapped around him, reminiscent of the gowns that flew behind students on bicycles at Oxford, or Cambridge.

Tony already had a chair ready for him. 'What will you have, Ivor?'

'Nothing right now, thank you. I got home this afternoon and heard all these terrible things that have been going on.'

It was inevitable that Alex wondered how the man could *not* have heard already.

'Such a shock, my boy,' he said to Elyan. 'Your poor family, and your dear sister. Such a tragedy. I'd like to go to Green Friday, if you think it would be appropriate. I never want to make people uncomfortable or, perish the thought, angry.'

Elyan shifted uncomfortably. 'I'd like to sound them out first. No offence, Reverend.'

'Well,' Ivor said, 'I've been quite busy since I got home. My wife said you'd asked to use the choir piano but it's, well, you know where it is. And the police still have everything taped off and officers keeping a look out. So I had someone help me move it to the other side of the altar, the other ambulatory where . . . well, you, know, it puts distance between you and what happened. If you feel you'd like to use it, the acoustics in St Aldwyn's are quite remarkable.'

'Yes,' Elyan said, 'I already noticed that. May I think about it?' Without waiting for a response he hurried out into the bar again and they soon heard the strains of *I Wish I Could Shimmy Like My Sister Kate*.

Annie had followed him out and she started to

sing the lyrics in a surprisingly rich and sultry voice.

Tony said, 'Wait till Dan hears the piano's been moved. You can bet Ivor didn't think to ask if it was all right.'

Thirty

In the room kept for her use at the Black Dog, Alex did her best to sleep. Some hope. The bed was comfortable but her brain wouldn't slip into neutral. Bogie had stayed with her and slept on a fat heap of blankets on the floor.

Tony had gone up the hill to check out her house and his own and they decided it was best for him to stay there tonight.

When Bogie got restless, Alex put on a cotton dressing gown and carried him downstairs and outside. He made a good job of hopping around on three legs but he made no attempt to explore very far.

At the bottom of the stairs, he balked but when she went to pick him up, he did his hobble, hobble, shuffle toward the kitchen and got a drink from his bowl. Afterward he sat looking from her to his empty food dish, a hopeful look in his black eyes.

'You shouldn't be eating at this time of night,' she told him, but found a few pieces of cooked chicken she'd saved for him.

A key turned in the front door to the inn. It

opened, closed and footsteps started across the restaurant toward the stairs, then stopped.

She straightened. The detectives had come back and they'd seen light shining from the kitchen. If she stood still they might carry on upstairs without checking. It wasn't unusual for a light to be on here and there in the building.

But would they tell her anything if she asked a direct question or two?

Footsteps went upstairs, but only one pair.

Dan appeared from the bar. 'I was afraid I'd shock you,' he said.

'No. I heard you come in. You must be worn out. May I get you something?'

'No, I just need sleep.'

So why had he come back there?

'Bogie's looking pretty good,' he said, crossing his arms and leaning against a counter. 'I'm glad he's bouncing back. We haven't had any luck tracing who caused the accident. There must be two Range Rovers for every household around here.'

She smiled.

'Did you see the press conference earlier?'

'Of course. I think everyone in the village did.'

He stared at her until she looked away. 'Aren't you going to ask the big question?'

'Nope. You wouldn't tell me anything.'

'Not much. But you'll find out it was Wells Giglio we took in.'

She thought about that. So Wells was definitely somewhere in the frame. 'You said you were arresting someone.'

'He's been taken in.'

247

Her legs felt rubbery.

'He knows more than he should but he doesn't know everything we know about him. I don't think he ever thought he'd be taken into custody, but he set himself up.'

'How?'

Dan shook his head. 'I couldn't tell you that.'

'Not till you've got the test results on Mrs Meeker? But I'd make a bet he likes to make anonymous phone calls.'

'You're too quick for your own good. If there's some brandy you can get to easily, I wouldn't say no. If you join me in a drop.'

Alex considered that. Why not? Perhaps she'd shake something loose. 'Of course. Let's sit in the up-room – it's comfortable.'

He waited until she led the way with a glass in each hand and slid into one of the high-backed banquettes.

'What do you think of Wells?' he said, after taking his first swallow from a snifter. 'Any idea what he wants? I mean here, with the Quillam family.'

'To bask in reflected glory,' she told him, without meaning to. 'That's not kind. He may have been in love with Laura, in which case, he's grieving and that's a personal journey.'

'How close was he to Mrs Meeker?'

Alex pursed her lips. He was searching for something. 'I don't really know. The only comment he made about her that I found odd was that she knew everything about everyone. I never heard that they didn't get along. Anyway, he was in no condition to do whatever happened to her last night.'

Dan took off his jacket and loosened his tie. He was an appealing man and she hadn't missed the interested signals he sent her way.

He raised his eyes to hers. 'What I'm going to say is for you and only you. You've got a mind I need, a mind to help me through the undergrowth of the way people behave – and why. What if I said I didn't think Wells was too drunk to do mischief last night?'

The prickles didn't come so often now, but that sent a charge up her spine and into her scalp. 'I saw him, Dan. When he came back he was paralytic. Sonia had to help him into Green Friday.'

'Sonia?' He swirled his brandy and watched the gold fire twirl.

'Mmm. She helped him get into the sitting room. He all but fell into the house. He'd been sneaking off to drink in a bathroom all night. I don't know why he didn't put his car up a tree when he drove down here.'

He gave a lopsided smile. 'Because he wasn't really as drunk as we were all supposed to believe?'

Alex spread her hands. 'I don't know. I have no way of knowing that. I do know what I saw.'

'He had a blood test.'

She frowned. 'When?'

'After he got back to Green Friday. He did a helluva job staying in character. You'd have thought he didn't know what was happening. Said, yes, when we asked and there you have it.'

'And.'

'His blood alcohol level was elevated, but not nearly as much as he wanted us to believe. From one report, he was seen in the Dog car park tipping up a bottle, but he didn't look smashed. His readings showed he'd had a few – a couple too many – but nothing like he wanted us to think.'

Alex lifted her glass to the light. 'Why would he do that?' She sipped.

'What do you think? Did he want us to think he was too shattered to do anything to Mrs Meeker?'

Alex put her elbows on the table. 'Did Mrs Meeker take those pills willingly?'

He shook his head. 'If this comes out, I'll know who let the cat out. In Laura's case the drug was liquid mixed with a strong liquor. We expect to get a similar result from Mrs Meeker. But it looks as if Laura drank the stuff either all on her own, or at least willingly. We have learned she enjoyed her gin and lime, or whatever. Mrs Meeker has bruises where she was probably held and forced.'

Alex put a hand over her mouth.

Dan took hold of her wrist. 'You okay? I thought a long time about sharing anything with you but you seem to have an extra sense about some things.'

She didn't pull her arm away. His steady strength settled her jumping nerves. 'I'm okay, thanks. Laura loved Mrs Meeker. They'd been around each other since Laura was born.'

'There's something off,' Dan said. 'It's been off from the beginning. Something we've missed. We had help missing it, that I'm sure off.'

'Do you think Wells did this?'

'I honestly don't know. He could have – but I

can't imagine that. I only met him a couple of times and he didn't seem the type.' She felt horrible, giving opinions on someone else's propensity for ultimate violence. 'No, he couldn't have.'

Dan leaned across the table. He smiled, closing his eyes a little, and tapped her bottom lip with a forefinger. 'Your problem is that you're too nice.'

'I'm not too nice.' Not too nice to enjoy a little flirtation with a very appealing man. 'But I have to be careful and fair.' She sat far enough back for him not to be able to reach her. Tony deserved better than this. She wanted better than this for him.

Dan drank more brandy. 'It's good. This is nice.' The look in his eyes gave her no doubt that the comment had more than one meaning. 'Wells went out of his way to make it look as if he was leaving the room to go to the bathroom while he became – as far as anyone could tell – more and more plastered. I don't yet have proof if he did anything untoward to Mrs Meeker, but I will. I already know there are no fingerprints on the digitalis bottle. A lime liquid designed for those who don't take pills well. The bottle had been wiped clean. We don't have a final on the glass. We do know Mrs Meeker has bruises on the back of her neck and on her left wrist. We believe she was left handed.'

Alex digested that. 'I see where you're going but it doesn't have to be neat like that.'

'No it doesn't, wouldn't it be nice for people like us if it was always neat.'

251

She didn't miss the 'us'. Did he think of her as a sort of partner? She got those prickles up her spine again.

'Couldn't it be that even if he planned everything the way you think he did, he had no intention of killing her? What if he was afraid of being implicated and he tried to make himself look innocent. He could be innocent and probably is.'

'Possibly.'

'I've got to think about this, Dan. A lot.'

'And while you do, think about the other people in that house last night. There were definitely motives for getting rid of Mrs Meeker. But I don't really know what they were.'

'Money,' she said, before thinking enough. 'I mean, perhaps there could have been a money issue. Laura was to come into a lot of money when she was twenty-five, wasn't she?'

He gave her a genuine grin. 'We'd make such a team, lady. You're thinking straight along the lines I'm thinking. All we need are the individual motives, evidence of enough will to carry out murder for profit, and an eye into how it was pulled off.'

'Which means you don't think Wells did it.'

'I didn't say that.' He kept on smiling. 'We should both get some rest. Is Tony upstairs?'

She went on alert. 'He'll be back when he's taken care of his dog.' Not an entire lie.

'Good,' he said, but his eyes didn't echo the sentiment. 'I'd better say goodnight, then.'

Alex made to get up. 'Elyan was here tonight, with Annie. He played the piano. Not for long, but it was lovely.'

252

'Really?' A speculative expression changed Dan. 'I thought his father and Sebastian were going to nail his toes to the piano pedals and make him practice until he dropped. That was the impression I got before I left the house. That boy has a heavy weight on his shoulders. He's their meal ticket.'

'We see that in the same way,' she told him. 'I think Reverend Ivor threw Elyan a wobbler by offering him the choir piano. Elyan said he couldn't stand being at Green Friday or around his father and Sebastian. He didn't take Ivor up immediately, but I got the impression he would think about it.'

'Bit macabre when his half-sister more or less died playing the thing.'

'Yes, but Ivor said he'd had someone help him move the piano to the other side of the altar to make it easier on Elyan.'

Dan fell back in his seat. 'Fuck.'

Thirty-One

'You're joking,' Bill Lamb said, keeping his voice down. He sat across from Dan O'Reilly in the inn restaurant. They were the only ones already down for breakfast.

'I bloody well am not,' Dan said. 'I've got to clean up my mouth.' He wasn't pleased with what he'd said in front of Alex the night before but the language went with the territory and he hadn't

253

asked her to involve herself, not in so many words.

Damn, he was glad she had involved herself and he had to back away from that, or risk making a complete fool of himself.

'So the damage is already done,' Bill said. 'Those cretins guarding the church have let the horse in.'

Dan screwed up his face. 'What horse, for God's sake?'

'Language, remember,' said Bill, looking a bit smug. 'Trojan horse, of course. While our lot pattered about outside like flaming idiots, they let someone give aid and comfort to the enemy. Just let them in. Amazing.'

'Finish up,' Dan said. 'We've got to get over there. When does the shift change?'

Bill checked his watch. 'Any time now, I should think. It'll be back to the day shift but I don't know who's in the rotation.' He wolfed down the rest of an egg on tomato, on cheese, on toast and finished his large mug of coffee. 'Ready when you are.'

At once, Dan got up and walked out of the building without looking back.

Bill drove Dan's Lexus. Dan had never been an enthusiastic driver – cars were just a means of getting from place to place.

'We're going straight to the church?' Bill asked.

'Pull over,' Dan said at once and they drew in to idle beneath a hawthorn tree in full red bloom that overhung a wall a short distance from the Black Dog. 'Careful is the watchword. No broad statements. Pleasant manner, even comments and

254

questions tentatively couched. Remember it would be natural to allow the reverend into his church. We can work out later if someone should have taken note of any minions he took in with him. I want to be casual and friendly. Stroll around inside. But keep your eyes and ears open. Any little remark could be important and anything that doesn't look right could be the lead we're waiting for. Anything.'

'Got it, guv'nor.'

Dan wasn't sure what he thought of Bill's attachment to calling him 'guv' or 'guv'nor' but had decided to take them as a form of respect, even if respect had never been Bill's strong suit. He did know that Bill Lamb wanted to move up the ladder but it wasn't happening for him. Dan wasn't sure why.

'Let's get on with it,' Dan said and Bill put the Lexus in gear.

Constable Frost, whom he hadn't seen for some time, was at the main entrance to St Aldwyn's. She looked fresh and competent – and confident.

'Morning, sir,' she said, and nodded to Bill. 'Morning.'

'Were you here yesterday?' Dan asked. 'Toward evening?'

'Yes, guv.'

'Anyone go in or out of the church?'

She frowned. 'Not that I saw.'

'Thank you.' He and Bill walked around to the door nearest the area where the choir practiced. The door was taped from jamb to jamb but there was no officer present. Bill raised a brow when Dan looked at him.

Wicks, looking scrubbed and on task, appeared from the back corner of the church. He started to greet them, but Dan cut him off. 'Wicks, were you on yesterday?'

'Yes, sir. A good part of the day.'

'Are you doing some sort of patrol, man? Leaving one door to look at another?'

'Yes, sir. But it doesn't take me more than a few minutes to go between the two and we're a man short.'

'I see,' Dan said, swallowing the bellow he'd like to give.

Bill turned the stiff metal handle that opened the door, ducked under the crime tape and went inside.

'Am I being too hard, Bill? Expecting these people to do as they're told?'

'No, guv,' Bill said and Dan picked up on the edginess in the man's voice.

'Mmm. Well, it's so damn quiet around here it probably doesn't matter.' He looked down, past the choir stalls, to the stone-flagged floor already painted pastel hues by the sun streaming through the stained-glass window. 'No piano. Reverend Ivor really did move it. I was praying he was still planning to do that in the future.'

He loped down to the main floor and set off around the altar, past gleaming brass – no doubt the work of diligent ladies of the parish – and stiff floral arrangements, to an area that mirrored the one they'd left except it held kneelers in front of a small altar rather than risers for choristers.

'I wanted it all left as it was when Laura died.

I don't see why that was so much to expect. Not that it's made much difference, or not necessarily.'

Out of habit, they began to search. Inch by inch, flagstone by flagstone, they paced off each area. 'The music stand was moved, too,' Bill remarked when he passed Dan yet again. 'Not that it matters.'

'This doesn't feel good to me,' Dan said. 'Something's out of place, and not just the piano.'

At last they stopped by the piano, which had been placed in much the same position as it had been on the other side of the altar, and Dan sat on the bench. 'All dusted, right?'

'Yes, guv.'

Dan couldn't play but he did his childhood rendition of chopsticks and Bill put his fingers in his ears.

'Sounds awful,' Dan said. 'And not just because I'm playing it.'

'Bagpipes running out of wind,' Bill said and laughed. 'Used to think I'd like to play those things just to annoy my old man.'

Dan didn't comment. His partner rarely said boo about any member of his family and Dan thought it best not to draw attention to it when he did.

'You play a fine chopsticks, guv,' Bill said. 'My old man played the piano. Played in a pub to make extra money. He was good, too. Nasty blighter.'

Holding the ledge under the keyboard, Dan stood up. The instrument was old and carved with acorns along a garland of ivy leaves. Making sure he didn't drop the thing, he lifted the front half of the lid, lay it back on its hinges and peered inside.

'Never saw inside a piano before,' he said, and turned his head sharply, thinking. 'Was it open or closed when we first saw it?'

'I don't remember,' Bill responded.

'I think it was open, at least at first. Not that it matters.'

He had no idea what he was looking at. Hitting a key, he watched a part rise and hit another part and almost winced at the sound. He tried several more. Who had possibly dreamed up a piano?

'Do you play?' he asked Bill.

'No, guv. My old man hated it if I even touched his piano.'

Bill's old man sounded like a real winner.

'Hammers and strings and who knows what. Amazing.' He reached to close the lid again.

In a front corner, on the left, dropped straight down and wedged there, was something red. He knew what it was before he took an evidence bag from his pocket to lift the thing out.

'Look what I found,' he said, swallowing against the heavy, fast beat of his heart. 'What do you suppose this is?'

Bill came to his side at once, watching the red thermos bottle with a tartan sleeve around it, come into view.

'I'll be damned,' was all he said.

Thirty-Two

Mary Burke patted Sybil Davis's hand. 'You finish up that tea and you'll have the first cup from the new pot. We'll get you set up in no time.'

'I shouldn't have troubled you,' Sybil said before dutifully drinking the rest of her tea before Mary whisked the cup away.

'Rubbish. Women have a special bond. Women who think the same way about things like kindness and duty, good manners and doing the right thing. Don't they, Harriet?'

'In many cases,' Harriet said, taking the cup and refilling it from the fresh pot she'd just made. 'But we still can't make the mistake of letting past experiences color a new situation. All men are not insensitive and those who are insensitive fail to understand some things in different ways, one man from another. In other words, we can't put all men in one category and say they're obtuse.'

'I agree,' Sybil said. Her hair was starting to show threads of gray but it was thick and wavy and Mary had always thought her an attractive woman, even if she did wear rather modern clothes for a vicar's wife.

When Sybil called and asked if she could visit them, Mary had been surprised. The only previous time had been right after Reverend Ivor took over the parish.

'You're sure Alex won't mind coming over?' Sybil said. 'I expect their late-morning business is heavy.'

'Alex makes her own hours,' Harriet said. 'We can all trust Alex to bring a clear head to things and she's more worldly than some of us. Logical, too. She and Tony have been so helpful with past troubles.'

Sybil nodded. 'I'm very fond of her. But I don't want anyone to think I'm being disloyal to Ivor. He just isn't . . .' She laughed a little. 'He isn't one of those worldly people you mentioned. Indefatigable, yes. Impossible to shock – I'd say so. But if it's a case of finding fault with someone, he has to do a lot of thinking about that and I don't think there's time in this case.' Her voice grew higher as she talked.

'Here she comes,' Harriet said from her post by their sitting-room window at the front of the building. She leaned out and called, 'Helloo, come on up. The door isn't locked.'

Mary noticed that Max and Oliver were asleep together in Max's bed. It rather ruined her excuse for taking him to the pub with her but she'd think of a plausible cover.

Downstairs, the door slammed, followed by the sound of Alex rapidly climbing the stairs. She came into the flat with a cake box that made Mary frown. Why would Alex bring cakes?

'I can see your mind working,' Alex said, wagging a finger. 'I brought some steak and onion pies for you to try at lunch. George says they're a new experiment.'

Harriet accepted the box with a slight sniff.

'One wonders what could be innovative about a steak and onion pie, but thank you and we shall pass along our opinions.'

Alex took in the three women in the room. Sybil definitely appeared anxious and ill at ease.

'Thank you for inviting me to join you. This is lovely. And yes, Harriet, I'll have some tea, please.' She smiled and wondered if she misinterpreted Harriet's skeptical glance at Sybil.

'Are we celebrating something?' She went to one of two cat beds where Oliver and Max curled together in the bliss of cat oblivion. 'That's so sweet,' she said softly.

'They never do that normally,' Mary said quickly. 'Oliver's a bit under the weather or he would never allow Max near him.'

'Yes, well, we asked you to come and hear what's happened to Sybil,' Harriet said, with a sour look at her sister. 'She's had a most unpleasant time of it with those detectives who should be ashamed of themselves.'

Alex sat in a straight-backed rocker with plum-colored corduroy cushions. She didn't remember seeing it before but didn't want to slow the conversation by mentioning it.

'Oh, no. You mustn't let them upset you. Their manner is always brusque – comes with the occupation. This morning Elyan was telling me how rude and upsetting they are. But he may be too sensitive to be logical at the moment.'

Three pairs of eyes became sharper. 'Elyan was back at the Dog?' Mary said. 'I was so disappointed when he didn't play any more last night but the poor boy must be very unsettled. Did he

261

know who the police arrested? I know I shouldn't ask anyone, but we're all waiting to find out.'

'The police will tell us when they're ready – if we don't read it in the papers first.' She didn't like being deceptive. 'Elyan is upset. He practiced something very ominous sounding this morning. Rachmaninoff and something to do with Paganini. Doc James would know.'

'Rachmaninoff *Rhapsody on a Theme of Paganini*,' Sybil said. 'Absolutely gorgeous and very difficult. I wish I'd heard it.'

'All the customers listened,' Alex said. 'I think they know they're getting something extraordinary. And it is a bit like watching the impossible made possible. He was still there when I left but he was giving them a few jazz and blues pieces. I'm sure his father would faint at that. I think Elyan's nerves are frayed. I told him we'd talk when I get back, if he wants to and he hasn't left.'

'He should be practicing on his own piano,' Sybil said. 'No offense, but I wonder the one at the pub doesn't just collapse under the onslaught. That's why I wanted to tell him to use the piano in the church. It's a good instrument and kept in tune. He could be alone there.'

'I don't think he minds the audience, odd as it may be for him,' Alex said. 'But I agree with you. Tell me what's happened with the detectives.'

Sybil's eyes shone too bright. 'They wanted to see Ivor but he's out visiting the sick. So they talked to me and they began to sound really angry. Detective O'Reilly said that even someone like me – as if I were some species other than human – should know what crime scene tape means. I said I did and he told me he knew I had talked to Elyan and that I probably encouraged Ivor to move the piano so Elyan could play on the far side from where dear Laura died.'

'Why was he so angry? They haven't found any evidence – or nothing that seems to have helped them. Why didn't the wretched thermos turn up?'

Harriet made the rounds with her teapot, bringing a little china tray with sugar and milk. 'I think he's off his stride,' she said. 'He hasn't had any breaks, or apparently not. I thought better of him than that he should lash out, especially at a lady like Sybil. It sounds as if they're desperate.' She stood very straight. 'I wonder if there's a real danger of another murder.'

Sybil gave a little cry and covered her mouth.

'I know,' Mary said. 'This is all frightening but we have to stay strong. We hear things the police would never hear. It's our responsibility to listen closely and see if we hear anything helpful that should be passed on.'

Alex felt an unexpected flash of anger. Shame on Dan for being nasty to Sybil. She would have expected better of him. 'I'm going to see Dan O'Reilly myself,' she announced. 'He doesn't have license to slam his plod-sized feet on the necks of the gentle people in this town. Whatever has, and is happening, came here with incomers. Anyway, we're not mind readers who know everything he wants of us. No, he's going to get a piece of *my* mind.'

'I don't think that's such a good idea,' Sybil said. 'Ivor wouldn't like it.'

'It isn't Ivor I intend to take apart into little

263

pieces. Don't worry, I will protect you. I'm as good at unnamed sources as any newspaper. I've had it.'

'Is that someone going to the rectory?' Harriet said from a spot by the window that overlooked the churchyard.

Alex looked, but only saw someone walk into the shadow of the church building, just as she had before. 'Did you see what he looked like?' she asked Harriet.

'No, I was listening to what you were saying and I didn't even really take in there was someone there until he was too far away.'

'Could be anyone. That lane back there branches out and goes all over the place. Sybil, did the police tell you anything I should know?'

'Oh, dear.' Sybil laced her fingers tightly together.

'Men,' Mary said. 'They really don't understand the finer nuances of communication. Stop worrying, Sybil, and trust Alex to do whatever is for the best.'

'I'll get back to you,' Alex said, already dialing Dan O'Reilly's contact number as she went downstairs and opened the front door.

Thirty-Three

On a bench near the pond on the village green, Alex regarded bobbing ducks and a single autocratic swan sweeping slowly up and down in their midst as the ducks cried out to one another.

She'd left several messages for Dan and spoken with Tony who had a heavy day at some local farms. She assured him she'd keep him up to date, without mentioning her planned chat with their favorite detective.

When she'd got back to the pub she'd been disappointed to find that Annie had arrived and Elyan had left with her.

Dan wouldn't have made what sounded like a nuclear attack on Sybil if he were himself. A nagging conviction that things were shifting within the case intensified her need to know what was going on.

'So, popular, am I?' said a voice approaching from behind. 'Must be nice to be able to hang out on a bench and twiddle your thumbs.'

Her irritation climbed a notch higher but she didn't argue with his assessment. 'It is. And I get to do it so often. Try a little relaxation sometimes, Dan – makes you sharper.'

He sat beside her in shirtsleeves and jeans. She had never seen him casually dressed before. Not for the first time she wondered if he really was completely unattached. For an instant she could imagine him helping a child sail a boat on the pond.

'You don't think I'm sharp enough?' He was grinning. 'Probably not, so I just have to do the best possible with what meager skills I have. But you didn't search me out to make small talk.'

'You made a big mistake this morning, Dan, and it got back to me. I'm disappointed in you.'

That got her a frown. 'Too much talk goes on in this village, Alex. It's annoying. It borders on obstructionism for us.'

'I haven't seen anyone obstructing you. You ask questions and people answer. Too bad the same can't be said for you.'

He seemed to relax a little as if stoking her ire satisfied him. 'Could we get to your point quickly? I must get back to Gloucester.'

'To carry on grilling Wells Giglio?'

'Yes,' Dan said, staring straight ahead. 'We're making considerable progress and should have a break in the case shortly. By the way, he's being held for questioning. Not under arrest.'

'Really?' Alex stared at him. 'It's not like you to make announcements like that. Sneaking up at the crucial moment is more your style. Was it this new and exciting break that made you behave like a bear to inoffensive little Sybil Davis? Bad show, Dan, really bad.'

He turned slowly toward her. 'I'd rather get along with you,' he said, oddly distant. 'But you make my life difficult. Your name, and Harrison's, come up at every meeting. I don't like the implication that without you I'd never get anything around here solved.'

'Oh, come on! You're exaggerating.'

He leaned to dig a stone out of the grass and shied it into the pond. 'I don't exaggerate.'

'If you throw stones in the pond you'll hit the birds.'

'Hmm. Sitting ducks,' he muttered.

'Feeble,' Alex retorted. 'So, do you still think Wells Giglio killed Laura and Mrs Meeker?'

'I didn't say that.' He found another stone and tossed it far away from the ducks. 'And, of course, we didn't have a conversation last night, remember?'

266

She swiveled on the bench, leaned toward him. 'Don't treat me like that. No one would believe we've been through some of the things we have – not when you treat me like a snotty-nosed kid who can't be trusted to hold her tongue.'

'I didn't—'

'Dan, I am not the enemy. Tony isn't the enemy. In general, you don't have an enemy in this town. We've had some really awful things happen around us but you know as well as I do that Tony and I have only tried to help.'

He stood and faced her, blocking out the sun. 'You were never asked to interfere. And from now on I'm warning you not to get in our way.'

'Warn away.' Her heart thumped. Alex hated the way he'd taken the advantage of standing over her, making her feel even smaller in comparison to him than she already was. 'You're afraid someone will think you *need* help from me. Enough of this. Just try to be a bit careful with the Sybils of this world. They aren't tough enough to take hounding from bullies.'

'Oh, my god. You don't get it at all. No one bullied Sybil Davis. She's very gentle and felt hounded. I'm sorry for that. I'll be more careful. But the piano was moved in what is still an active crime scene. That sort of thing would drive any copper berserk.'

'Right.' This was pointless.

'Would you like to know what we found today?'

Her legs shook and she clasped her hands to stop them from trembling visibly.

When she didn't answer, he sat beside her again. 'The thermos, Alex. We found the . . . we found it.'

Her palms were wet. 'Wells had it?'

'It was inside that piano. Lodged down in a corner. The cap we all thought would be there had been screwed back on. We're hoping for prints.'

'But, Dan – did Wells tell you it was there?'

'No. But we're going to find out if he put it there.'

'It should have been found during the search,' she pointed out. Now there was hope of getting to the bottom of all this horror.

'*If* it was there then. But it wasn't easy to see, not where it was. I think it got jostled and moved about inside the piano.'

Alex studied the backs of her hands. She didn't care anymore if he saw them shaking. 'I wonder if Ivor and whoever helped him caused the thermos to shift so it could be seen while it was hidden before?'

'Maybe they did,' he said mildly. 'You are the master of getting the last word.'

Thirty-Four

It was a good thing Alex had returned to the Dog. They were having a busy lunch trade. And there was no doubt that talk about the arrest announcement the day before was as much a reason for the business as hunger and thirst.

Big, bluff Kev Winslet, gamekeeper at the Derwinters, held court near the bar. He had the

usual group clustered in close, including Major
Stroud who had taken to giving Alex poisonous
glances from time to time. When there was a
chance, she'd have to sort it out with him.

She caught his eye and smiled.

He looked into his glass, but slowly a tight
smile appeared and she took it as a good sign.

Her mum came and leaned across the bar. 'Can
you come into the restaurant, Alex? Have you
got enough help here?'

'Be right there.' She took Hugh aside and he
said he, Liz and Juste, who was in for an extra
day, would manage just fine.

When she walked through the room, she felt
watched. Most of them really thought she had an
inside track to information from the police.

In the restaurant, near the stairs, stood Doc
James. 'Is Tony around? I couldn't reach him.'

Lily indicated a corner table well away from
the smattering of lunch guests, and left when they
were seated.

'Tony's delivering a sheep baby today – I mean
a lamb.' She giggled. 'I'm a basket case.'

'Ah,' Doc said, unsmiling. 'That'll be why he's
switched off his phone. I'm in an awkward position,
Alex. I don't think Molly Lewis – the police surgeon
– knows Tony is my son, or that you and I are old
friends. She's coming to me for any pointers I can
give on the Meeker case. It's a baffling one and
I'm the only medical link she has between the two
deaths. She's trying to get some backup for something she's going to suggest to O'Reilly.'

Alex waited while a server passed by. 'I don't
understand why it's awkward for you. You can

269

only say what you know and you never saw Mrs Meeker after she died.'

'True. But I saw her before she died.'

For an instant, Alex didn't understand. 'Yes, but . . . you mean as a patient?'

Doc hesitated, but said, 'Yes.'

'We would never expect you to break patient confidentiality, Doc.'

'I know. But I see you two getting sucked in – as you usually do – and I don't like it. Someone's playing deadly games with drugs – at least they did with Laura. Or so it looks. The perfect place to do that would be right here, in a bar, particularly when it's really busy and you can't watch everyone at once. Drinks are easy enough to spike. Please separate yourselves from this one. Don't be seen talking to the police, or holding chit-chats with Mary and Harriet and anyone who gives them information.'

The server passed again.

Alex laced her hands on the table. 'Are you talking about Sybil being with me at the Burke sisters' place?'

He nodded, yes.

'Who told you? Who's watching me? It's maddening.'

'I'm not telling you who. All I'm asking is for you to carry on as if nothing different has happened. Spend more time here and be careful who you're seen with. People carry grudges and look for ways to satisfy them. Keep that in mind.'

Triplet lambs were rare and Tony was glad the delivery was over. Before the three live and healthy lambs were safely in the world, he'd resorted to tying pieces of colored thread on feet to make sure nothing got muddled up on the way out.

He had sluiced off at the farm but wanted a shower. However it would have to be at the clinic. He'd left Alex without wheels, something he only remembered while admiring the three wet newborns, and their mother's efforts to care for the overload.

Arms waving overhead on the last bend in the hill brought him a grin. Alex, toiling uphill, didn't try to hide her relief that she wouldn't have to climb all the way up on foot.

'Where are you going?' he called through the window when he was beside her.

'To find you.' She looked cross. She wore a red tank top that must belong to Lily, but still had on jeans and boots and must be hot. 'Turn your phone on when you aren't in the middle of a procedure.'

'Sorry about that.' There was no point in raising her already bubbling ire by pointing out that as the queen of self-sufficiency, she hated being told what to do.

She climbed into the Range Rover but stopped him from driving off again. 'We're well enough off the road. We need to talk.'

Sun through the windshield was heating up the interior of the vehicle but she didn't seem to notice as she poured out what had been said at the visit from his father.

'So what do you think he was saying and trying not to really say?' she finished.

271

Tony looked at the tall grass beside the road, standing straight with no breeze to move it, and the scattering of wild flowers. He put the side of a fist to his mouth and went through what she'd said in his mind.

'I think we'd better take notice of what Dad's said. Stay away from any of the Green Friday crew.'

'Why? I have my own theories but I want to hear yours.'

'You're first, Alex.'

She looked up into his face, her green eyes intense and unhappy. 'Okay, but no laughing. I think Mrs Meeker saw Doc because she's got some sort of heart problem, too. And I don't care how sneaky we have to be, I'm going to find out if that's true. I already know the liquid digoxin is used mostly with children or for people who can't swallow pills. And if you think back over everything that's been said, we don't know for sure that Mrs Meeker didn't have pills and not the other stuff. Dan only said the death was much the same as Laura's. But what if Mrs Meeker *was* one of those with swallowing problems and she was the one who had the stuff that killed Laura? What if she caused Laura's death deliberately, someone found out and killed her, too, out of revenge?'

'We don't know if any of that is right,' Tony told her. 'But I think some of it could be. How can we find out if Mrs Meeker had trouble taking pills? They found a bottle on the floor by her bed. I assumed it was a pill bottle, but it could have been the liquid.'

272

'Tony!' Alex grabbed his upper arm in both of her hands. 'That's it. Mrs Meeker depleted her own drug supply on Laura then had to get a refill prescription from Doc. Let's go straight to . . . to O'Reilly. I was going to say, Dr Molly Lewis but she probably wouldn't even see us.'

'I want to know what Dad prescribed – or even if he prescribed at all. Making fools of ourselves may not be very important, but we can't do this, not walk in and state facts we don't have.'

She took his face in her hands and made him look at her. 'Come on, my love, let's just do it. Or the chemist's. There's only one in Folly.'

'We . . . no, we can't waltz in and ask them.'

'Mm . . . nope, we can't. Especially since the prescription was probably filled by a chemist in a bigger town.'

'This may seem inappropriate timing, but I think it will help us relax.'

Kissing Alex had never relaxed Tony, quite the reverse, but it always chased any other thoughts from his mind, thoughts other than how much he enjoyed kissing her – and what a perfect prelude to the real event it was.

Deciding to avoid any acts of public indecency, they eventually sat, leaning together and very disheveled.

'You take Doc,' Alex said when her breathing slowed down. 'We just want to know if Mrs Meeker used the same stuff Laura took.'

He rolled his head toward her. 'And you think he'll give me a straight answer?'

'If you wiggle around the question he might

give a hint. If he doesn't, plead about what a nasty position we're in. Say you're worried about me and how someone could slip me a mickey.'

'Don't even say that.' He looked angry.

Alex coughed to hide a smile. 'We have to do it, Tony. I'll find Elyan and remind him we were supposed to have a chat. When I saw him this morning, he said he'd like that. I'll just find a way to mention Mrs Meeker and pills, and hope he corrects me. He'd know what she took, wouldn't he?'

'He might. Why are you so determined not to leave it to the police to figure all this out?'

Why? Alex glanced at Tony. 'Because I can't. I don't trust them to get to the bottom of it quickly enough. And it's my responsibility. I was there when she left . . . I mean, died. I found Laura's body and I can't stop feeling I should find out who killed her.'

Thirty-Five

'They're picking us off one-by-one,' Elyan said. 'Wells is back. They couldn't have had grounds to hold him any longer. He's as shaken up as hell, and now they've taken Sebastian. How do you try to think about people you've known forever as murderers?'

'I don't think you do,' Alex told him. 'If there was anything that stood out, you'd remember.'

She had called him and he picked up on the

first ring. And he'd been so eager to get out of the house, he had suggested they meet at the public library in Broadway, a few miles away, as soon as they could get there. He'd found it on an earlier visit when he was researching abandoned railways and he said there were very few people there on that occasion, but they could always go somewhere else if it was busy this time.

The library was modern and on Leamington Road with its rows of fresh detached houses and flower-filled gardens.

In the library, half a dozen people seemed to be holding a reading group and were completely engrossed in their whispered discussion.

Alex and Elyan sat at a table with great chunks of silence hanging between them.

When she got there, he already had several books in front of him. 'I've been a railway nut since I was a kid. Or I have when I could steal the time to get into them,' he said. 'The Cotswolds are criss-crossed with disused tracks.'

His enthusiasm made her smile. 'I can see that being interesting. I suggested we get together because we'd mentioned having a chat. If I can help you in any way, all you have to do is say so. I get the feeling you're pretty much alone in all this – apart from Annie, of course.'

'She's wonderful. I wish she wasn't going through such a bad time. It's bad for her as well as for me and her parents aren't helping. They don't think she should come to see me until it's all over.' He rested his chin in his hands. 'I've been told not to go up to London. I asked that

O'Reilly chap and he said, no. What does he think I intend to do on a little run up to London?'

'I've seen this with the police before,' Alex said. 'They like to keep all the case principals in one place, or as much as possible.'

'Annie and I are going to get married just as soon as we can.'

Alex couldn't help smiling. They seemed so young but she'd felt the force of their feelings for one another. 'I think you'll make a great couple.' She barely managed not to say, *When you're older.*

'Yes.' His eyes looked into the distance. 'Poor old Meeker said that. She was a good person but I took her for granted. I took Laura for granted too, come to that. She thought Annie and I should just run off together but she didn't know any more about the ins and outs of that than we do. Annie's got school anyway and she loves her parents.'

'Had Mrs Meeker been ill?' Alex asked, feeling like a snake. 'She looked so fit, didn't she?'

With a forefinger, Elyan made lines on the table. 'I suppose she did. She took medication regularly, I know that. But from what the police say, it can't be anything to do with that. Do you know if parents can do anything to stop a marriage, or nullify it?'

Alex's heart sank. 'I'll try and find out.'

'Would you? Thanks. I'd do it but I wouldn't put it past my father, or even Sebastian, to have ways to follow whatever I do on the computer.'

'There are computers here,' she pointed out, nodding to the stations in the library.

'I just don't want anyone to know it's on my mind. If someone decided to follow what I've been doing lately, they could find out I was here and even if I used a computer. They'd flip out and find ways to make our lives impossible. Look, I haven't asked Annie to do it, yet, so you won't . . .'

'Of course not. You must miss having Laura to talk to.'

He blinked rapidly. 'Of course I do. She was healthier than when she was younger. She told me that. The past couple of years she'd seemed much stronger.'

She scrambled for the right response.

'My father didn't seem to recognize that. He just kept on treating her like an invalid. Sometimes I've wondered if she really needed the medicine anymore.'

'Perhaps illness frightened him. Some people are like that.'

When he seemed lost in thought, Alex gave him time. Outside, darkness was settling in, leaving streetlights to illuminate flowers along the pathway and pick out dogs trotting ahead of their owners.

'Meeker said that was the problem,' Elyan said. 'And she thought he was frightened of losing Laura. Meeker never mentioned her illness to him.'

Alex could have kissed him. 'Not her own, I'm sure.'

'Oh, no. He's almost paranoid about getting sick himself.'

'Did you say Mrs Meeker had to take pills

regularly? What was wrong with her? She seemed to be on top of everything.'

'I saw her take pills,' Elyan said. 'But it wasn't something you'd think of asking about. But how would I know? Just pills to me.'

Alex weighed her response. She must not alert him to her fact-finding mission. It was clear Elyan didn't know exactly what had killed Laura, or Mrs Meeker, but there was nothing to suggest the housekeeper had any difficulty taking pills. The methods of the two deaths didn't sound as if they matched – but they could, couldn't they? There was no way of being sure until they knew what killed Mrs Meeker.

'Did Wells talk about the police questioning?' She frowned in what she hoped was a distant, thoughtful way. 'This all needs to be over so things can get back to normal for all of us.'

'All Wells said was that his fingerprints weren't found on anything in the church. He said they wouldn't be since he'd never been inside the place. But he's still not allowed to leave Folly. He's back at the house and my mother is all jumpy about that. She's scared someone will try to hurt her and I suppose she's already tried Wells and found him guilty of murder. She won't listen to me.'

Alex's mobile vibrated and she excused herself to take the call when she saw it was Tony. She went outside the library and stood under a street-light where Elyan would see her and know she saw him, in case he was tempted to slip out.

'Tony,' she said. 'I'm at the library in Broadway with Elyan. The police let Wells go but now they've taken Sebastian in.'

278

He let out a sigh. 'The trouble is they may be looking in the right places but without evidence to back up theories.'

'What does that mean?' A Land Rover was parked at the corner. Dark blue and very muddy. It reminded her of the accident on the hill. 'Tony, what did you mean?'

'Mrs Meeker died of a digoxin overdose. She was already taking the drug regularly. Then she ingested a big additional dose – and a fairly hefty amount of whisky.'

'The cocktail tumbler . . .'

'Yes. Sounds as if she might almost have been drowned with the stuff. She had bruises consistent with someone strong holding her by the base of the skull, and her arms were bruised as if she fought.'

'Doc told you this?' Alex saw Elyan get up and start toward the door.

'No.' Tony cleared his throat. 'He left a set of records open on his desk and left the room for water.'

'Are you telling me they were Mrs Meeker's notes?'

'Yes. Not a lot there but enough to tell us what we want to know.'

'Elyan told me she wasn't well. He's coming out, Tony. I'd better go. At least, we'd better not say anything telling. Here he comes. Hi, Elyan, are you leaving?'

'I should get back. My father will be foaming at the mouth again by now.'

'Right,' Alex said. 'Let's touch bases again. I'll see what I can find out about what we discussed.'

'Thanks.'

'Is he still in earshot?' Tony asked.

'No, he just walked to the corner and got into a dark blue Land Rover.'

Thirty-Six

The instant he realized Sonia was attached to the Quillams who wanted to lease Green Friday, he should have backed out of the agreement.

If he was honest with himself he had to admit he'd been curious at the thought of seeing her again. That made him a stupid git who still let his dick get the better of him. He'd never stopped recalling sex with Sonia, even after she'd left him without so much as a note. She'd been nineteen and a knock-out – and he'd actually thought he loved her.

Damn, why hadn't he stuffed his curiosity away with the rest of the best-forgotten memories?

'Hugh! Over here!'

He turned, deliberately slowly, to watch her clack her backless high-heels up the center aisle of the tiny church she'd designated. Not far from Naunton, she had told him. Still, he hated meeting her there and feeling the specter of dead Laura Quillam as if she were watching. And he had loathed the way ancient gravestones had been leaned against crumbling walls around the church-yard like so many discarded and forgotten lives. The dark green lushness of the grass seemed

somehow ominous. A sparse scattering of dande-
lions were all that was mildly cheerful.

'Hugh, thank god you came.'

'I said I would. But why here? It looks as if
pieces of the place could cave in at any moment.'

She laughed and hitched a handbag over her
shoulder. A sleeveless deep blue dress swirled
around her pretty legs and her hair was loose. 'If
you had Norman bits, they might fall off at any
moment, too,' she said, reaching him. 'I chose it
because I remember it from a visit to Naunton
as a child, with my father. He loved searching
out old churches. Said trying to find some of
them was like being a detective following clues.'

Her father, whom he had never met, was of no
interest to him. 'I've been away from the pub
too long already,' he told her. 'What is it you
must talk to me about, *in complete privacy*?'

'This will be difficult for both of us,' she said,
pressing the palm of one hand against his chest.
He felt the warmth through his cotton shirt. 'I've
borne it all alone as long as I could. Now I need
help – from you.'

'You might as well be speaking another
language, Sonia. I don't understand you.'

'You will. When Percy married Laura's mother
he went from pretending to be rich to being filthy,
stinking rich – sort of. She let him have whatever
he wanted but she had come into a huge
inheritance.'

Hugh selected a rough-hewn stone pew and sat
down with a wary glance at the roof. 'What does
this have to do with me?'

'Just listen. In her will she left three quarters

281

of her estate to her then baby daughter, Laura, and the rest to Percy. When she died, Percy was in easy street, only he can spend money like no one you've ever seen. Elyan's been a big help but he's not at the top of his game and there's been a fairly dry period.'

He crossed his arms. 'Laura was worth—'

'She would have been when she turned twenty-five but she pre-deceased Percy so it all went to him.'

It was impossible not to stare while he stumbled around for the next answer.

'Exactly, if Percy isn't the main suspect in her death, he should be. And Meeker knew all those details which made her a danger.'

'Percy wouldn't be so stupid. He'd know the police would look at him first.'

She swung around, sending her skirts whirling. 'He told them all about the will right away, as soon as Laura was killed. You're right, he isn't stupid. And he talked about Wells trying to get Laura to marry him so he could get his hands on the money. I don't know if that's true but it might as well be. Anyway, they've let Wells go so they're back where they started.'

Hugh slapped his knees and got up. 'I don't come from a planet where I can think about a man killing his daughter for money and that's what you're suggesting.'

'Yes, it is. Percy gets very drunk and says more than he should – to me. He didn't say he poisoned Laura, not that, but he told me about the will. And he told me that after him, everything goes to Elyan, for his music.'

'Which leaves you, where?' That hadn't been the best card to play now but he couldn't stop himself. 'Or surely there's a nice fat accommodation made for you so why worry?'

'Why are you being so mean to me?'

He didn't answer.

'Nothing for me. It would be up to Elyan to look after me. I'd be dependent on my son for an allowance and a roof over my head.' Tears glittered in her eyes. 'It's not fair. I gave up everything for him. I gave up you. I never loved anyone but you, Hugh.'

'Stop it. You'll always land on your feet. There are more immediate things to worry about. Do you really think there's a chance Percy is responsible for the deaths of Laura and Mrs Meeker.'

She held her head high and sniffed. 'Yes.'

'Then why haven't you gone to the police and made sure you got Elyan away?'

'He would never hurt Elyan. He reveres him. His prodigy. He made him – that's what he says. No, Elyan's safe and he won't hurt me because that would really focus all eyes on him. Sebastian's wife overdosed, did you know that?'

'Oh, my god, I'm in Neverland. Are you sure of that?'

'Sure enough. He hasn't said this but Percy let the police know about it and that's why they've taken Sebastian in. Never mind that the woman had serious mental health issues and had tried before. And she'd just lost her mother. Apparently she adored her mother – something I can't imagine.'

'Forget yourself and your family, Sonia. This has to go to the police. Now.'

She rushed at him and flung her arms around his neck. 'No, we can't do that. For Elyan's sake.'

'You've just explained why he'll be fine, except for the crippling trauma he'll go through when he finds out his father's a killer.'

'I don't want to stay with Percy.'

He almost laughed. 'You're not going to have the chance. He'll be behind bars – unless you're making this all up.' And it wouldn't be the first time she'd spun him a fantastic yarn.

'You've made things up with your family, haven't you? I'm glad, Hugh. You deserve real peace and happiness.'

'Where did that come from?' He wasn't about to discuss his business with Sonia. 'We have to get back.'

'No, you don't understand.'

With finger and thumb he rubbed tired eyes. 'I don't care. You're going to go to the authorities with the truth and then we'll all see what happens. Elyan will be all right and he'll take care of you . . . at least until there's someone else in your life.'

'You don't understand.' Her voice rose until it broke. 'We can't let this happen. I want you to help me decide if the best thing to do is to hire someone to get rid of Percy. I know there are lots of people who do those things properly if they're paid well. And I know how to make enquiries without involving us.'

'That's madness.' He narrowed his eyes. 'Us? There is no us and never will be again. I'm asking

284

you to get these wild ideas out of your head and do the right thing.' He didn't add, 'for once.'

'It may take a while for the estate to be settled on Elyan, but it will be and then there'll be nothing else to worry about. We'll all be set forever. And I think Green Friday is beautiful. We can make it the social center of the Cotswolds. Everyone will come to our parties. And I'll go back to my music, too.'

He studied her eyes, looking for signs that she was high on something.

'Haven't you figured it out yet,' Sonia said, holding her hands, palms up, toward him. 'We can't let anyone know the truth about Elyan. If we do, he won't inherit.'

Hugh shook his head, no. 'I haven't figured it out. I don't know what will happen if Percy's in jail and can't get his hands on the money from Laura but it'll be worked through until it goes to Elyan.'

'We've got to do this before he does something really stupid and runs away with Annie. He doesn't think I know what he's planning, but Meeker did, poor gullible Meeker, and she told me, the way she did with everything.'

He gave up and stood quiet, letting her run on.

'Hugh, Elyan's not Percy's son, but no one has to find that out. Help me keep his future safe.'

'And yours,' he said under his breath.

'Think about it. Look at him. He's yours, Hugh, your son and they're all going to find out if we let them. He'll lose everything.'

285

Thirty-Seven

The parish hall did not improve with familiarity. Grotty still described the place perfectly, even if Sybil had buried her anxiety about the police and brought in vases of flowers to put around. And there were home-baked flapjacks on a tray covered with fancy paper doilies.

'Your Sybil Davis brought the flowers and the goodies,' Dan said, indicating the roses on his desk. 'Nice lady.'

'Yes, she is.'

'I do regret being hard on her, Alex, but old habits die hard.'

She didn't respond to that. 'I came by to see if you could find something out for me.' Passing a piece of paper across his makeshift desk, she added, 'Dark blue Land Rover. It would be nice to know who owns it.'

Tony put a hand on her shoulder. 'Could be the vehicle that forced her off the road. She's not at all sure but she did see it and think it was familiar.'

'Thank you, Tony,' Dan said, in a not particularly pleasant tone. 'Bishop, follow up this plate, please.'

A woman arrived at a trot and whisked the number away.

Alex sat balling a Kleenex in her hands. 'You have Sebastian in custody.'

Dan allowed his head to drop forward. 'Yes. I won't bother to ask how you know.'

'Thank you. You don't think Sebastian had anything to do with this, do you?'

He remained quiet.

Alex said. 'Did his wife commit suicide, or was—'

'No, she wasn't. And yes, she did. He's still being questioned.'

'Where's Daisy?'

Dan was silent so long, she stared at him until he met her eyes. 'You're a nice woman. You need hobbies – safe hobbies. You're neglecting your painting and your first edition collection. Daisy will be fine. A message came in for the two of you. The Misses Burke would like to see you when you have time.' He pushed a memo sheet to Alex.

Alex stuffed the paper in her pocket.

'I wonder what you know that I don't know you know,' Dan said.

'Remember you made an offhand comment about wondering if there were one or two killers?' Tony said. 'Did you decide anything?'

'Sit down,' Dan said, 'you're hurting my neck. Doesn't seem much point in holding back what I think you've already found out but if you make my life any more difficult than it is, you'll wish you hadn't. I can put a lot of persons of interest behind bars for a few uncomfortable hours.'

Tony grinned and pulled at the front of his hair. 'I think I've been warned.'

'This is my own theory, but it's getting harder to believe one person did both of them. They're more different than they're the same. With the exception of . . . well.'

'The digoxin?' Alex said and winced, avoiding eye contact with Tony.

'I'm not sure it would be possible to keep anything under wraps in Folly,' Dan said, but didn't sound perturbed. 'And it being mixed with alcohol in both cases – to speed up the result. This will be one of those cases where the pieces fall like dominoes once the first ones are shaken loose.'

Bishop returned and handed another piece of paper to Dan. 'I think it's all there, guv'nor.'

He mumbled something resembling thanks and stared at what she'd written. He looked up sharply. 'Where are you staying at the moment, Alex?'

'I've been at the Dog,' she said, puzzled. She thought he already knew.

He turned to Tony and looked strained when he said, 'I think it would be a good idea if there was someone around Alex at the moment. Can you stay in the village?'

'I'll make sure she's not on her own tonight,' Tony said, and Alex frowned at him.

'You should know what this is about,' Dan said, flapping the paper he'd been given. 'The Land Rover is a rental from Moreton-in-Marsh. A Mr Percy Quillam picked it up on the Wednesday evening of last week, after he arrived on the train from London. He said he needed it for at least a week or so. He gave his London address. Said that was best because he was on vacation here.'

'We do think Elyan Quillam could have been driving it earlier this evening,' Tony said.

Thirty-Eight

Bogie made his 'step-step, hop-and-tap, step' way across the empty bar room. He seemed blissfully happy that his convalescence was taking place at the pub although he got impatient while he waited for his favorite customers to show up.

He went to stare at the door again, sighed, and tucked himself under the entryway settle. Tony had gone out on a call, taking Katie with him, and neither Hugh nor the detectives had come down yet.

When Hugh did appear and movement started, Bogie would cheer up. He wasn't to know how early it was.

Alex's eyes felt as if they'd been rolled in fine grit. She had used some generic drops and blinked frequently but what she needed were several nights of uninterrupted and deep sleep – and to stop worrying that someone, maybe her or Tony, could accidentally swallow potential death.

You had to get an overdose and be susceptible or already weak to suffer real damage, but time also counted and the one defense for that outcome was never to be out of sight of help.

She was getting paranoid.

It would do her good to drink bottled water and nothing else for as long as it took to know they were safe. Even the coffee in her mug took on sinister shadows, although she'd made it herself with instant boiling water and coffee granules. But what about other people? Should the entire village be warned?

That was the job of the police and panic didn't accomplish a thing.

Elyan was someone she couldn't help worrying about. She didn't believe he had tried to harm her on the hill. Perhaps no one had. The driver might not have seen her. Elyan could also be in the killer's sights.

Alex pulled out her mobile and entered Elyan's number, hoping he didn't leave his phone on when he was sleeping.

She need not have worried. He answered after two rings. 'Hi,' she said. 'It's Alex. I just wanted to make sure you were all right. Was everything okay last night? Did you make it in without any trouble?'

'Yes, and I'm already practicing like a good boy.' He was quiet for an instant. 'But don't be surprised if you find me working in a London club shortly. A man has to earn his keep.'

No snappy answer came to mind. 'Don't you wake the whole house when you play this early?'

'I'm not sure any of them even notice. I play all the time.'

Asking questions about the Land Rover was out of the question.

'I was going to call you,' he said. 'Do you remember I told you about being interested in the old railway lines? There are lots of disused ones around here.'

'Yes, I do. You sound excited. Does that mean you've made a find?'

290

'I think so. On the computer after I got home last night. I'm going to check it out. I think there's a railway graveyard a few miles from Moreton-in-Marsh. Sounds as if you might need wilderness gear but I'm going to take a look later this morning. My father rented a Land Rover to take fishing and hunting and I thought I'd borrow it. He'll never actually go hunting or fishing, of course.' He laughed. 'I like driving bigger vehicles and a four-wheel drive could be useful for this.'

Alex had heard every word he said but stopped thinking when he blithely talked about a Land Rover.

'Would you like to come?' Elyan said, and when she didn't answer added, 'of course you wouldn't. I used to try dragging poor Laura along on my expeditions. She'd go sometimes. I think she felt sorry for me.'

She heard him swallow. What a horrible time he'd had, and he was likely to go through a lot more.

'When does Annie come back?' she asked for something to say. He was a lonely kid. Eighteen, but not very worldly. Being kept away from people his own age added to that problem.

'This afternoon.' He sounded instantly cheered up. 'I just want her to get here.'

'I'll come with you this morning,' she said and instantly felt rash.

It was his turn to be very quiet.

'If you still want company?'

'Well . . . yes, I'd really like that. Okay. How about ten? Where will you be? Where shall I pick you up? At the pub?'

When would she learn she couldn't rescue everyone who was unhappy? 'I'm going to Wilkins' on Hillop Street about half-nine and I'll be through there by ten. It's the dairy. Do you know it? I could wait outside if I get through early. I won't drive.'

'See you there.'

She'd heard a definite lift in Elyan's tone and felt better about trying to cheer him up.

Sounds came from the restaurant kitchen and she walked back expecting to see Hugh. She hadn't heard Lily come in but she was there making coffee while the woman who helped with breakfast for the inn turned bacon rashers in a frying pan.

'Mum! When did you get here?'

'You were on the phone so I didn't interrupt. Our two eager beavers are down for breakfast. I'm glad Mrs Butters is on top of things.'

'Dan and Bill are down already?' Alex smiled at Mrs Butters who wore a yellow gingham wrap-around apron over her clothes.

'They are,' she said comfortably.

Alex hurried into the restaurant and found the two men at the isolated table they preferred when they didn't eat in the snug. 'I won't interrupt you for long,' she told them. 'The mystery of the Land Rover and Elyan driving it is solved. He came right out and told me his father rented it to go hunting or something. Elyan says that's never likely to happen but he enjoys borrowing the Land Rover. He wouldn't have told me that if he'd been driving the vehicle that ran me off.'

'Help is on the way,' Lily said from behind

292

Alex. 'Coffee, gentlemen.' She turned up their mugs, got an extra one from a cart and filled all three. 'Breakfast will be up shortly.' Lily glided away on the high-heeled black shoes she favored.

'Join us,' Dan said.

'I've already had a cup.'

'And you don't need more than one in the morning? I envy you. Please sit and explain how you found out about Elyan.'

'The more I think about what happened to me, the more I think it was an accident and the driver never saw me,' Alex said. 'I could only guess at the color anyway and I didn't see a license plate on the hill. It probably wasn't the same one.'

'Yes,' Dan said. 'How did you happen to be speaking with Elyan, did you say?'

'He's interested in the old railways,' Alex said and got ready to fib. 'So am I, and he called to tell me he tracked down this railway graveyard. You know, one of those places they take old carriages to keep in case they can be sold for parts, or because someone decides to buy one to open a mobile coffee stand at boot sales. You know the sort of thing.'

'I suppose he's a trainspotter,' Bill said, straight-faced. 'I wonder how many numbers he's got.'

'I doubt he was ever allowed to do things like that,' Alex said. She sat and put cream in a mug of coffee. 'He says he likes driving this rented Land Rover because it's a good off-road vehicle. I think I just made the wrong connections, don't you . . . when I saw him in it?'

'Could be,' Bill said. 'Might not be.' He looked at Dan.

'Different subject,' Dan said. 'Do you carry a liqueur called Jenever?'

She thought about it. 'We do have a bottle but it's probably a bit old. Good grief, what do you want that for?'

'It was added to the digoxin overdose that killed Laura Quillam. To cover up the taste.'

'Dutch courage,' Alex said almost under her breath. 'It's a spirit, not a liqueur. Old relative of gin and very strong. I understand it has the taste of gin or some say vodka. It couldn't have come from here but I'll check just to make sure. Was it . . . no it couldn't have been in the tumbler Mrs Meeker . . .' Some things were just too hard to say.

Dan nodded. 'Sorry to bring that up but we need to check. Laura drank the white one. I'm told they come in all kinds of flavors and they put a lot of odd stuff in it. Like herbs. Strange thing for a young woman to drink early in the morning – especially when she was singing.'

'There was a lot of honey in it,' Bill added.

'They put a lot of different ingredients in it. There are berry kinds, too. Did she think she was taking something for her throat?' Alex said. 'She didn't sound as if she had a sore throat.'

'Could you check . . .?'

'Yes, right now.' Already on her feet, Alex turned back to the men. 'I can't remember who, but someone asked for Jenever recently. Hugh might remember who it was.'

The detectives had left before Hugh showed his face, his puffy, red-eyed, grey face, which he would not even admit looked any different from usual. He recalled finding an almost empty bottle of Jenever when Elyan said Sonia liked it a lot.

Alex stared at him and felt like sitting down. That's right, it had been Sonia who had a thing for Jenever.

'What is it?' Hugh said. 'You look worried.'

She thought about it. 'Nothing. Just a thought I had.' And it was nothing, just one of those coincidental . . . She'd been caught out by coincidental things before. 'Would you let Dan O'Reilly know we do have some Jenever, or a very little bit of it. If he has more questions, don't hold back. He always has more questions.'

Hugh turned his head as if he hadn't heard a word she said and Alex shrugged. 'I'm going out for a few hours. Elyan's taking me to a railway graveyard.' She grinned. 'I'm broadening my education.'

He snapped his attention back to her. 'What?'

'I'm going out with Elyan Quillam to look at some railway carriages. The old ones are his hobby. In a rash moment I said I'd go with him. I felt sorry for him because he's been through so much lately and we seem to get along well.'

'Thank you,' he said, which made her frown.

'I'm happy to do it.'

She spent the next hour going over orders with her mother before setting out for the dairy. Some discussions were best had in person. Somehow she wanted a nice way to let them know she loved their products, but not the racket they made early in the morning. Lily had been getting complaints from guests.

When she got through to Tony, she was only yards from the loading bay at the dairy and leaned against a wall while she talked to him. She told him where she was going, expecting him to have too many questions – which he did. Turning the conversation to the detectives' questions about Jenever distracted him.

'She didn't ask for the stuff,' Tony said. 'Sonia, that is. It was Elyan who asked.'

Alex smiled. 'He asked because Sonia likes it.' Sonia was the kind of woman men felt a need to defend, even when there was nothing to defend, and evidently Tony felt defensive of her, too.

'I don't feel good about any of this,' he said. 'The potential suspects have become a shorter, tighter, list but I still don't have it narrowed all the way down. Wells or Sebastian seem the most likely, but which one and why?'

'Or Percy,' she said. 'I don't like saying it. I don't even know the man but looking at all this from the outside it seems as if he's the one who wants to control everyone. Or am I missing something?'

'I don't know. I feel as if I don't know anything, except I want you here with me. Where are these railway carriages?'

'Near Moreton-in-Marsh. It's not far. I know we can't be gone long because he'll want to be back in time to meet Annie. She's coming down from London this afternoon. I'll call you again later.'

She rang off and went inside to greet Mark Wilkins, the grandson of the original owner of Wilkins Dairy.

Less than half an hour later she re-emerged

296

into a sunny day under a cloudless sky, just in time to see Elyan's red and white Mini come along the road that lay behind the High Street buildings and turn onto Hillop Street.

He pulled up and leaned to push open the passenger door.

'I thought this was going to be a Land Rover off-road expedition,' she said, hesitating before climbing in.

'Father wanted to play with it today so I didn't ask. Off we go. Should we stop for lunch on the way?'

'I'm not going to be hungry for a while. But if you are . . .?'

'Nope. I want to see those carriages and it shouldn't take too long to get there. Should we go into Moreton-in-Marsh to eat afterward?'

'Let's see how we feel.' She wanted to get back.

'The building where they're keeping the carriages isn't far from that arboretum that's supposed to be so good. It's a big old rail shed – or it is now. I don't know what they used it for initially. I suppose they put down rails to keep them on, but I don't know. Seems they'd be difficult to move otherwise.'

Why had she pretended to be interested?

Because she was a softy! For once she needed to give herself a break for wanting to make everyone feel better. 'Do we stay on this road?'

'As far as Upper Swell. Here, I sketched this. There isn't a cartridge for the printer so I copied it off the computer screen.'

She looked at his stylishly drawn map and smiled. Elyan was unlikely to do anything poorly.

He drummed his fingers on the wheel, rocking back and forth to music – or perhaps just a beat – he heard in his head.

Elyan took his eyes off the road to tap the map. 'Do you see Sezincote House there? There should be a sign to it soon. Then, very shortly, there's a marker for something called Bishop's Nob. A right turn. It's there.'

'The house sign,' Alex said. She leaned forward and peered toward a little turn between tall firs. 'We just passed it. Is this Bishop's Nob? We're coming to it.'

Elyan made the turn sharply and she grabbed the dashboard. 'Show me the map,' he said.

Alex held it up, aware of how close the trees were on either side of them.

'Yes, I remember that,' Elyan said. 'Look at this in here. It's so beautiful. Absolutely peaceful. I bet no one ever comes here. They don't want peace, not one of them. More and more of everything is all that gets them going.'

Her heart took a jump. 'They?'

'Everyone. They have to get stuff around them so it blocks out the mirror. They can't see themselves in the mirror, just their stuff. They forget who they were before. Look at this place. It's a cathedral of trees. It's good here. No one paid to make it look like this but they don't believe that's possible. I don't want any of it anymore. Just Annie.'

Alex pressed her lips together and hung on to an overhead strap. As he talked – shouted – Elyan waved his arms, sometimes both arms. The car skewed and bumped.

'All I wanted was for everyone to leave me alone.' He gave her a wild-eyed look. 'I played for them. I played for me but not as much as I played for them. They took anything I wanted for myself. I was never a kid – that would have taken too much time. If I talked they told me empty vessels make the most noise. If I didn't talk they told me still waters run deep. I was always wrong.

'Laura was the best of them. The best. The very best . . . and now she's gone. I had a model of a steam engine made of brass. I found it in an old trunk and cleaned it till it glittered. And I put it in the music room. I was fourteen. You could take it all apart then build it back, piece by piece, to make the engine again. It taught you how a steam engine went together. My father saw it and went mad. He took it away and then it was gone, like anything I wanted.

'He wouldn't tell me why but Mrs Meeker did. My father's grandfather worked on the railways. He drove a train. And he taught young men who wanted to do the same thing all about how they worked. My father was ashamed of that. He was ashamed of a grandfather driving a train.

'I should have killed *him*.'

Alex sat very still. Her eyes stung at the pain in this young man, but she was also afraid of him. She made up her mind. 'Please stop.'

'What do you mean?' He looked blank and kept on driving.

'Stop the car, Elyan. We have to talk.' Alex touched his hand lightly.

He did as she asked, stopping in the middle of

299

the small track with a jolt. 'Are you all right? What is it?'

She buried her face in her hands and shook her head.

'What?' he said loudly, sounding panicky again.

'Elyan, I think we need to turn around.'

The sharp angles of his face seemed accentuated in the shadows thrown by the tunnel of trees. He was very pale. 'Why? I don't understand.'

'Just turn around. I'll explain why I need to go back as we go. If you still want to come and do this, we'll come back another time.'

'We're almost there.'

'It doesn't take long to get here. Half an hour or so. We can even get back today if . . . well, let's see how it goes.'

Elyan nodded his head up and down, up and down, up and down until Alex wanted to grab him and make him stay still.

'Is that okay, Elyan?'

'You don't understand anything. I've lost my whole life and all you care about is how you feel. Everything I wanted has slipped away. It's been taken away. And I can't get it back. Other people's ambitions. Their wants. Their needs. Perform, perform – like a sideshow freak. I wanted to believe I'd been wrong about you. I wanted you to be different and I just wanted to see the trains and forget for a bit, but you couldn't even let me have that.'

She swallowed the retort that he sounded like a spoiled child. 'I'm sorry to disappoint you, but this isn't right.' Her throat was so tight she struggled to get her words out.

'She wasn't supposed to die,' he said and started to cry. Still gripping the wheel, he sobbed and rocked his forehead from side to side on his hands. 'They wouldn't listen to her and without my father's say so, Laura didn't have a penny of her own. She wanted to go back to London. She hated it here. Her friends are there and she could have had gigs. She was offered gigs. Wells wanted to help her, too. I think they planned to get together.'

Alex sat very still. The engine was still running. Elyan's foot still rested near the gas pedal. If she tried to get out and he accelerated, the door might catch her.

'I'd like to get out and walk for a bit,' she said. 'I feel awful.'

'*You* feel awful? My sister is dead because we weren't careful enough. We thought she'd pass out and everyone would think she'd tried to kill herself. They were supposed to say she could go back to London and then leave her alone. She was even ready to agree to a shrink just to keep them off her back.

'And Annie and I could have been alone when she's here instead of always having Laura around. We wouldn't have to have her with us all the time in London, either. She'd have made a good life for herself. Oh, my god, it all went wrong.' He kept his head down but looked sideways at her. 'She had her regular dose. She'd taken it for so long we didn't think it would be a big deal. We even thought she might have to fake passing out. But I came back and you were there. And she was . . . dead.' His voice rasped.

301

What he was saying began to seep in. 'You two agreed to fake attempted suicide?'

'Yes. If I'd got there earlier, I might have saved her.'

'I don't think so, not from what the doctors said.'

'I might have.' He scrubbed the tears from his face. 'I dropped the thermos bottle in the piano. Then I couldn't get back in to take it away. If I'd taken it away, no one would ever have had any proof of what killed her.'

'Why not just tell the truth now?' The words were out before she could stop them.

'When did telling the truth ever make anything better? No one believed what Laura wanted. No one believes what Annie and I want. I can't go back there.'

He put his foot down and drove, his body heaving with his dry sobs. Coughs wracked him. He veered wildly, one way, then the other, barely missing trees. 'They would never let me be happy. I was the goose with the golden egg. Practice, practice. Now it's over. I'm going away with Annie and never coming back. My mother used me like everyone else.'

'It can be sorted out, I tell you,' Alex said. She didn't want to plead but heard her own desperation.

'Laura could never get pills down so it was easy to use the medicine. My mother had Jenever and Laura always liked the stuff. It was perfect. She drinks gin and tonic. She loves it.' Fresh tears streamed down his face. 'We put too much in, didn't we? I didn't think we had, just about half the bottle, but it was too much.'

302

Through a cut to the right, he drove, a cut barely wide enough for the car to pass, and into a sloping field open on the downhill side. A bleached, grey wood building was falling in on itself to the left. The roof sagged and holes gaped. It looked as if it had been put together from discarded lumber – and many years ago.

In front of great double doors that hung at angles, Elyan stopped the car. 'Get out,' he said, and when she didn't move, he yelled, 'get out!'

She did what he said, looking around, trying to work out how to get away. All she could do was run, but run where?

'You can't get away,' Elyan said. 'I knew when you asked all your clever questions about pills and what Mrs Meeker took, that you were going to be trouble. I hoped you wouldn't be, but I knew it was only a matter of time before I had to do something about you.'

Mrs Meeker.

Alex didn't say a word, only watched and waited.

'Aren't you going to ask any more questions?' he said.

'You didn't set out to hurt Laura. You both did a stupid thing but it's not as bad as if you'd deliberately killed her.'

'Like I did Mrs Meeker?'

Alex closed her eyes, closed out the world. 'How could you have done that?'

'Someone did, why not me?'

'You're not very well.'

'But I'm not mad, if that's what you're hinting at. I had the other half of Laura's bottle of medicine. Meeker knew everything. Laura talked to her about what we planned! I couldn't believe it when Meeker said she knew and now everything had gone wrong she was deciding what to do. *She was deciding what to do about my life.* She would have made sure I lost Annie, too.

'It wasn't easy. Meeker fought and I had to force the stuff down her throat with whisky. She liked whisky.' He stared at her. 'She didn't like it then.

'The idiot police were in the house. I played my own recording while I did it. I fooled them.'

He reached behind the driver's seat for a small backpack and threw it over his shoulder.

Alex started to run, downhill, legs and arms flying, but he was on her before she had gone any distance.

'Stop it,' he said, holding her down when she struggled. Her fists were useless. 'All I want is to see the carriages. Then we'll go back.'

She didn't believe him.

Elyan dragged her to her feet. 'Where's your mobile?' he said.

'In the car.' It all felt hopeless.

'It's in your pocket. You always carry it there. Give it to me.'

He took it from her jeans' pocket himself, turned it off and threw it away. She watched it arch through the air. They could still follow those things, couldn't they? Triangulate the position?

If they knew they needed to.

When he worked one of the doors open enough for them to squeeze inside, she didn't resist. It was unbelievable that he would try to kill her but if he did, she would need what strength she had to fight. And she would fight.

The holes in the roof let in plenty of light to show four filthy, deteriorating rail carriages standing at different angles. There were no tracks. They had been moved in there somehow and left.

Alex felt the beat of her heart under her skin. Her fingers and toes had their own hard, tingling beat. 'Elyan, what are we doing here?'

'Looking at these old carriages. Too bad there isn't an engine. That would be really interesting.'

He pulled her along by an elbow until she drove her heels into the dry, cinder-covered ground and leaned away.

'What's the point of that?' he said. He didn't sound mean or angry, just resigned.

'Are you going to kill me?'

He bellowed at her, 'Don't say that. Shut up. Don't talk any more.'

One carriage looked in better condition than the others. Alex noticed at once that it had no windows and no doors in the sides. Elyan towed her to its back door and pulled down a complicated-looking handle – long, jointed at its center, as if it were intended to be closed, then snapped into place as one solid bar.

'How about this?' He pulled the door open with ease. 'A security car for moving valuable things. Get in.'

'You've been here before,' she said. 'That's been oiled, hasn't it?'

The sadness on Elyan's face wasn't feigned. He sighed and lifted her to kneel just inside the door. Inside was only blackness and a few pinpricks of light where floorboards were rotting. 'I came here,' he said. 'But I didn't know I would need it for this. I don't want to need it for this.'

Bracing, waiting for a knife in her back, or a felling blow to the head, Alex remained on her knees. 'Let me go, please. I can help you explain what happened. It all got away from you. It'll be bad, but it doesn't have to be . . .'

'Be quiet. If you pray, pray. Pray you outlast what's going to happen here. I want you to – after Annie and I are away and they can't catch us. These are for you.'

Beside her on the filthy floor, he set down a torch and extra batteries. Then he slid a red thermos bottle beside them. 'We can live for a long time without food. Not so long without water. I hope someone will find you before you have to give in and drink.'

Thirty-Nine

'*Do* something.' Tony heard his own voice but it sounded like a stranger's. He crossed the parish hall toward Dan who stood, surrounded by Lamb and other officers, around a whiteboard.

'It's dark, damn it. She's somewhere and she's scared. She's got to be. And you stand there scribbling on your bloody board.'

A clatter, like mini-machinegun fire, followed.

Dan had thrown a handful of dry markers at the board. He crossed his arms and shoved a hand into his hair.

'It may look as if nothing's happening,' Bill Lamb said. 'That's an illusion. We've got people out searching. Many people. And dogs. You name it, it's out there. And it's dark.'

'Cadaver dogs?' He heard his own words again and felt his knees start to give out.

'Search dogs,' Dan said, meeting Tony's eyes. Worry etched deep into the detective's face. 'A blue Range Rover with a known license plate doesn't just disappear. Bill forgot the choppers. We're going at this from every angle we've got.'

One of the phones rang and a constable snatched it up. 'Yes. Yes. Yes, sir. I'm listening. But . . . the parish hall, that's right.' The constable hung up. 'Some geezer who has to tell us his information in person. On his way in. Didn't give a name. Didn't register one at this end.'

'Could be another damn joker,' Bill said.

'She's been gone all day and it's coming up on nine,' Tony said. 'Percy Quillam's been sedated. Dad said they haven't heard a word from Elyan and they're all in their rooms like they're mourning the death of another family member.'

'Nobody else has died,' Dan said, his face stony. 'You said you couldn't believe Elyan would hurt Alex.' He looked at Tony.

'I can't. So what's happened? Are they in a ditch somewhere? What other explanation can there be?'

'The search will go on until we've got them,' Bill said.

Dan's mobile gave a jarring beep and he slapped the instrument to his ear. 'Yeah?'

'We should be back out there looking,' Tony said. They'd searched with crews since mid-afternoon. Sometimes one or two of them had broken away to go alone and check an idea. But every time they'd ended back here.

Dan said, 'Thanks,' and returned the mobile to his pocket. 'Sonia Quillam thinks Elyan's passport is missing.'

'Oh, my god,' Tony muttered. 'The airports, then. Buses, trains. He could be in London, St Pancras, taken the Eurostar and be in Europe . . . he could be all the way there already for all we know. If he didn't have anything to hide, he'd have contacted us by now.'

'Unless the passport isn't missing and he's unconscious,' Bill said.

Through the doors came Major Stroud, more bedraggled than Tony had ever seen him. His hair stood up as if he hadn't combed it recently and his Barbour hung away from wrongly matched buttons toward one shoulder.

He approached and sat in the first metal folding chair he came to. 'Time to come clean,' he said in his clipped tones. 'When a man's wrong, he owns up. Honorable thing to do. Shouldn't have blamed that girl. Not her fault.'

For an instant no one moved, then he was surrounded and Dan kept a hold on Tony's arm. 'Give him time,' he said. 'Hear him out.'

'What is it, Major?' Bill asked. 'Have you seen Alex Duggins?'

'Hurt pride, that's what it is. Disappointment.

Harry always a disappointment. Then that other business earlier in the year and all the trouble. Just about killed his mother, I can tell you.'

Tony wanted to shake the man and make him get to the point.

'I was angry. She said she understood the boy. Said other people hadn't given him the benefit of the doubt. Then she didn't stand up for him after all. I wanted to get back at her.'

A slow, heavy beat began at Tony's temples. Dan's fingers dug into his arm but he let it hurt, let it give him a focus.

'I didn't set out to do it, y'know.'

Moving away from Dan, jerking his arm free, Tony sat on another chair.

'I'd been saying asinine things to her ever since. Then I saw her on the bike. I just wanted to give her a scare. Didn't even know she'd taken a tumble till the next day. But it was wrong. Got to turn myself in.'

Like a marionette on broken strings, Tony let his head and hands hang between his knees. How would Alex know the difference between Range Rovers in the dark, and when she was trying not to fall off the damned bike?

He got up, scuffed to the door and outside. The major's vehicle was badly parked on the verge opposite the hall, just one of many in this place. More time wasted.

When he got to his own Range Rover he was too numb to jump at a tap on the shoulder. 'I've been all over,' Hugh Rhys told him. 'No one even heard of a railway graveyard anywhere near Moreton-in-Marsh.'

'Get in,' Tony said. 'I'm going up that way again. We've missed something. Do you think Elyan Quillam would be capable of doing something to Alex? I don't know what else to think but I don't see it, I just don't see it. Why would he?'

Hugh looked over his shoulder as Tony backed up. 'What do any of us know? How do we know what we're capable of? I talked to his mother and she thinks they're both badly injured somewhere. Hysterical. Doc James gave her a shot. It's a house filled with silent shock. Sebastian's back and apart from he and Daisy, the place might as well be empty. Wells went off to check every pub with a piano – like someone wouldn't have noticed Elyan playing in some bar. I've called all over.'

Rather than respond, Tony concentrated on getting back to the High and heading for Hillop Road.

'Where are we going?' Hugh asked.

'The last place I heard her voice from. Then toward Moreton. Shit, I don't know where to go but I can't sit around.'

Rain sent a fine mist across the windshield. Tony put the wipers on low and peered ahead through the headlight beams.

Hugh alternately peered around and put his face in his hands. Tony glanced at him repeatedly. 'You care about Alex, don't you?' It occurred to him that the other man could take that wrong. 'I mean, you feel really badly about this.'

'She's a special lady,' Hugh said. 'Sometimes she tries too hard to look out for other people and gets herself into trouble. But you know that. You shouldn't be punished for being decent. What's that? Over there?'

Tony followed Hugh's pointing finger and saw what looked like the top of a car in a ditch. They were only a couple of miles from Moreton-in-Marsh but he had to stop and pull over.

Out of the ditch climbed a couple and for an instant his breath wouldn't go in or out of his lungs. 'Is it them?'

'I don't get it,' Hugh said. 'It's . . . Tony, we've got to keep it steady or we could miss the chance we need. It's Elyan. But that's Annie with him.'

Hugh was out of the car before it fully stopped and running toward Elyan and his girlfriend. 'Where have you been?' he yelled. 'Where's Alex?'

'Wait.' Tony scrambled after him and grabbed Elyan by his shoulders. He began to shake him. 'Where's Alex, you little shit? Where is she?' Elyan's eyes kept closing. He slumped against Annie and would have fallen if she hadn't held him around the waist.

'Please,' Annie said. 'We should go now. Leave him. He's not himself – I'm not sure who he is anymore. I know where Alex is. We can't waste time. She . . . I don't know what could happen to her. Elyan only said she was in a railway carriage. I made him come back.'

'From where?' Tony said, dragging Elyan to the Range Rover and opening a back door. 'You sit with him, Hugh. Make sure he doesn't try to get away.'

'He wanted us to run away together,' Annie

said. She cried quietly and steadily. 'We were in London by the time he told me what he'd done. He has to have help. Please just drive on.'

Before they'd gone three miles, a police car screeched up behind them, lights flashing, and pulled them over.

Tony recognized the policewoman at the wheel as Constable Bishop. Wicks was with her. He gave them a message for Dan, looked at Elyan's condition and asked that he be transported back to Folly where the detectives could detain them.

When they all but lifted Elyan from the Range Rover, Annie said, 'I know exactly where to go. Elyan took Laura and me there.' She made a visible effort to pull herself together. 'They won't hurt Elyan, will they?'

Tony opened his mouth to say that as far as he was concerned they could do what they liked to him, but Hugh leaned from the back seat to pat the girl's shoulder. 'They're very careful about things like that,' he said.

They drove too fast for the narrow roads but had to slow down when they finally turned onto the even smaller tracks Annie led them to. 'Bishop's Nob is where we turn right,' she told them. 'It comes up suddenly. Oh, Elyan.' She cried louder.

Tony met Hugh's eyes in the mirror.

'He just wanted us to get away. He's been so poorly treated. On the outside it all looked rosy, but I've known. I knew how poor Laura suffered. I have to tell it all now, don't I?'

Tony wanted to insist she did and right now

but he said, 'You should try to settle down and let's concentrate on finding Alex.'

'Elyan and Laura were going to pretend she attempted suicide,' Annie said. 'They had it all worked out but got it all wrong.'

Tony almost slammed on the brakes.

'Then it all got worse and worse and the church was taped off and guarded so he couldn't get the thermos back. It would have been all right if the police never found it.'

In the space of a few minutes, while they made the right turn at Bishop's Nob and threaded through tall, very dark trees, Annie told an extraordinary story so bizarre it had to be true.

'They won't put him in jail, will they?' she said. 'He isn't himself. He's not the Elyan I know. He needs to be helped.'

'Right,' Tony said, not trusting himself to say anything else.

Through a gap Annie pointed out between trees on the right, they slithered into a field. Tony couldn't see how big it was or where they were supposed to be going, but went in the direction Annie pointed out. The rain was heavier and he had the wipers on full.

When the headlights picked up a large wrecked wooden building, he knew what was meant by having your heart in your throat. He couldn't swallow.

'It's in there,' Annie said. 'The carriage on the right, he said. The one with no windows. I forget what it was for. Please, please let Alex be all right. Elyan said she tried to be kind to him. He didn't think she understood.'

313

'You can bet your boots she didn't understand and if—'

'Tony,' Hugh interrupted. 'Let's go.'

The outside doors were hard to open since they'd dropped down on their hinges, but soon enough there was space for them to squeeze inside. Tony and Hugh shone torches around and picking out the right carriage was easy. Tony put a finger to his lips and they all listened, but heard nothing.

In the distance came the sound of sirens. Tony didn't know if he was glad. If they needed help, he'd be pleased to see them, but he didn't want to need help.

A heavy, well-oiled and jointed closure on the back of the carriage opened under several well placed thumps.

Hugh looked at Tony.

Annie withdrew to the doors of the shed.

Using both hands, Tony pulled the door open, and howled. He received a solid crack over the head from a hard object.

'Hold up,' Hugh cried. 'Alex, stop.'

He was too late to save Tony from a second blow, this one to his shoulder, but Alex's pale face, illuminated in the ghostly uplight from the torch with which she was assaulting Tony, went lax. Her mouth opened and closed before she threw herself into a slightly staggering Tony's arms.

They clung together, rocking, laughing and crying, while Alex spilled the horrors of the darkness in the carriage and how she'd tried to pick a hole through rotting boards in the floor. To demonstrate, she held up broken and bleeding nails and fingertips.

Annie had asked, piteously, to be taken back to Green Friday. She wanted to tell Elyan's family how much she loved him and would always love him. And she wanted, if she was allowed, to stay there till morning and they all knew what the next steps would be with Elyan.

Tony capitulated, but only because Alex insisted. 'Unless you want me to start spouting about the quality of mercy, you'll drive there now. Those poor people have suffered so much.'

The police who arrived in the field too late to help or hinder followed them back to Folly and up the hill to Green Friday.

'No,' Alex said as they drove toward the house. 'Has something else happened here?' Official vehicles were parked on both sides of the driveway and in front of the house. No emergency lights showed but the dark shapes of police stood around.

It wasn't until Tony opened his door that they heard the sound of music coming from the house, piano music.

Annie climbed out to stand with Alex and the two men and they went inside together, but Dan, just inside the front door, put a finger to his lips. With his mouth close to Alex's ear, he whispered. 'They brought him because I was already here. He's no threat, except to himself. We're waiting for specialists to get here.'

Before they could stop her, Annie darted away to the open door of the music room. Dan went quietly to stand behind her and the other three followed suit.

At the piano sat Elyan, playing as if possessed, transported far away from the moment. Sebastian stood beside the piano and gave the group in the doorway a thin smile. Daisy sat, cross-legged, on the floor and put a finger to her lips when she saw them.

'Rachmaninoff,' Dan said quietly, impressing Alex.

She didn't remember feeling so very sad other than when she lost her baby girl.

Tony put an arm around her and said, very low, 'This is the only piece of classical music O'Reilly could name and that's only because Harriet Burke told him. Please could we leave now?'

Dan heard and nodded.

'Yes,' Alex said.